SECRETS

OF A

SEAMSTRESS

BY

VANESSA HERBERT

HEMINGWAY
PUBLISHERS

Table of Contents

Preface

"You are safe now, my love," said the Earl in his most tender voice. "I have never been so thankful to see you, my lord," softly speaks Nicolette while gazing into the sapphire blue eyes of the Earl. "I am truly sorry that I did not listen to Lord Watson. I do not know what I was thinking, my lord. You have every right to scold me."

"I will not scold you, Nicolette. You are not a child." Quickly, he leans towards her face, places his lips on her warm lips, opens her mouth with his tongue, and kisses her with a passion that sets his body on fire.

CHAPTER 1

England 1865

Primrose Estate

"That was quite the ride today, Lady Anne. This new side saddle father purchased for us seems to suit you much better than the last one did when we took the horses out for a ride. Don't you agree, Lady Anne?" she asked with a hopeful smile.

"I do agree that the side saddle does suit me much better, Lady Miranda," Lady Anne replied, pausing to sneeze, "But I can't help but sneeze every time we gallop across these woodlands and meadows where all these lovely yellow flowers are growing wild."

"It must be the Primrose flowers that grow everywhere this time of year," Lady Miranda replied thoughtfully. "After all, we do have more than our share of them."

"Well, I do have to admit the flowers are very pretty with their vibrant yellow blooms," Lady Anne commented as she wiped her delicate nose with her lace handkerchief.

"There is no doubt in my mind that I must get used to them, and hopefully sooner, the better," she mused, gazing at the sprawling meadows.

"Once your brother Lord Austin takes me as his bride, I will be able to call this my home one day, Lady Miranda. But it is rather apparent that your brother, the Earl of Primrose, prefers to drag his feet on this matter," she added, her voice tinged with frustration.

Then she continues to explain, "It has been a couple of years since our fathers came to a marriage agreement between the Earl and me. It appears as if our fathers want to keep close family ties with one another, so they thought that a marriage between the Earl and me would be a way to carry on a bloodline between our families once our children are born. Even though the cotton textile industry they own in London has taken a hit since the Civil War broke out in North America, they are still profiting from their wheat fields. I do realize that the Earl has been traveling quite often the past few years and our chances of being in each other's company have been less than what I so desired. But I have to admit his reputation as an Emissary for our government has been extremely honorable," she admitted with a note of admiration.

"Now that he has taken a leave of absence and is spending time here at Primrose Estate, I have wanted to visit here more often. Even though I enjoy your company Lady Miranda, I do love to spend time with your brother. The few times that we have been fortunate enough to be together, he barely holds my hand, and once in a while, we share a few stolen kisses when we go for our walks in these lovely gardens. Therefore, Lady Miranda, I'm beginning to wonder if he will ever ask me to be his bride," she concluded, looking earnestly at her friend for reassurance.

Lady Miranda was the first to dismount her horse and hand the reins over to the groomsman. She then breathlessly spoke to Lady Anne, "You don't have to worry, Lady Anne because I overheard the Earl tell your brother, Lord Atticus, yesterday after your arrival here at Primrose Estate that they would officially be brothers-in-law soon."

"Well," said Lady Anne, releasing a sigh of relief. "I surely hope so. He kept me waiting long enough."

"Oh golly, speaking of the devil himself, there he comes towards us, Lady Anne," she exclaimed. The bright yellow sun was shining so brightly overhead that they had to shield their eyes with their hands so they could see the Earl and Lord Atticus walking swiftly towards them.

"Good Afternoon, Lady Ashton, the Earl spoke as he stopped in front of Lady Anne.

"Do you recall that I mentioned on my last visit here that you may call me by my given name, my Lord? I would be delighted if you would call me Lady Anne, my Lord," she suggested with a polite smile.

"Why, of course, my dear, I would be honored to call you Lady Anne," he agreed warmly. "And may I add that you look so lovely today, my sweet. Lord Atticus and I would be delighted to walk you ladies back to the Manor for our afternoon tea."

Lord Austin, the Earl of Primrose, took Lady Anne Ashton by the arm and guided her through the entrance of the exquisite gardens that lead to the Mayfield Manor. Lady Miranda first broke the silence between her and Lord Atticus, "I truly hope you are finding your visit here at Primrose Estate a pleasant one, my Lord," she inquired kindly.

"I do find my visit to be most pleasant, Lady Miranda," replied Lord Atticus, starting to walk side by side with her towards the Manor.

"I can't help but hope that my brother and Lady Anne will spend more time in each other's company on this visit," she mused. "Prayer tells. Don't you agree, Lord Ashton? It's about time those two wed. Everyone is beginning to talk and speculate about those two. I've even heard gossip that the Earl doesn't really want to marry her because she is not attractive enough or witty enough for him. And if he did marry her to honor our father's wishes, he would surely take on a mistress much lovelier than her. But we both know my brother too well, and he would never dishonor Lady Ashton by taking a mistress," she tried to explain by looking at his eyes to find reassurance.

"I suppose he is an honorable man, Lady Ashton, and he would honor his bride," quietly spoke Lord Atticus, a half grin forming on his handsome face. "But we all know that the ladies find him quite handsome and desirable."

"Well, I have to say, Lord Atticus, that the Earl is taking a long time to ask for your sister's hand in marriage, and I can tell that Lady Anne is getting more impatient by the day," she remarked with a knowing look.

Lady Anne could tell that her spirits were somewhat lifted, and her mood was more pleasant now that she was in the company of the Earl. She had to admit that he was the most handsome and muscular man she had ever been this close to. Every time she came this close to him, she could smell his distinct manly scent. It was a scent that made her want to touch him, lay her head on his muscular, bronzed chest, and inhale the heady fragrance of musk and leather. But unfortunately the spell was broken when they heard horse's hooves and the wheels of an old open carriage come to an abrupt halt on the graveled road right beside the manicured tapestries in the Mayfield gardens.

"Lord Mayfield! Lord Mayfield!" a voice called urgently. "Would you please come and help us? That new farm hand you hired is causing trouble. He's done stirred up old Cyrus, and now Cyrus is threatening to burn down his farmhouse, sir."

"Please come follow me, Lord Atticus," the Earl suggested urgently. "We shall go to the horse stables to get the horses ready and grab my pistol. We will immediately ride out to old Cyrus's farm if that is okay with you, my Lord." The Earl and Lord Atticus both hopped onto the back of the open carriage and then Lord Atticus responded to the Earl.

"Excuse us, ladies, we shall return soon." the Earl called out. "Please be safe, my lords," Lady Anne spoke out loud as the carriage hurried towards the stables. "Come, Lady Anne, we must hurry to the Manor. Mother and Father are probably waiting for our arrival. Everyone will be gathering in the parlor for the afternoon tea," Lady Miranda urged. Quickly, both ladies lifted their lovely gowns and hastened to the Manor.

Once Lady Miranda and Lady Anne entered the front hall of the Manor, they couldn't even make it to the front parlor. Both ladies stopped dead in their tracks upon hearing a loud knock on the front door of the Manor. They turned their pretty heads to watch Oswell, the family butler, open the front door. He was greeted by a messenger who handed him a letter in a sealed white envelope. They overheard the messenger say that the letter was intended for Lord Austin Mayfield, the Earl of Primrose Estate. After Oswell closed the front door, Lady Miranda motioned for him to approach her. Immediately, Oswell walked towards Lady Miranda and announced that he had a letter for her brother, the Earl.

"You may hand me the envelope, Oswell, Lady Anne, and I will be glad to deliver the letter to the Earl when he returns," Lady Miranda said decisively. Oswell handed over the envelope to her and politely excused himself. "We are ready for our tea now, Lady Anne. We shouldn't keep Mother and Father waiting," Lady Miranda stated as they prepared to join the others.

When the ladies entered the front parlor, they were surprised to find Lord Jared, the younger brother of the Earl, and Lady Miranda standing at the front window. They also noticed that Lady Miranda's father, Lord James Mayfield, the Marquis of Primrose, was seated in his usual chair by the fire. Lady Constance Mayfield, the wife and mother of the Mayfield children, was sitting on a blue velvet settee next to the youngest of the Mayfield children, Lady Katherine.

Lord Jared was the first to greet his sister and Lady Anne when they entered the parlor. "Good afternoon, Ladies. I was beginning to wonder if everyone except Mother, Father, and Lady Katherine had mysteriously disappeared on me. It is lovely to see you, Lady Anne and I sincerely hope you are enjoying your visit here at Primrose to be a most pleasant one," he said with a warm smile.

"I find that my visit here so far has been most pleasant, my Lord. It is kind of you to ask," Lady Anne softly replied, her voice carrying a note of genuine appreciation.

"Good afternoon, Mother and Father. We are sorry if we kept you waiting. The Earl and Lord Atticus are dealing with a mishap that has taken place at old Cyrus's farm, but I am certain they should be arriving here soon," Lady Miranda explained, her tone apologetic.

"Please come and sit with me and I will pour us a cup of hot tea. I am extremely parched right now, and I imagine you are as well," Lady Constance suggested, beckoning them over with a gesture towards the settee.

As the ladies took their seats on an ivory settee near the large fireplace, Lady Anne gently reminded Lady Miranda that she was still holding the letter in the white envelope in her gloved hand. Lady Miranda turned her head towards Lord Jared, who was staring out the front window, and interrupted his thoughts as she softly spoke to him. "I am holding a letter that is addressed to the Earl, and it arrived as we were about to enter the parlor. I shall make sure he gets the letter when he returns," she assured softly.

"Do you happen to know from whom and where the letter came from, lady Miranda?" Lord Jared asked, his voice filled with curiosity.

"I did overhear the messenger tell Oswell that the letter was from North America, and a gentleman was mentioned by the name of Mr. Richard Harrison of Virginia," Lady Miranda relayed, recalling the details.

"Ah, that name sounds familiar," Lord Jared replied, nodding thoughtfully. "The Earl has spoken to me on several occasions about Mr. Harrison of Virginia. He happens to be a horse breeder of some mighty fine Arabian horses, and the Earl is very interested in one of his stallions.

"At first, I thought it might be a letter from the British government since our brother is an Emissary for our government. But now that the war in North America is finally winding down and the British government has issued a Declaration of Neutrality to signify its official stance on the American Civil War, the Earl has not made too many visits to America lately," Lord Jared continued, his tone reflective.

"Since he has the opportunity to be home now, he has mentioned that he is interested in horse racing once again, and he has his eye on this Arabian stallion in North America," Lord Jared concluded, his eyes lighting up with enthusiasm.

Before anyone had a chance to utter a word, the Earl and Lord Atticus walked in. "Sorry we are late for tea, but there was an urgent matter that Lord Atticus and I had to attend," the Earl announced apologetically.

"So what happened at old Cyrus's farm?" the Marquis asked loudly, gesturing for the servants to pour hot tea in a cup for the Earl and Lord Atticus.

"The new farmhand, Jacob, who was recently hired, has had his eye on Cyrus's oldest daughter, Sara," the Earl began, his tone serious. "Cyrus kind of suspected that something might be up with those two when he decided to make a surprise visit to Jacob's farmhouse. When Cyrus arrived at Jacob's house, he knocked on the front door, and no one answered, so he decided to do some snooping around," the Earl continued, pausing for effect.

"That's when he spotted the small stables on the far side of Jacob's farmhouse. Since old Cyrus was alone, he decided to quietly walk to the stables and peep inside," the Earl explained, his voice lowering.

"At first, he heard girlish laughter, and when he stepped further inside, he saw Jacob and Sara in each other's arms, kissing one another. Immediately, Cyrus ran right up to Jacob, grabbed Sara, and pulled her out of the way. The next thing Cyrus knew, he was punching Jacob in the face, and without thinking, Jacob punched him back. Before a bad fight breaks out between them, Joshua, Cyrus's son shows up suddenly and pulls them apart. Cyrus takes Sara by the hand and starts to walk out of the stables, but before he does, he threatens to come back and burn Jacob's farmhouse down if he comes anywhere near Sara again," the Earl added, his tone grave.

"When Lord Atticus and I arrived at Cyrus's farm, we tried to explain to him that it wasn't Jacob's fault that his father had a bad reputation. I told Cyrus that Jacob wasn't anything like his father, and Jacob was sober, trustworthy, hard-working, and kind-hearted, unlike his father. He would make a good suitor for his daughter Sara. I advised him that when you left there, you would go visit with Jacob and tell him that you do not want him to see Sara for the time being. But you need to think this over, Cyrus, because those two could possibly be in love, and you and I either don't want to hear that they ran off together somewhere on their own. So give Jacob a chance. He's a good man," the Earl concluded, his gaze steady.

After the Earl finished speaking, Lady Anne rose to her feet and walked towards the Earl and stood before him. "Well, you do have a soft heart and a romantic side to you, after all, my Lord," Lady Anne observed softly, a slight smile playing on her lips.

The Earl took Lady Anne's slightly trembling hand, lifted it towards his face, and spoke aloud, "What made you think maybe I wasn't those things, my Lady? Have I given you cause to think otherwise?" his voice tinged with a mix of curiosity and concern.

At that moment, Lady Anne didn't know whether to just stand there in front of him in shame or to run out of the parlor door, her heart racing. She couldn't believe she had spoken those words. Now, she was holding her breath, just like everyone else in the room. At the same time, all she could do was stand there and wait on his wrath, but she knew she had to come up with a quick answer soon.

"I have noticed on previous visits here, Lord Austin that you hardly make time for us to spend time together. You are always running off to someone or someplace else," Lady Anne confessed, trying to hold on to the situation.

"If I am guilty of such behavior, my Lady, please allow me to make it up to you," the Earl softly spoke in a deep masculine voice.

"If you like, I will have the cook prepare us a lovely picnic basket of your favorite food and wine since tomorrow will be your last full day here at Primrose Estate," the Earl offered a hopeful note in his voice.

"That sounds like a marvelous idea my Lord, but may I suggest the pond on the east side that is the farthest from the woodlands where so many of the Primrose flowers grow. It has come to my attention on previous visits here that I am quite sensitive to their fragrance," Lady Anne suggested with a thoughtful expression.

"I know just the perfect spot for us, Lady Anne, and I am looking forward to our gathering tomorrow. But right now, I would love to sit and join you for a cup of hot tea, my lady," the Earl said, his eyes brightening with the prospect. At that very moment, it seemed as if everyone in the room let out a sigh of relief.

Lord Jared moved away from the window in the parlor and took a seat by the fireplace. "I believe you are still holding a letter that came for the Earl, sister," Lord Jared reminded Lady Miranda, finishing his last sip of tea with a curious glance.

Lady Anne stared down at the letter she was holding in her gloved hand and handed it to the Earl. The Earl walked over to a small desk in the room and grabbed the letter opener to open it. He appeared to take his time reading it while everyone in the parlor was eagerly waiting for him to say something.

The Marquis was the first to break the silence, addressing the Earl, "I suppose you will let us know who, what, and where the letter came from, my boy."

"Oh, I'm sorry to keep you waiting, but I do have good news," the Earl began, his eyes alight with excitement. "The Arabian stallion that I have had my eye on for some time now is ready to be purchased if I am still interested. Indeed, I am still interested, and I will send a letter immediately to Mr. Harrison to inform him that I will be sailing to North America in a few days from now. The ship that I will be sailing on will dock in Baltimore, Maryland, when it reaches America. It will probably take about two weeks to arrive there. The return letter should be in his hands before then on a carrier ship that will leave tomorrow. He can bring the horse to Baltimore, and I will meet with him there, and hopefully, I will be bringing home a winner," he continued, his voice filled with hope.

"I have decided, father, that I would like to venture into horse racing once again. Since I am home now, I will have the time to devote to my interests. May I ask you both to do me a favor while I am away, my Lords?" he requested, turning to face them directly. "I would like for you to find me the best horse jockey you can find. So when I get back with my horse, we can get started immediately preparing for the Epsom Derby. The Arabian stallion has already been trained to be a racehorse, and all we have to do is train it to be the best. I am aware that your family, Lord Atticus is well known for horse racing in the past.

"I realize that your father is getting on up there in age and no longer participates in the sport, but your knowledge and Lord Jared's popularity with all of London's elites can bring us access to all the well-known horse jockeys around. So what do you say, my Lords, can I count on you?" the Earl asked, looking expectantly at Lord Jared and Lord Atticus, who both nodded in agreement as he walked towards the door.

"Will you please excuse me," he said as he glanced over at Lady Anne and smiled his most charming smile her way. "I shall see you all at dinner. I am looking forward to the picnic tomorrow, but for now, I have many preparations to make my lady," the Earl announced, his tone light yet earnest.

They couldn't find a more perfect day to have a picnic by the pond. The sun shone brightly, and the sky was as blue as the bluebirds that flew over the clear, shining waters of the rippling pond. The Earl and Lady Anne dismounted their horses and left them tied to a tree near the pond where they would enjoy their picnic. Lord Atticus, Lord Jared, and Lady Miranda chose to continue riding their horses across the open meadows near the wheat fields instead of joining the Earl and Lady Anne.

They all agreed that the Earl and Lady Anne needed some time alone together, even though it wasn't suitable for a lady to be alone with a suitor. Of course, neither one of them would ever tell another living soul about this arrangement. Once they reached the pond, the Earl found a soft grassy spot where they could spread their blanket. "This seems like a lovely spot to sit by the pond. Don't you agree, my lady?" the Earl inquired, seeking her approval.

"It is to my satisfaction, my Lord. You have picked a lovely spot because we are most fortunate to have this large Oak tree near the pond to give us some shade. The sun appears to be brighter than usual today, my Lord," Lady Anne responded, her tone appreciative.

After spreading the picnic blanket, Lady Anne carefully lifted her lovely yellow satin gown and sat beside the Earl. The Earl reached into the picnic basket, took out a bottle of Lady Anne's favorite wine, and began to pour it into the wine goblets that were also in the basket. Lady Anne's slender body had been trembling slightly, but after drinking the wine, she began to relax. She started to ask the Earl about the Arabian horse that he had his eye on in America, but she was interrupted when he leaned over, placed his muscular arm around her, and drew her close to him.

She felt her body stiffen suddenly, and before she knew it, he leaned in closer, and his mouth found hers. He parted her lips and kissed her with his tongue, delving inside her mouth. "This kiss was different," she thought. It was different from some of their previous kisses. Again and again, he pressed his lips to hers and retreated. This time, he wanted her to reciprocate and she did it without being ashamed. All she could feel at that moment was pure pleasure.

"Yes," he murmured as she wrapped her hands around his neck. "Yes, that's the way," he encouraged softly. Suddenly, she realized that he was teaching her how to kiss and be responsive to his kisses. But then he paused to draw his breath and pulled away from her. *Oh, don't stop. Don't stop,* she thought desperately. But that is exactly what he did. He gazed into her dark brown eyes and smiled with his own, his expression tender. She hadn't known that kissing could be like this. She knew that this was dangerous but yet so wonderful. She also understood why he had to stop.

She reached up to touch her swollen lips when she realized she was still wearing her gloves. Despite the fabric barrier, she could still feel the warmth from his neck where she had placed her hands.

The Earl lowered his eyes and stared at her gown; it was bunched in a pile between them. "Please take my hand, my lady, and I will help you to your feet so you can smooth out your gown," the Earl offered, extending his hand toward her.

In a polite tone, she replied, "It is not necessary, my Lord. It will be just fine."

"Then why don't I peep inside the picnic basket and see what we have to eat? I'm certain the cook has prepared us something delicious," the Earl said eagerly, as he was trying to distract from what had just taken place between them.

What am I doing? She is going to expect a proposal of marriage from me, and I am not ready. I'm not sure if I will ever be ready. What shall I tell my father, the Marquis, and her father, the Earl? I don't want to disappoint them, but I'm not sure that I will. I just need more time, and going to America will give me the time that I need. Until then, I shouldn't allow my desires to go this far, but after all, I am a man, not a saint.

"Lord Austin! Lord Austin!" she called. "Are you with us, my lord?" echoed through the air.

"Oh, sorry, my lady," the Earl replied, distractedly reaching into the basket to pull out some cheesecakes, beef sandwiches, and fruit turnovers.

"This all looks delicious, my lord, but I don't appear to be very hungry. I will try one of the cheesecakes, though," Lady Anne conceded, making an effort to partake. The Earl nodded, handed her one of the cheesecakes, and poured another goblet of wine for each of them. Lady Anne had barely taken a few bites of her cheesecake when the sound of distant thunder reached her ears. As she reached for her goblet of wine, she once again heard the sound of thunder. She quickly drank the rest of her wine and suggested to the Earl that it might be time to leave. The Earl agreed and started gathering up their belongings. As they were mounting the horses, he noticed the sad look on Lady Anne's pretty face. There was no doubt in the Earl's mind that he had disappointed Lady Anne once again. Therefore, he observed that she chose to ride in silence the rest of the way home.

It wasn't long after Lady Anne returned to the guest quarters of the Manor that she realized the rain never came. She really didn't care that she wanted to leave the picnic suddenly. The fact that they heard a thunder was a good excuse for them to leave. Once again, the Earl did not propose marriage or even mention a future with her. There was no doubt in her mind that one day, he would honor their father's wishes because he would never want to disappoint the Marquis. But at this point, she wasn't even sure if she could be happy knowing that he didn't feel the same way she felt towards him. But he is a man after all, and tonight, when they gather for the evening meal, she will look her best. She planned to give all her attention to Lord Jared and ignore the Earl completely. *"I will wear one of my finest gowns. I believe the red silk gown with the very low-cut front will do just fine,"* which she felt would be just perfect. "Please come, Nora, and get my bath water ready. Instead of the lemon oil, I would prefer the rose oil this evening and pull my red silk gown from the armoire. I feel like wearing red tonight," Lady Anne instructed her maid with a decisive tone.

It was no surprise that Lady Anne was awake at the crack of dawn the following morning. Before dressing, she decided to take a quick look out of the bedroom chamber window. It was obvious that the rain had come during the night, and now the morning sun was trying to peek out from behind the clouds. A soft knock at her door preceded the arrival of servants, who brought a tray of breakfast to place on a small table near her four-poster bed.

She purposely asked for her breakfast to be brought into her room so that her brother, Lord Atticus, and she could get an early start on their trip back home to Old Wood Manor. The truth, however, was that she wanted to spend less time in the company of the Earl. She still had her pride, and she wasn't about to let the Earl see any sign of disappointment on her lovely face if she could help it. She was waiting for another knock on her chamber door from the servants, knowing that this time, they would be announcing that the Ashton family carriage was ready and waiting in front of the Mayfield Manor to escort her and her brother back home to Old Wood Manor. She had to admit that she was famished this morning, so she ate every morsel of her delicious breakfast. As Nora, her lady's maid was putting the last pin in her light brown hair, the knock came at the door, informing that Lord Atticus and the carriage were waiting for her to come.

When she stepped outside, she saw the Earl looking as darn handsome as ever, standing beside the Mayfield carriage, which was ready to escort him to London so he could make plans for his trip to North America in a few days. The Earl saw Lady Anne, and he walked over to stand in front of the Ashton family carriage. Lady Anne first stopped in front of the Mayfield family and said her goodbyes to each and every one in the family. Upon reaching the Ashton family carriage, she was greeted by the Earl and Lord Atticus. The Earl took her hand and pulled her closer. She expected him to either kiss her hand or give a quick peck on her rosy cheek, but instead, he surprised her with a warm kiss on her soft lips. The Earl felt her body stiffen beneath him, but he also felt the warmth of her kiss. When he let go of her embrace, he said, "Goodbye, for now, Lady Anne. I shall visit with you when I return home from my trip to America, my sweet. I wish you well, my lady." Then he took her hand to lift her inside the carriage. Lady Anne did not care to look him in the face instead, she softly spoke, "I wish you a safe and well trip to America and back home, my Lord." The carriage pulled away, heading towards Ashton Manor, and the Earl just stood quietly, staring off into the distance.

CHAPTER 2

Spring 1865

"Good morning, Lady Townsend. I must say it is lovely to see you and your daughters out and about this morning. Since that horrible storm we've all endured the past several days on the Royal Princess Ship heading to America, we are most fortunate to be standing here on the top of this deck, enjoying this bright and beautiful sunshine this very morning, my lady." Said Lord Mayfield with a wide smile.

"I agree, Lord Mayfield. We are ever so fortunate to even be alive after being so confined to our staterooms and holding on to any furniture we could find. It was most dreadful, to say the least, my Lord." The Earl continued to walk along the rails of the deck, basking in the glory of the bright sunshine. When he glanced into the open sea, he was glad to see the calm waters of the Atlantic Ocean. Unfortunately that was not the case for the past few days as the ship kept sailing along. The raging waves of the sea kept rising over the hull of the ship, almost flooding the inside of the turbulent ship.

It has been a little over a week now since the Royal Princess Steam Ship left London, England, heading to Baltimore, Maryland,

and after that, would be heading to Charleston, South Carolina. The Earl was leaning against the rails of the ship, patiently waiting for Lord Atticus to join him. He thought about the plans that he and Lord Atticus made before they left England. He remembered Lord Atticus telling him about the letter his mother, Lady Margaret Ashton, received while he and Lady Anne were recently visiting Primrose Estate. His father, Lord Gerald Ashton, the Earl of Old Wood Manor, agreed with his wife, Lady Margaret, that they would help her sister, Lady Elizabeth Braxton, and her two adult children come to England and stay at the Ashton family Manor and work in London as a tailor and a dressmaker. Lady Braxton was introduced to Thomas Braxton of Charleston, South Carolina, a tailor who owned a shop in Charleston. They got married and had three children, but unfortunately, the youngest daughter died several years ago due to scarlet fever. That left them with two now: Nicolette, the oldest daughter, who happened to be a year younger than the Earl of Primrose, and Daniel, the younger brother of Nicolette. Not only was Thomas Braxton a well-known tailor in Charleston, but he was also a Confederate soldier in the American Civil War. It didn't take him long to move up the ranks to Lieutenant Thomas Braxton. But unfortunately, Lt. Braxton was killed in the Civil War. Since then, the family has been trying to recover from his death and the hardships that the war has left in its aftermath. The Earl remembered the look on Lord Atticus' face when they were back in England, and he informed him of this terrible tragedy. After hearing that Lord Atticus was planning on sailing to Charleston, South Carolina, to help the Braxton family board the Royal Princess Ship in Charleston and sail back to England, he decided to meet with Mr. Harrison in Baltimore about the Arabian horse first and then he would help Lord Atticus with the Braxton family. They had even less than a week before the ship would dock in Baltimore. He unfastened a few more buttons on his white tailored shirt and raised his face up high towards the bright yellow sun. In that very moment, all he had on his mind was a dark Arabian stallion that would soon be his.

The next few days promised smooth sailing on the Royal Princess. The sea remained calm except for a very mild storm that passed over them very quickly. It was the last evening for the passengers and the crew to spend on the ship before it docks in Baltimore the following morning. The Royalty or Nobility had their own separate dining room. When they gather this evening for dinner, they will be able to enjoy music and dancing as well. "Oh, there you are, Lord Atticus. I hope you don't mind that I made an arrangement earlier today to have the Townsend family join us at our table for dinner this evening. Since there would be dancing this evening, I thought we should ask the Townsend daughters to dance. It has come to my attention that they are probably among the fairest of ladies aboard. Don't you agree, Lord Atticus?"

"Well, thanks to you, my Lord. The evening looks rather promising after all," replied Lord Atticus with a slight chuckle in his voice.

When the Earl and Lord Atticus opened the French doors to enter the dining room, all heads turned to stare at them. The Earl looked quite dapper in his long, black tail coat, white waistcoat, black silk vest, white trousers, and black dress boots. His hair looked dark black and shiny to the point that it reflected a blue tint. When he walked by the tables, he politely smiled at the other passengers, especially the ladies. There was only one other gentleman in the room who could come just close to the looks and charm of the Earl, and he was Lord Atticus. His evening attire was just as appealing to the eye as the Earl's. Lord Atticus wore a long, dark brown tailcoat, ivory shirt and waistcoat, light brown silk vest, ivory breeches and dark brown dress boots. His light blonde highlights glowed in his dark blonde hair when the bright yellow sunlight reflected. Once they reached their table, they noticed that Lord Townsend was sitting at the table, but his wife and daughters had not arrived yet. The Earl and Lord Atticus politely spoke as they greeted Lord Townsend, "We hope you are having a pleasant evening, Lord Townsend?"

"Yes my Lords, I find my evening to be quite pleasant and even more so now that I see Lady Townsend and our lovely daughters." The Earl and Lord Atticus remained standing when they glanced across the room and saw Lady Townsend and her two daughters walking towards the dining table. Lady Claudia, the oldest daughter was nudged in the side by her mother to take the dining chair at the table that was next to the Earl's. When she approached the chair, the Earl pulled it back and helped her into the seat. "You look quite lovely this evening, my lady. The light green color you are wearing brings out the lovely green shade of your eyes." Lord Atticus took the seat across from Earl next to Lord Townsend, his wife and youngest daughter Mary. After everyone was seated, the servants began to serve them delicious food and wine. Everyone ate their food until they were satiated. The orchestra began to play some familiar tunes. Lord Townsend and his wife were among the first to step on the dance floor. Some of the others from another dining table quickly joined them on the dance floor. Moments later, the Earl stood to his feet, glanced over at Lady Claudia, and politely asked, "May I have this dance, my Lady?" Lady Claudia looked up at the Earl standing there looking so handsome that she could hardly speak. But she did manage to answer him, "It would be my pleasure to dance with you, my Lord." He took her by the hand and led her to the dance floor. She began to feel a little weak in her knees. She somehow managed to gain her strength back when they started to switch their dance partners back and forth. Lord Atticus came in front of her, and she danced with him for a moment. She noticed that he had the same effect on her. Lord Atticus was just about as handsome but not quite as charming as the Earl. *So what was a lady supposed to do?* She thought out loud. But there's one thing for certain, she was indeed the most fortunate to be in the company of both the gentlemen. Suddenly, the music stopped and the Earl took her by the hand and led her from the dance floor. She saw Mary coming her way and noticed Lord Atticus beside her. They appeared to be laughing at something rather funny. They told her what they were laughing about when they approached her. "Do you remember meeting Lady Chambers, her only daughter Prudence and her three sons when we first boarded the ship in England?" Mary asked her sister once she caught her breath from laughing so hard. "Yes, I do remember them, Lady Mary, especially those sons of hers. They are always staring at us when we move past them."

"Well, everyone knows by now that Lady Chambers gossips about everyone around her. She even makes up stories about others from time to time and never has anything good to say about anyone. So, while they were dining at another table across the other side of the room this evening, she was complaining about the shoemaker back home in England showing interest in her daughter, Prudence. She complained that he wasn't wealthy enough or handsome enough for him to be a suitor for Prudence. But those who know of the shoemaker speak very highly of him. He is the best shoemaker in London, and has established quite a fortune from this trade. Of course, the ladies find him to be most handsome and charming. Well, earlier, when Lady Chambers was on the dance floor, her heel broke off, and she nearly fell to the floor. But fortunately, Lord Atticus was standing there and caught her before she fell to the floor. She cursed the shoemaker out loud for doing this to her shoe on purpose. Everyone on that side of the room happened to witness this incident. Lord Atticus and I are grateful that he was there to help her, but we couldn't help laughing at it once we were able to get away." Moments later, they heard a rather loud feminine voice and someone wobbling their feet out the door. They turned their heads to see who it was, "Please come, Prudence. We are leaving, and that shoemaker is going to pay dearly for this, if it's the last thing I do." Once the orchestra began to play another tune, everyone's attention was back on the event. The evening was now coming to an end for Lady Townsend and her daughters. They said their goodbyes for the evening. Lady Claudia and Lady Mary couldn't help but be sad because they knew it would be their last evening to spend with the Earl and Lord Atticus. Once the ladies left the dining room, the Earl and Lord Atticus joined a few other gentlemen in a small room to drink brandy, smoke their cigars, and play a few hands of poker. They planned on retiring soon because the ship would be sailing into Baltimore very early in the morning, and they wanted to get off the ship as early as possible.

The following morning, the Earl woke up at the crack of dawn. His groomsman, Jackson, informed him that the Royal Princess was safely docked in the Baltimore harbor. After letting out a sigh of relief, he decided to get dressed early and have a quick breakfast in his stateroom. Jackson and Mobley, Lord Atticus Groomsman, went to see if their baggage had been sent over to the Harbor Inn, where they would be staying for the next couple of days while the ship was docked here. Lord Atticus was to see him on the top deck of the ship soon, so the Earl grabbed his coat and headed that way. When he reached the top deck, he noticed the air was rather cold for early April. He was glad that he had chosen a light wool gray and long tail coat to wear. The morning was much cooler than usual. He predicted the air to be warmer through the day since the sun was out. As he strolled along the top deck, he thought about his lunch meeting today with Mr. Harrison, owner of the Arabian stallion. Lord Atticus and he were supposed to have lunch at Harbor Inn before they went to look at the stallion that he had brought with him. The Earl has been eagerly waiting to see this beauty of a horse, and now the time has almost arrived. The Earl and Lord Atticus met at their usual place, "Good morning, Lord Austin. I hope the morning finds you well. I know that you are quite anxious to get settled in at the Harbor Inn, and looking forward to your meeting with Mr. Harrison today." Before the Earl could reply, he spotted Jackson and Mobley in the distance, already standing beside the carriage that would escort them to Harbor Inn on Thames Street. "Please come, Lord Atticus. I see that our carriage is waiting. I just now spotted our groomsmen waiting beside the carriage."

It was late morning, the Earl and Lord Atticus rested comfortably upstairs in their rooms at Harbor Inn. The Inn was one of the finest and most regal of all the places in Baltimore. The room had a rather large poster bed that would have been fit for a king. He was stretched out on it at this very moment, but it felt very lonely and empty. He couldn't help but think about his last visit with Lady Anne. He could tell that she was highly disappointed that he did not ask her hand in marriage. There were no doubts in his mind about the time running out, yet he kept finding reasons not to propose to her. In a lot of ways, he was thankful that he received the letter from Mr. Harrison. This trip to America gave him another reason to avoid doing what he really wasn't sure about, and that was to marry Lady Anne Ashton.

"Please come in, Jackson," the Earl managed to say when he heard a knock at his door. He must have drifted off to sleep for a short while, but it was time to meet Mr. Harrison for lunch. They were to meet Mr. Harrison downstairs in the private dining room. Immediately after lunch, they were to visit the nearby horse stables, where he would see the Arabian stallion for the first time. The Earl raised himself up and reached for his gold pocket watch placed on the small table to check the time. He quickly nodded his head to Jackson and politely said, "We must hurry, Jackson. We must not be late for lunch."

Lord Atticus was already waiting for the Earl in the large front foyer of the Inn. He walked up to Lord Atticus, "I am sorry if I kept you waiting. I laid down to rest and fell asleep, my Lord."

"No, my Lord, you have not kept me waiting. I came downstairs just a few moments ago. I was hoping to be on time and not keep you and your guest waiting since I was running late myself," replied Lord Atticus. When they entered the private dining room, the two gentlemen were standing near the dining table located in the center of the room. The tallest of the gentlemen with a short brown haircut and mustache was the first one to turn around and greet them, "I must assume you are Lord Mayfield. It was a pleasure to meet you." The Earl walked over to the dining table and waited for the servant to pull out a chair for him. Lord Atticus sat down. Mr. Harrison and the gentleman joined them at the table. "I am most eager to make your acquaintance, Mr. Harrison. I can't wait to lay my eyes on that stallion you brought with you," said the Earl with a slight grin on his face. "But first, let us enjoy this delicious meal I'm seeing in front of us. I don't know about the rest of you, but I am quite famished."

Once they finished their lunch, they got inside the carriage that took them to the horse stables in town. The stables were dark and dank, like a cave. Only a small shaft of light came through the barn. The Earl and Lord Atticus noticed a blizzard of dust motes whirling around in the air. At Mr. Harrison's order, the groom opened the door of the Arabian stallion's stall and released him into the yard. The horse began to shake himself, nostrils flared and his head swung side to side. The groom jerked lightly on his halter and the stallion began to settle down. The Earl walked softly towards the stallion and began to circle the horse. His shiny black coat had been raked nicely with a currycomb. The stallion's grooming was impeccable. There was no doubt he had an impressive example of horseflesh. His high, taut haunches and long, arched neck showed his Arabian ancestry. Then the Earl circled the horse back to the front again and stood to the side of the horse, allowing the animal plenty of space to see him and investigate his scent. The Earl saw the stallion's large dark eyes pleased him. He saw spirit and arrogance there. He removed his gloves and tucked them beneath one arm as he approached the stallion. After extending his hand out for him to nose and inspect, he laid it against the horse's withers and gave it a rub. The horse turned and nosed his palm. It tempted the Earl to saddle the beast and ride him straight out of the yard. Instead, the Earl walked over to Lord Atticus and asked his opinion, "Well, what you think of the stallion, my Lord?" All of a sudden, Lord Atticus gave out a soft whistle, startling everyone there. "That, my Lord is one magnificent animal!"

"He is," said the Earl with pride in his voice. "It would make me proud to take him home to Primrose Estate." The Earl glanced over at Mr. Harrison while the groom led the stallion into the stables and told him that he wanted to make an offer for the stallion. But before Mr. Harrison could answer the Earl, all three gentlemen turned their heads towards the entrance of the stables when they saw the groomsman leading another Arabian horse into the yard and halted the horse in front of them. "What do we have here," asked the Earl in a rather startled voice. "This is a mare, Lord Mayfield. I thought I might bring her along in case you might be interested in purchasing this fine looking Arabian mare. She is solid white and her color coat is just as rare as the black coat of the stallion. If you want to take both horses, I will gladly offer you a deal you can't resist, my Lord."

The Earl stood there quietly in deep thought for a moment before he decided to walk towards the Arabian mare. He circled the horse once and then circled back again to the front, where he stood beside her so she could eye him and smell his scent. He held out his hand, and she began to nose his palm. She was a beauty, no doubt and she could probably breed some of the finest horses in England. The Earl started to rub her pure white coat when he heard Mr. Harrison softly say, "Well what do you say, my Lord. Do you want to make an offer on both the stallion and the mare?"

"My answer is yes, Mr. Harrison. I must say you have most certainly taken me by surprise. I was not expecting to leave here with two Arabian beauties, but I am truly pleased." The Earl made his offer and Mr. Harrison agreed. Mr. Harrison promised the Earl he would have the horses ready to board the Royal Princess Ship later that day, even though the ship wasn't scheduled to leave Baltimore for a couple of days. The Earl wanted the horses to be settled in before the ship sailed to Charleston. Not only did he want the horses to get familiar with their surroundings, but he wanted them to get familiar with him and Lord Atticus. Now that everyone was in agreement, they walked towards the carriage that would take them back to Harbor Inn. Suddenly, out of nowhere, they felt raindrops on them. The sun was still in the sky but was hiding in the gray clouds. Fortunately, they were all safely gathered around the large fireplace at Harbor Inn when it started to rain heavily. The deal between the Earl and Mr. Harrison for the purchase of the Arabian horses was sealed and everyone in the room shook hands and went their ways. The Earl and Lord Atticus had planned on visiting some men's shops the rest of the day before they returned for the evening meal. So they decided to keep their seats by the fire in the front parlor of the Inn until the rain let up. Lord Atticus went over and stood by the window. He watched as the rain kept pouring against the window panes. He thought about the Arabian horses that the Earl had just purchased and found himself starting to get excited about the prospect of taking an interest in horse racing, as he did so many times with his father in the past. But his father's health was deteriorating quicker than he wanted to admit, so he gave up the sport a few years ago. The Earl cleared his throat and glanced over at Lord Atticus as if he could read his thoughts.

"I believe you are just as excited about bringing those magnificent horses home with us as I am, my Lord."

The rain finally ended, but it was too late for the Earl and Lord Atticus to take a shopping trip, so they retired to their rooms to freshen up for the evening meal. Neither one of them was very hungry so they had a light dinner and headed to the nearest saloon on Thames Street. When they entered the saloon, they could see clouds of smoke in the air and the smell of whiskey. They found a table with a couple of vacant chairs and sat. There are four other gentlemen already seated at the table playing a hand of cards. The Earl ordered a round of whiskey and asked to join the other gentlemen in a hand of poker once they finished with that hand of cards. The Earl and Lord Atticus gulped down a couple of shots of whiskey when they heard a loud, familiar voice coming from the far side of the room. They turned around to see Mr. Harrison seated at a table, playing cards, grinning from ear to ear. Evidently, he is grinning because he must be lucky this evening. "It is too bad we are not sitting at the table with Mr. Harrison, Lord Atticus. I am certain that we could most likely win back some of that money he got from me today. Don't you agree, my Lord?"

"There is no doubt in my mind, my Lord," replied Lord Atticus as he watched two lovely females heading towards their table.

After winning a few hands of poker at the saloon, they decided to retire early this evening. When they rode in the carriage that took them back to Harbor Inn, they witnessed the streets being rather crowded and noisy that evening. The streets were still slightly wet from the rain earlier in the day but it had turned out to be a lovely evening after all. They got back to the Inn and said their goodnights. Moments later, when the Earl was starting to undress himself to get in bed, he heard a soft knock at his door. *Who could that be,* he thought? When he opened the door, he was surprised to see one of the women who were at the saloon earlier this evening. "Hello, Lord Mayfield. My name is Emily. I was paid and sent here by a gentleman named Mr. Harrison. May I come inside, my Lord? I guarantee you won't regret it." While he was standing there, he heard a knock at Lord Atticus' door. He grabbed Emily by her arm, pushed her inside, and quickly shut the door.

CHAPTER 3

Spring 1865

“I notice that you are somewhat later than usual for breakfast this morning, my Lord,” said Lord Atticus to the Earl with a sly look on his handsome face. “You must not be very hungry, or perhaps your appetite has already been satisfied,” he teased. “Isn't that called the pot calling the kettle black, Lord Atticus,” replied the Earl as he took his seat at the dining table.

“I can see that you have barely touched the food on your plate, Lord Atticus. May I suggest that you eat all you can because we have got a busy day ahead of us?” The Earl suggested. He continued, “Jackson and Mobley have arranged for a carriage to take us around the city today. At three o'clock today, we will be able to board the Royal Princess Steam Ship once again. The ship will be fueled and ready to set sail to Charleston, South Carolina, this evening. I am most anxious to check on the Arabian horses and see if they are adjusting well.”

“I sincerely hope they are adjusting well, my Lord and I am also eager to get to Charleston. It has been a while since I saw my Aunt and cousins,” Lord Atticus commented in between delicious bites of hot cakes and ham. "It is like I said before Lord Atticus, I am here to help you with your family in Charleston in any way that I can. Rest assured; between the two of us, they will be in safe hands, my Lord," the Earl reassured him.

The sky was a deep shade of blue today, with a few white puffy clouds lingering around. The cobblestone streets of Baltimore were much more crowded than usual today. They were filled with more visitors than normal. Many folks were in town, ready to board the Royal Princess sailing to Charleston that evening. The Earl and Lord Atticus had already settled into their staterooms and met one another below deck where the horse stalls were located. The Earl was the first to arrive at the stall of the Arabian horses. He brought some apples that Jackson had purchased at the market earlier that day with him. He slowly walked over to the stall where the black stallion stood, glaring out at him. After a couple of attempts, he managed to calm the stallion. The Earl immediately began to rub his coat and extended his palm downward with an apple he had in his coat pocket. The black stallion devoured the apple and allowed the Earl to rub his coat once again. When the Earl reached into his pocket once again for another apple and looked up, he saw Lord Atticus standing beside him. "I can't keep my eyes off this black beauty of a horse, my Lord. He is as dark as night, and his coat is as shiny as silk," commented Lord Atticus with pride in his voice. "That is brilliant what you just said, Lord Atticus," replied the Earl. "What did I say," asked Lord Atticus. "You have just come up with the perfect name for the stallion. We shall call him the 'Dark

Knight!'" the Earl declared enthusiastically. "Well, I have to admit, I certainly do like that name, my Lord," Lord Atticus agreed.

"Then it is settled, Lord Atticus, his name is Dark Knight," the Earl confirmed. A moment later, Lord Atticus took the apple from the Earl, placed his hand palm down with the apple on it, and fed it to the Dark Knight. He continued to rub his shiny coat while the Earl walked over to another stall where he could set his eyes on the white Arabian mare. He reached inside his pocket, pulled out another apple, and placed it in his hand, palm down. The mare nosed the Earls hand and eagerly ate the apple. He rubbed her solid white coat and noticed how much more affectionate she was compared to Dark Knight. He knew that he had made the right decision when he decided to purchase the mare. She was a beauty, and there was no doubt in his mind that she would breed some mighty fine-looking Arabian horses. "I can't think of a name for this white mare, Lord Atticus," said the Earl. "But I'm sure we will think of something soon," he added optimistically.

The following days on the Royal Princess seemed to pass by rather quickly. The Earl and Lord Atticus spent most of their time below deck with the Arabian horses when they were not enjoying card games, drinking brandy, and engaging in small talk with the captain of the ship and some noble passengers. Unfortunately, Lady Claudia Townsend and her sister, Lady Mary, were not on the ship. They stayed in Baltimore, visiting other royal members of the Townsend family. After spending their first evening back on the ship, the Earl and Lord Atticus realized how much they had enjoyed Lady Claudia and Lady Mary's company. But they both knew they would see them again. After all, the Townsend family was part of the London elite. The Earl knew that he shouldn't even be thinking about spending time with other ladies since he was supposed to marry Lady Anne, but he was thinking about other ladies and he couldn't seem to change that.

"Ah, there you are, my Lord. I've been looking everywhere for you," said Lord Atticus as he was trying to catch his breath. "I just finished speaking with the captain Lord Atticus. We are only a few hours away from Charleston. They sent a messenger around the ship to inform the passengers to get ready to depart the Royal Princess in a few hours from now," the Earl explained. "Let us go now and check to see if Jackson and Mobley have received the news. After that, we could go check on the horses and make sure everything is okay since we will be departing the ship once we dock in Charleston."

After the Earl and Lord Atticus found Jackson and Mobley, they made sure everything was in order for them to depart the ship soon and went to check on the horses. The Earl was very pleased with the care the ship's grooms were providing for the horses. When they dock in Charleston, the Earl and Lord Atticus would only be departed from the ship for a few hours. Once they visited the home of Harry Braxton and his wife Lucy, they would be returning to the Royal Princess Steam Ship with Lady Elizabeth Braxton, her daughter Nicolette, and her son Daniel.

The Braxton family had been staying with Lady Elizabeth's late husband's brother, Harry, for the past several days after selling their family home. The letter that Lord Atticus and his family received while he and Lady Anne were visiting the Mayfield family. It also mentioned that the tailor shop, which was owned by Thomas Braxton and then handed down to his son Daniel, was recently sold as well. The letter further stated that Lady Elizabeth owned one of the finest seamstress shops in all of Charleston. She and her daughter Nicolette designed and created the loveliest gowns in the city, although the war had taken its toll on both their business and their lives.

Lord Atticus couldn't help but feel somewhat anxious about seeing the Braxton family since the decease of Thomas Braxton. But he knew that he and the Earl would do everything in their power to ensure their safety back to England. There, for a moment, Lord Atticus pondered about what Nicolette and Daniel might look like now. He remembered Nicolette with her blonde plaited hair, big blue eyes, and a young girl who was not yet a woman. And Daniel was the younger of the two but the most well-behaved.

"It shouldn't be much longer now before the ship should be sailing into the port of Charleston," the Earl said to Lord Atticus while he was standing on the top deck looking out to sea. "I agree my Lord; it does look as if we are inching closer to this lovely city. But I have to admit I am somewhat skeptical of what devastation we shall see from the aftermath of the war," Lord Atticus added with a frown.

"I feel the same as you, Lord Atticus. But don't you remember a while ago that news of General Sherman's invasion of Columbia and Charleston, South Carolina, traveled all the way to England? There was news that Sherman spared Charleston. Rumors had it that Sherman had a soft spot in his heart for the city because he spent time in the city when he was stationed at Fort Moultrie in the 1840s, and rumor has it that he enjoyed all the times he had spent there. But it won't be long before we shall see it with our own eyes, Lord Atticus," said the Earl as he placed his hand on his forehead so he could cover his eyes as he kept starring out into the open sea.

Both gentlemen just stood there in silence as the steamship gently glided over the waves of the sea. The ship was now getting closer to the harbor, located between the Ashley River and the Cooper River, and they could see that the remaining forts and batteries had been evacuated after the city's recent surrender. The Earl broke the silence between them when he said out loud, "It looks as if there are more passengers on board the ship than I had even realized, Lord Atticus. It appears that they are all on the top deck, anxious to see this lovely city as much as we are anxious, my Lord."

"It is extremely noisy here, my Lord. I can barely hear what you are saying. Of course, I did have my attention elsewhere for a moment," replied Lord Atticus. "Where was your attention, Lord Atticus, or should I ask?" the Earl inquired with a raised eyebrow. "My attention, my Lord, happens to be only a few feet away. I'm surprised you haven't noticed before me. Please turn around and look over there where I am pointing my finger," Lord Atticus suggested, pointing discreetly. The Earl turned around and saw four lovely ladies standing in the crowd. There was an older lady and three younger ladies dressed in elegant gowns, and it appeared as if they were of noble descent. The Earl and Lord Atticus looked at each other and it was as if they could read each other's mind when they both started walking towards the ladies. But before they reached the ladies they stopped walking when they saw a young gentleman approach the ladies and take one of the younger ladies by her hand and lead her away. Afterward, the Earl and Lord Atticus approached the remaining ladies and introduced themselves with a pleasant demeanor. "Good morning, ladies," said the Earl in a deep, masculine voice. "I hope you are finding your morning thus far to be as pleasant as mine?" the Earl continued. "Good morning to you as well, and we are finding our day to be most pleasant," replied the lady in the gold satin gown and bonnet with the shiny copper hair.

"Please let me introduce myself," said the Earl with a slight smile on his handsome face. "I am Lord Austin Mayfield, and this is my friend, Lord Atticus Ashton," he continued, gesturing to his companion. All three ladies bobbed a curtsy towards them and began to introduce themselves. The older lady, Julia Devereux, is the mother of three lovely daughters and the wife of John Devereux. He was a famous architect and builder known for his designs in Charleston, South Carolina. Her eldest daughter, Elizabeth Devereux, had just walked away with her husband. The middle daughter with the copper hair was Charlotte Devereux, and the youngest daughter introduced herself as Emma Devereux. "It is my pleasure to make your acquaintance, ladies," said the Earl and Lord Atticus with a charming smile on their handsome faces. "Do I have your permission, ladies, to inquire about your trip on the Royal Princess Steam Ship," the Earl politely asked.

Charlotte was the first to answer the Earl as she stepped closer to him, "We have been to Baltimore, Maryland, visiting with my mother's family, Lord Mayfield, and now we are back home in Charleston where our father and the rest of us will come back on board to sail to London, England when the ship sets sail from Charleston tomorrow evening. We will be staying with Lord Chamberlain and his family while we are in London. Lord Chamberlain is a good friend of my father, John Devereux and they both are horse breeders and participants of horse racing. I sincerely hope that my answer satisfies your curiosity, Lord Mayfield," she concluded earnestly. "I am pleased to say that you have most graciously satisfied my curiosity, Miss Devereux," the Earl acknowledged with appreciation. "Now it is my turn to ask you the same question, Lord Mayfield. Will you be staying here in Charleston, or will you be sailing to England?" she inquired. The Earl stared into her lovely hazel eyes and said in a deep voice, "Lord Atticus and I will be sailing home to England once we take care of a most important matter that we came here to do Miss Devereux. I sincerely hope that you and your family have a pleasant and safe trip, Miss Devereux. Lord Atticus and I will be honored if our paths cross once again."

As soon as the Earl and Lord Atticus stepped off the ship, they spotted Jackson and Mobley up ahead. They quickened their pace so they could catch up with them. Their groomsman noticed a coachman up ahead who was motioning for them to come to the carriage that was waiting to escort them to Harry Braxton's home. Once they caught up with one another, they hurried to the carriage and set off their way to meet up with the Braxton family. When the Earl glanced out the window of the carriage, he noticed the streets of the city near where the ship was docked were crowded. But when the carriage turned the corner onto the next street, he detected the faint smell of gunpowder and noted how empty the street looked. He observed a few Union soldiers occupying the empty streets but there were no Confederate soldiers left in the city. The captain of the ship had informed the Earl and Lord Atticus during one of their few trips to the captain's station that the Confederate soldiers were ordered to evacuate on February 18 this year. There were no Confederate soldiers left in Charleston except for the wounded, who were either in the hospital or with their family and friends.

The next street over was Meeting Street, and that was where the carriage slowly pulled up in front of a lovely two-story brick home with large white columns on the front porch of the lovely home. Lord Atticus and the Earl stepped out of the carriage onto the sidewalk located in front of the home. They stretched their arms and legs briefly for a moment and began walking towards the front door. Before they even knocked at the door, it opened, and there stood a gentleman who looked as if he was the Braxton family butler. "Please come follow me, my Lords. I will escort you to the drawing room where the Braxton family is waiting on your arrival," the butler said. Upon entering the drawing room, they were greeted by a rather tall gentleman with light brown and slightly gray hair. "It is a pleasure to see you once again, Lord Atticus. It has been a while since our last visit with you and your family," said Harry Braxton as he stepped forward to give Lord Atticus a warm, friendly hug. "Who is this gentleman you brought with you, my Lord," Harry politely asked Lord Atticus. Before Lord Atticus made his introduction of the Earl, he quickly glanced around the room and saw Harry's wife.

He saw his cousin Daniel and Lady Elizabeth Braxton, but he did not see his cousin Nicolette. "This gentleman happens to be my friend, the Earl of Primrose. I would like to introduce you to Lord Austin Mayfield. Lord Austin I would like for you to meet the Braxton family of Charleston," Lord Atticus announced. "It is a pleasure to make your acquaintance," said the Earl as he took his seat in a chair beside Lord Atticus. "I would like to extend my deepest sympathy to all of you for the tragic loss of your loved one. I promised Lord Atticus I would be honored to help in any way I can," the Earl expressed solemnly. "We are most grateful to have the Ashton family willing to open up their home to me and my children. Now I am also grateful for your kindness as well, Lord Mayfield," softly spoke Lady Elizabeth as she smoothed out a large wrinkle in her black satin gown. "I want to personally thank you, Lord Atticus, for taking the time to come here and help us have a safe trip to England. Our trunks and other baggage are ready and waiting on the Braxton family carriage that will escort us to the ship," she continued. "Daniel, my son, would you please go tell your sister that her cousin has arrived and we are ready to leave?" she asked. "Yes, Mother, I will go tell Nicolette that we will be leaving soon," quietly replied Daniel with a rather puzzled look on his face. The Earl stood from his chair and told Lord Atticus that he would step outside and inform Jackson and Mobley to help the coachman load some of the Braxton belongings on the carriage that they rode herein. "That way, we will all have plenty of room to ride in both carriages," he explained.

When the Earl stepped out onto the walkway in front of the home, he heard voices coming from a lovely courtyard on the side of the large home. Once he informed the groomsmen to help with the baggage, he decided to walk quietly toward the small courtyard from where he heard the noise. When he got closer to a wrought iron gate that entered the courtyard, he heard soft feminine laughter. Looking a little closer, he saw a lovely young lady with light blonde hair who appeared to be about his age and a young lad dressed in a somewhat modest gray tailored suit. He saw the young gentleman put his arm around the lady and lower his head so he could give her a kiss. A moment later, he heard a meow and felt something rub against his leg. When he looked down he saw a large cinnamon and white fluffy cat at his feet. The Earl immediately hid behind a huge evergreen tree, but it was too late to hide. When he looked up, he found himself gazing into the bluest eyes her ever seen. Her eyes resembled those of a goddess, who must have emerged from the blue Mediterranean Sea.

He stood there frozen as if he were a statue. He couldn't move or speak for a moment. She leaned over, scooped the cat into her arms, and asked the Earl with a soft, angry tone, "Who are you, and why are you here? I shall have you arrested for trespassing and spying on me." As the Earl began to speak, he glanced into the courtyard and noticed the young gentleman was still standing there waiting for him to identify himself. "Please rest assured, lady, you do not have to have me arrested. My name is Lord Austin Mayfield, and I have traveled here from England with my friend Lord Atticus," he explained calmly. "Well, there you are, my Lord. I can see that you have met my cousin Miss Nicolette Braxton," said Lord Atticus when he swiftly walked up beside the Earl and Nicolette. "Hello Nicolette," said Lord Atticus as he placed a kiss on the top of her hand that wasn't holding the fluffy cat. "It is a pleasure to see you again. It has been a while since we last saw one another. I must say you are even lovelier than you were before, cousin." When Nicolette started to speak, the Earl glanced over in the courtyard and noticed the young gentleman who was standing there moments ago slipping out the back gate of the courtyard. The Earl decided to remain silent and not mention the gentleman he had seen kissing Nicolette.

"It is a pleasure to see you again, Lord Atticus, but the truth is that I'm not happy about leaving Charleston. I do realize the war has caused my family more heartache than we should have to endure, especially the loss of my father. But I shall miss all my dear friends and family that are left here. Although I am grateful to you and your family for being so kind to us in our time of need, my

Lord," softly replied Nicolette with a note of sadness in her voice. "My family and I are more than glad to help Nicolette. After all, that's what families do for one another. But I do understand your hesitation to leave your home but give it a little time, my dear. I believe that you will find your new home in England to be most satisfactory. So I've been standing here wanting to ask you, Nicolette. Is that your cat you are holding in your arms? I believe, if I'm correct, his name is Biscuit, and he was a small kitten the last time I saw him," Lord Atticus commented. "You are correct, Lord Atticus. This is my cat Biscuit, and I am surprised you remember his name. I must take him inside now and leave him here with my aunt and uncle. I shall miss him dearly, Lord Atticus," Nicolette spoke with a sad look on her face. The Earl, who had been standing there listening to the conversation between Lord Atticus and Nicolette, cleared his throat and asked Nicolette out loud, "Why don't you take Biscuit to England with you, Miss Braxton?" The Earl's sudden question startled her for a moment, and when she glanced into his sapphire blue eyes, she began to tremble.

She thought he was probably the most handsome gentleman she had ever seen and could hardly catch her breath to speak. "I suppose I would love to take Biscuit with me to England, Lord Mayfield, but Mother and I thought that it might cause some inconvenience for you and your family, Lord Atticus," Nicolette explained. "Nonsense," said Lord Atticus out loud. "This idea that the Earl just mentioned is an excellent idea," he added. "Why thank you both," kindly replied Nicolette. "I shall go and inform my mother that I will be taking Biscuit with us. You don't have to walk around to the front to enter the house, my lords. Just follow me through the garden, and we shall go inside the back door entrance to the home, and I shall be ready to leave soon." When they got inside, the Earl and Lord Atticus remained in the drawing room with Harry and his wife while the Braxton family were making sure they had everything packed and ready to take with them. Nicolette found her mother looking into a mirror in her mother's bedroom chamber when she walked into the room. "Mother, I want to let you know that we are taking Biscuit with us to England. It is Lord Mayfield and Lord Atticus's idea. I did not have to ask," Nicolette informed her. "Well, this is excellent news, my dear. I know that you don't want to leave him behind, and the truth is neither do I, Nicolette," her mother responded. "I must hurry, Mother, and go to my bed chamber now so I can make sure that I do not leave anything behind," Nicolette said, starting to leave. When Nicolette walked into her chamber, she looked around before heading straight to her vanity, where she could look into the mirror. She set Biscuit down on the floor beside the vanity and stared into the mirror.

She couldn't help but notice a curl that had fallen down, so she placed another pin on her light blonde hair. Looking down at the vanity table, she noticed her father's blue bell that he had kept on the counter inside his tailor shop. The customers would come into the shop and ring the blue bell when her father and Daniel were not in the front room of the shop. She remembered ringing the bell when she was a young girl because it had a lovely sound. She let out a sigh of relief when she saw the bell there. Obviously she forgot to put it in her trunks when she was packing her belongings.

She saw her drawstring purse on the vanity and decided to slip the blue bell inside her purse that she was carrying with her on the trip. *It will have to do for now until we get into our staterooms on the ship,* she thought to herself. Suddenly, she heard a knock at the chamber door, and her mother entered the room. "Are you ready to go downstairs, my dear," Lady Elizabeth asked Nicolette when she glanced down and saw Biscuit at her feet. Nicolette stood up, put on her bonnet gloves, and picked Biscuit up into her arms. "Could you please grab my purse, Mother, and place it on my arm? It has the bluebell inside of it because I forgot to pack it inside the trunk but I do want to take it with me," Nicolette requested. During that moment, all she could see in her head was a very tall black-haired Earl with sapphire blue eyes, and she could feel a slight tingle of desire as her cheeks began to blush.

It was noon when they heard the church bells ringing from Saint Michael Church as the Earl, Lord Atticus, and Daniel were stepping out of one of the carriages that stopped in front of the Meeting Street Café. The second carriage, escorting Lady Elizabeth, Nicolette, and most of their belongings, pulled up behind them. Lord Atticus and the Earl strolled over to help the ladies from the carriage. There was plenty of time to have lunch and a short visit with the nephew of Mr. Henri Ashford and the cousin of the late Jonathan Wagner of Baltimore, Maryland, before boarding the ship to England. They all enjoyed each other's company and a delicious meal at the café. The Earl sat on the other end of the table, far away from Nicolette. He was famished, and he didn't want any distractions. He almost groaned out loud when he admitted to himself that she was indeed a significant distraction.

She had a beauty like no other he ever knew. It was a beauty that came from deep down into her very soul. And those big blue eyes of hers mesmerized him to the point where he could be lost in her beauty for eternity. However, he knew that he had to avoid her as much as he could, but that was going to be impossible since they would be traveling on the same ship to England. She was the cousin of Lord Atticus, and he promised to help Lord Atticus with the safety and care of the Braxton family. While he was gulping down the last of his wine, he thought to himself. *Damn, how in the world am I going to manage to get through these next two weeks sailing on the Royal Princess Steam Ship with this lovely goddess? I am certain that Lord Atticus will inform Nicolette of the marriage arrangement between his sister, Lady Anne, and me. Then maybe she won't notice when I can't keep my eyes off her lovely body because she will know that I have been promised to another.* "Are you ready to leave, my Lord," anxiously asked Lord Atticus to the Earl. "We shall go for a short visit with Jack Ashford since he is expecting us around 2 O'clock today," the Earl responded.

When they arrived at the Ashford home, the men gathered in the drawing room while Nicolette and her mother waited in the front parlor of the lovely two-story home. The gentlemen discussed the cotton industry. Now that the war was winding down, they discussed the shipping of cotton to England since the Earl's and Lord Atticus's fathers owned a cotton textile industry together back home in England. All the gentlemen in the room, along with Daniel, seem to have had hopes that, once again, the cotton industry would thrive now that the war was ending. It was getting close to the time for them to board the Royal Princess Steam Ship, so they said their goodbyes to Mr. Ashford, helped the ladies in the carriage and got into their own carriage. The sun was bright and warm in the afternoon sky as they boarded the ship. Daniel carried the wooden crate holding Biscuit, the cat. Lord Atticus and the Earl ensured the ladies found their staterooms while Jackson and Mobley made sure their belongings were safely on board and placed inside their rooms. Once Daniel was settled into his stateroom, he brought Biscuit the cat to Nicolette. She immediately opened the wooden crate with the holes in it and set Biscuit free. She stretched across her wooden bed, allowed Biscuit to lie down on the bed beside her, and she fell fast asleep dreaming of a man with sapphire blue eyes.

CHAPTER 4

April-May 1865

"N icolette!.." Said Lady Elizabeth, "Nicolette, you awake, my dear? It is time to get ready to go to the dining room for the evening meal," asked Lady Elizabeth as she hurried into Nicolette's stateroom. Nicolette slowly opened her sleepy blue eyes upon hearing her mother's call. "What time is it, Mother? I must have fallen asleep." Nicolette glanced around the room and noticed that Biscuit wasn't there. "Where is Biscuit's mother? Do you see him anywhere?" Nicolette asked. "While you were sleeping, your brother and I quietly entered the room and took Biscuit below deck so he could be taken care of along with the other animals, my dear," Lady Elizabeth explained gently. "I certainly hope they will take good care of him, Mother," Nicolette expressed with a hopeful tone.

"You need not worry, my dear; Lord Atticus informed me that Lord Mayfield has hired the best grooms in England to sail with him on this trip," Lady Elizabeth responded. "And why would he do that, pray tell," asked Nicolette as she stared into the vanity mirror near her bed. "Because, my dear, it has come to my attention that the Earl purchased two Arabian horses in Baltimore,

Maryland, when this ship docked there several days ago. The horses are below deck in their stalls and Lord Mayfield's grooms are taking care of them. Lord Atticus and Daniel took Biscuit below deck, and the Earl requested his grooms to look after Biscuit," Lady Elizabeth reassured.

"Well, I must say, Mother that is very kind of the Earl to have his groom take care of him, but Biscuit belongs here with me, and I shall let him know that as soon as possible," Nicolette declared firmly. "That won't be necessary, my dear. Biscuit will have to stay below deck with the other animals. Those are the rules, Nicolette," Lady Elizabeth stated flatly. "Whose rules, Mother? Are they Lord Mayfield's rules?" Nicolette questioned sharply. "No, they are the captain's rules, my dear," Lady Elizabeth clarified.

"I hope you remembered to put the jasmine oil in my bath water, Mother?" Nicolette asked hopefully. "You have no idea how glad I am that you decided that it's time we get out of these black mourning gowns, Mother. I still miss my father more than ever, but I need some color. I honestly believe my skin is beginning to look as dull as these gowns I've been wearing for so long. Why don't I wear my sapphire blue silk gown that is low cut and has off the shoulder puffy sleeves? What do you think, Mother? I don't want to go too bold with color right away," she asked, looking hopeful. "I think the sapphire blue gown will be perfect for this evening, my dear. After all, tonight is the captain's ball, and you wanted to look your best," replied Lady Elizabeth as she was getting Nicolette's gown out from the armoire. "I shall return soon, my dear and help you get ready for the ball. I am going to my room now to bathe and I shall return with my gown and accessories so you can help me get ready as well. I think I shall wear my cornflower blue gown that we designed and made at our seamstress shop before we had to sadly let it go. I must hurry and leave now. I shall be back soon, dear," Lady Elizabeth announced briskly.

It is almost as if there was a sprinkle of magic in the air that evening. The gas lanterns on the Royal Princess Steam Ship seemed to glow a bit brighter than usual, and the sea air appeared to be much clearer, too. All the passengers that were invited to attend the captain's ball were dressed in their finest apparel and there appeared at the top of the list was none other than the Earl and Lord Atticus. The Earl looked so handsome wearing his midnight blue long-tail coat suit with trousers to match, and Lord Atticus looked just as striking in his black long-tail coat suit and trousers that matched his coat. The Earl stood near the bar that was set up for the passengers in the ballroom, enjoying his brandy.

He was glad that the evening meal was over because sitting at the same table with Nicolette and trying to avoid looking at her was absolute torture. Fortunately, she made it much easier for him to avoid her because she barely spoke or looked at him during the evening meal. He knew that she was still a bit angry with him after finding him hiding behind that evergreen tree, spying on her, and that young gentleman kissing in the courtyard. He also knew that the gentleman he saw was probably the real reason she didn't want to leave her home. "There you are, Lord Mayfield," said Daniel as he stepped beside the Earl. "Hello, Daniel," spoke the Earl as he watched Nicolette and Lady Elizabeth walking towards him. "I hope you are enjoying your evening so far, my ladies," said the Earl as he stared at how lovely they both looked in their beautiful blue gowns. Before they could even answer the Earl, Lord Atticus quickly stepped in front of Nicolette and asked her if she would like to dance. The orchestra began to play one of the most popular waltz tunes of the time. The Earl stood there, watching as Lord Atticus took his cousin by the hand and led her to the dance floor. Moments later, Lady Devereux and her two daughters, Charlotte and Emma, approached the Earl, who then introduced them to Lady Elizabeth Braxton and Daniel. The Earl asked Charlotte to dance, and Daniel asked Emma to dance while Lady Devereux and Lady Elizabeth remained standing there engaging in conversation with one another.

Once the waltz ended, everyone stayed on the dance floor and exchanged partners. The Earl and Nicolette suddenly became partners, as did Lord Atticus and Charlotte. When the Earl took Nicolette by the hand, her body began to tremble slightly. She hoped he wouldn't notice, but it was too late as he stared into her big blue eyes with those sapphire blue eyes of his and told her to relax. Now, he kind of wished that he hadn't said that to her because he could tell she was agitated with him. This state of agitation didn't flatter her complexion, but it did enhance the swell of her ample bosom. He could see that she was amply endowed everywhere, actually. There were generous curves pulled against the blue silk of her gown. Nicolette was the first to break the silence when suddenly she spoke in a soft feminine voice, "I will feel much more relaxed, Lord Mayfield, when you feel the need to apologize to me for hiding behind that tree and spying on me. I know that you saw George and me kissing, but you chose not to mention that to Lord Atticus. Why is that, my Lord?"

"All I can say about the matter, Miss Braxton, is that I do apologize for spying on you since I obviously allowed my curious mind to get the best of me and for that, I am truly sorry. But my choice not to mention it to Lord Atticus or anyone else was because I believe if the shoe were on the other foot, Miss Braxton, you would choose to do the same," the Earl explained. "But you do not yet know me, my Lord, so how can you be sure that I would not tell?" Nicolette challenged. "I know your kind, Miss Braxton?" the Earl stated confidently. "And what is my kind, my Lord?" Nicolette inquired curiously. "You are like me, Miss Braxton. No one tells the Earl what he can and can not do," the Earl declared. And then for a brief moment when the music stopped, he saw a mischievous smile on her lovely face when she bobbed a slight curtsy and swiftly left the dance floor.

The rest of the evening, before all the ladies retired to their staterooms for the evening, the Earl and Nicolette succeeded in avoiding one another as much as possible. The Earl chose to dance one more time that evening, and he chose to dance with Miss Charlotte Devereux. He couldn't help but notice Nicolette glancing his way once or twice while he was swirling Miss Devereux around the dance floor. After that, he noticed her dancing with Charlotte's brother, James and the only son of the Devereux family. While they were swirling around the dance floor with their partners, the Earl thought he heard Nicolette laugh out loud. *Damn,* he thought to himself, even her sweet laughter aroused his desire for her. *For Heaven's sake, how am I going to survive this trip home?*

There were a few new faces in the gentlemen's room, where they drank their whisky, smoke cigars and played their card games. The captain's ball was beginning to wind down, and most of the passengers started to retire to their staterooms for the evening. The Earl and Lord Atticus both were not having good luck in their card games that evening so they decided to retire to their rooms earlier than usual. They both had mentioned to each other that they were rather tired and sleepy. After all, they agreed it had been a long and eventful day. When the Earl finally crawled into his bed, he thought about the lovely Nicolette. He imagined how he would love to touch her rosy cheeks and kiss her luscious lips. But then he thought about Lady Anne and their marriage arrangement and how the prospect of fulfilling his father and Lord Ashton's wishes made him feel so uncomfortable. If he had his way, he would forget about ladies altogether for now and totally focus on the Arabian horses. But he knew that once he returned to Primrose Estate, Lady Anne would want to visit him again soon. *Well, I'm not going to think about that right now*, so instead, he fell fast asleep dreaming about a lovely goddess with big blue eyes.

"Daniel, will you please take me below deck after we finish eating our breakfast? I miss Biscuit, and I am sure he misses me," asked Nicolette in her most persuasive tone of voice. "I'm almost finished eating," replied Daniel. "Are you ready to go now, Nicolette?"

"That sounds like a wonderful idea, Nicolette," said Lady Elizabeth. "Would you like to come along, Mother," Nicolette responded. "No, dear, you go with Daniel. I promised Mrs. Devereux and her daughters that we would visit with them this morning. You can always join us later, my dear," Lady Elizabeth suggested. "Okay, Mother, I shall join you and the Devereux ladies in the gathering room after I go below deck to visit with Biscuit," Nicolette confirmed. She quickly followed Daniel down the stairs to where the animals were kept. When they reached their destination, she noticed large wooden crates scattered around and the sound of dogs barking here and there. When she and Daniel walked toward the back of the large area, they saw small horse stalls and stacks of hay lined up against the wall. The whole room gave the appearance of an upscaled country barn.

She couldn't keep her curiosity; she wanted to peek inside the horse stables. Daniel had mentioned that the Earl had two Arabian horses in the stalls, but she was anxious to see Biscuit right now. "There you are, Biscuit. I am so happy to see you again," said Nicolette as she reached into the small wooden stall where Biscuit was meowing. "I surely hope they are taking good care of you." Before she could say another word, she turned her head when she heard the deep masculine voice of Lord Mayfield. "You need not worry, Miss Braxton; my grooms are taking excellent care of Biscuit," Lord Mayfield reassured. "I am not worried, Lord Mayfield. I can see for myself that Biscuit has been well taken care of by your grooms. There is no doubt that I am truly grateful, my lord," Nicolette thanked gracefully. "Would you please excuse me, Miss Braxton? I must check on my Arabian horses," said the Earl as he quietly walked towards the stall of the Dark Knight. Nicolette stood there for a moment, holding Biscuit in her arms as she watched the Earl walk towards the horse stalls.

She couldn't help but notice how handsome he looked this morning without the usual long tailcoat suit. He wore a simple white tailored linen shirt with buttons undone to show off his bronze muscular chest, brown trousers and brown boots. Yet, even dressed in simple attire, she thought he still appeared as charming and arrogant as ever. Suddenly, Nicolette handed Biscuit to Daniel and asked him, "Will you please put Biscuit back into the crate for now? I would like to see the Earl's Arabian horse, Daniel. You do know how much I love horses and how much I cried when we had to sell my horse," Nicolette requested. "Yes, I will go with you to see the horses, Nicolette," replied Daniel. "I am sure the Earl won't mind."

"I don't care if he does mind. I shall go see them anyway," replied Nicolette in a rather sarcastic voice. When they reached the horse stall of the Dark Knight, they noticed the Earl inside the stall, standing beside his groom, combing the horse's shiny black coat.

Nicolette caught her breath for a moment when she first set eyes on the Arabian horse. "You have yourself a magnificent horse, my lord," softly spoke Nicolette. "I must agree with you, Miss Braxton. I am a most fortunate man to have found him." replied the Earl as he handed the curry comb to his groom and led the Dark Knight towards the opening of the stall. Nicolette stood outside the door of the stall, and the Earl handed her a carrot. She opened her hand palm down and the Dark Knight nosed her hand and quickly ate the carrot. Then she began to gently rub the Dark Knight, and the Earl could sense her fondness for the animal. He was close enough to her that he smelled that same fragrance he had noticed the previous evening when he had the pleasure of dancing with her.

At first, he wasn't sure what scent he smelled until he remembered the Jasmine flowery shrubs that grow in the gardens at Primrose Estate during the warmer months. He remembered, as a boy, that the scent of the Jasmine shrubbery was among his favorites and to smell it on her was intoxicating. But it wasn't just her scent that was intoxicating; the mere sight of her was just as overpowering. He thought she looked so lovely in her modest ivory gown, with her hair platted and falling down her slender back. "I hear that you have another Arabian horse, my lord," said Nicolette when she gazed into the sapphire blue eyes of the Earl. "Yes I do have another Arabian horse in the next stall over. Would you like to see my mare, Miss Braxton?" She nodded her head and replied, "Yes, I would love to see your mare, my lord. Please lead the way?" The Earl handed the reins to the groom and led Nicolette and Daniel to see the mare. When they arrived at the stall where the mare was located, she walked over to them, and the Earl handed Nicolette another carrot. The mare quickly ate the carrot, and Nicolette began to softly rub her head. "She is a beauty, Lord Mayfield, but I am wondering if she has a name yet," asked Daniel as he was standing there admiring the mare's beauty. "I know that you named your stallion Dark Knight, but I have not heard of a name for this mare, my lord."

Suddenly, Nicolette looked down and saw Biscuit at her feet. As she leaned over to pick him up, she dropped the drawstring purse that she was holding on her arm onto the straw-covered floor. Lord Atticus quickly appeared and leaned over to pick up Nicolette's purse. "There is a small wooden box lying on the straw that must have fallen out of your purse, Nicolette. I shall pick that up for you as well," said Lord Atticus. "I am sorry that Biscuit got away from me when I went to check on him earlier." When Lord Atticus leaned over to pick the small wooden box up, it came open, and a small blue bell fell out into the straw. "Why do you have a bell in your purse," Both the Earl and Lord Atticus curiously asked Nicolette simultaneously as they stood there staring at the bluebell. "Oh, for heaven's sake, I forgot to take the bell out of my purse when we first went aboard the ship yesterday. It belongs to my father and he used it in his tailor shop so the customers could ring the bell when he or Daniel was not in the front room of the shop. I have always loved this blue bell since I was a young girl," Nicolette explained. "I did wonder what happened to the bell, Nicolette," happily remarked Daniel. "I am relieved to see that you brought it with you, Nicolette." As Lord Atticus started to hand the bell to Nicolette, he began to ring it, and everyone glanced over at the white mare and noticed that her ears had begun to flare, and sounds were coming from her mouth as if she were talking. Everyone began to laugh out loud but quickly stopped laughing when Nicolette suddenly blurted out loud, "We can call her Blubelle Lord Mayfield!" The Earl stood there in silence for a moment, along with everyone else, before suddenly replying, "If you think that should be the name for my Arabian mare, Miss Braxton, then I shall call her Blubelle. What do you think about this name, gentleman?" Lord Atticus and Daniel both nodded their heads in agreement with the name Blubelle.

Nicolette continued to rub Blubelle and Daniel took Biscuit back to his wooden stall. Lord Atticus excused himself to go look over some important business papers that were given to him when they visited Henri Ashford's nephew in Charleston. Daniel returned and asked Nicolette if she was ready to leave now. The Earl noticed that Nicolette did not answer Daniel right away and she continued to give her attention to Blubelle. "I will be glad to escort you to wherever it is you need to be, Miss Braxton. It appears that you are rather fond of Blubelle and want to spend more time with her," said the Earl as he quietly opened the stall door and allowed Nicolette to enter the stall. Nicolette picked up a curry comb and began to comb Blubelle's shiny white coat and said to Daniel, "Please tell Mother that Lord Mayfield will see to it that I will be joining her soon." Daniel thanked Lord Mayfield and headed to the top deck. He couldn't help but notice the way that Lord Mayfield looked at Nicolette and the way she blushed every time their eyes met. He remembered Lord Atticus telling him about the marriage arrangement between the Earl and his sister, Lady Anne, last evening. Even though Lord Mayfield has not officially asked for Lady Anne's hand in marriage, he knew that it was inevitable. Lord Atticus mentioned that the Earl did not want to disappoint his father, Lord James Mayfield or Lady Anne's father, Lord Gerald Ashton. Daniel knew that he was going to have to inform Nicolette of this recent news and pray that Nicolette would keep her proper distance from the Earl. But he wasn't sure about how the Earl was going to act around Nicolette. The only thing he did know for sure was that he was going to have to keep a keen eye on those two.

According to the captain of the ship, there were only a few days left before the Royal Princess would be sailing to the shore of England. The weather had been somewhat friendly until a couple of nights ago. There was a severe rainstorm out in the sea that came close enough to cause havoc for those on board. The passengers were confined to their stateroom for several hours until the storm was over. The rain left an abundant amount of water on the top deck, and no one was allowed to go there until the captain gave his approval and permission. Nicolette was relieved that the storm had passed, and she was able to leave her room. She admitted that she was rather frightened at times, but having her mother share the room with her the past couple of days helped her feel more secure. While she was getting ready to go to the dining room for breakfast this morning, she thought about what Daniel had told her several days ago before the storm hit so suddenly. It didn't surprise her at all to hear that the Earl was promised to another.

After making a few trips below deck to visit with Biscuit and stopping by the stalls to see the Earl's Arabian horses the past several days before the rain storm, she still trembled every time she was close to the Earl. Sometimes, he would invite her into Blubelle's stall and let her join him while they would rub and comb her shiny white coat. They didn't seem to have any difficulty striking up a conversation with one another. It appeared as if they had a lot more to talk about than she first thought, and on several occasions, he would make her laugh out loud. But one thing she couldn't quite picture in her mind was the Earl and her cousin, Lady Anne, together. If there were ever two people who didn't belong together it was those two. She could see the way the Earl would look at her when their eyes met. It was a look of desire that she had never seen before. Even her beau George back home never gave her that look before. At this point, she wasn't sure whether she should be excited or scared out of her whit. The latter is what she should be feeling, but she felt excitement every time she was near the Earl. While her mother was busy lacing her undergarments, she told herself, *if I could just turn this ship around and sail back home to Charleston into the arms of George and pretend that I never set eyes on Lord Mayfield, I will be set free of this feeling that has come over me. But I know that I will never feel free again now that the Earl has enlightened a desire in me that I never knew existed. To have such a feeling is undeniably wrong, so this will be my secret forever. God forbid!* "Are you wearing the gray silk gown hanging over the chair beside the bed? I will go get it for you, my dear.

"Nicolette! Nicolette! Are you listening my dear? You seem to be a million miles away."

"Oh sorry, Mother, my mind is elsewhere," replied Nicolette as she came back to reality. "Why, it's nothing important, Mother. It isn't anything you will be interested in."

"Well, whatever you say dear, but you know I will always be here to listen if you need me."

"I do know that Mother, but for now please hand me the gray silk gown and I will finish getting ready because I suddenly realized that I am famished."

When Nicolette, her mother and Daniel entered the private dining room for breakfast this morning, they noticed a larger crowd than usual. It was obvious to them that most passengers on board were grateful that they were not confined to their staterooms any longer since the storm had passed. Once they reached their usual table to take their seats, Nicolette noticed that the Earl and Lord Atticus were not seated at the table. When she glanced around the room, she saw that they were not present. Since she was famished this morning, she quickly ordered her usual breakfast and sat quietly while the others seated at their table engaged in polite conversation. They were mainly talking about their traumatic experiences with the recent horrendous rainstorm. Once their food arrived, she ate most of hers and still noticed that there was no sign of the Earl and Lord Atticus in the dining room. Daniel was the first to speak to her, "Are you planning on visiting Biscuit this morning, Nicolette? I will be glad to walk you there. I would like to check to see if Lord Atticus and the Earl need any help. I hear that the Earl's Arabian horses got quite a scare when that horrific rainstorm came a couple of days ago. I assume that they are with the horses now, and that is why they are not with us now."

"I am ready to go now if you are Daniel," anxiously replied Nicolette as she stood to her feet.

As soon as Daniel opened the large wooden crate that held Biscuit, he immediately jumped into the arms of Nicolette. She could tell that he had been well taken care of, but he seemed a bit shaky. There was no doubt that he was still slightly shaking from the storm, but she could feel that he was beginning to relax in her arms. So Nicolette decided to keep holding Biscuit in her arms when she walked over to the horse stalls. She saw the Earl in Blubelle's stall when she got there. She had already heard noises coming from Blubelle before she even got there. It was obvious that Blubelle seemed restless and nervous. Nicolette stopped in front of the stall and waited to see if the Earl noticed her presence. "Good morning, Miss Braxton. I am glad to see that you and Biscuit have safely survived the storm. And of course, I'm glad to see you as well Daniel," commented the Earl as his sapphire blue eyes stared right into the beautiful blue eyes of Nicolette. "Thank you, Lord Mayfield. Daniel and I can say the same about you, my lord," replied Nicolette with a slight tremble in her soft feminine voice. It had been a few days since the Earl and Nicolette last saw one another, and all he could stand there thinking about was how damn beautiful she looked with her hair pulled up in the front and long curls cascading around her shoulders and down her back. At that very moment, he wanted to sweep her into his arms, kiss her rosy lips and lay her down on the bale of hay near his feet. He shook his head and realized that it was a good thing that Daniel was there with them because he was tempted to follow through with his desire. It was as if everything that he had promised himself that he would not think or feel when he saw her again just flew out the window.

Blubelle began to move her head back and forth once again when she heard Nicolette's familiar voice. Nicolette quickly handed Biscuit to Daniel and slowly walked into the stall towards Blubelle. She began to rub and softly speak to her and the Earl stood back while Nicolette performed her magic on Blubelle. It was obvious to both the Earl and Daniel that Blubelle had settled down. She appeared to be much calmer than she was before. The Earl could see the close bond between Nicolette and Blubelle, and he didn't want it to end when they got back to England. He wanted Nicolette to visit Blubelle at Primrose Estate as often as she could, but he already knew one major obstacle standing in her way, and its name happened to be Lady Anne Ashton.

CHAPTER 5

May-June 1865

"Well, here we are once again, my lord," exclaimed Lord Atticus as he quietly entered the Earl's stateroom. "I hope you have plenty of brandy in your room, Lord Atticus," asked the Earl as he stretched his long masculine legs across the large settee on the other side of the room. "It looks as if we are not getting out of our staterooms anytime soon, so please go get yours; I am starting to run out of mine."

"I do happen to have plenty of whisky left, my lord. But before I leave to get it, I want to tell you that I spoke to one of the security police on my way to your room. He informed me that they had just arrested the person who pushed that gentleman overboard late last evening. Fortunately, they have an eyewitness who got away from the killer. The officer told me that the fight broke out late last night while the other passengers, who were not of nobility on the other side of the ship, were sleeping. As you are aware, those gentlemen have their own room where they drink whiskey and play card games since they do not join us gentlemen of nobility. It so happens that they have a thief and a cheater among them, and now a murderer. Even though they have the killer in custody, they want all the passengers on board to stay in their staterooms until tomorrow morning."

"Well, I'm certainly glad they have caught this scoundrel, and everyone can feel safe once again," replied the Earl as he stood on his feet suddenly. "I can certainly say this has been one hell of a trip, but the good news is that the captain of the ship informed me yesterday morning that we only have a couple of days left, and we will be able to see the coast of England soon."

"I can hardly wait, my lord," said Lord Atticus as he walked out of the room. "You are not the only one who feels that way, Lord Atticus. The sooner, the better." But then the Earl thought about the lovely Nicolette and the Arabian horses. He knew the horses would keep him busy when he got back home, but the thought of not seeing Nicolette the way he wanted to made him feel weak and vulnerable. So, he asked himself out loud, *Why should I even care? She is already aware of the marriage arrangement between Lady Anne and me,* and I know for certain that Nicolette is a lady of integrity, *and she will honor this arrangement between her cousin and me. Therefore, the question is how long I will be able to hold out before I have to honor this marriage arrangement.*

The Earl walked over to a small table and poured himself another small glass of brandy when he heard a soft knock on his door. "Who's there?" asked the Earl out loud. "It's me, my Lord," replied Lord Atticus. The Earl strode over to open the door, took the wooden box of brandy from Lord Atticus, and noticed Daniel standing there with him. They came into the room, and they sat down at the small table to play their card games, drank their whiskey and waited for their late evening meal to arrive. After a couple of hands of poker and realizing that Daniel was more skilled at playing cards than the Earl had initially thought, he had to fold this time.

So that left Lord Atticus and Daniel to play the game. "I believe it's time for me to go check on Mother and Nicolette," said Daniel, glancing at his father's gold pocket watch. "I promised I would keep an eye on them often since everyone has been feeling somewhat less secure these days."

"That sounds like an excellent idea, Daniel," suddenly said the Earl as he stood up from the table. "Since you and Lord Atticus need to finish this game, I will be glad to check on the ladies." Without giving Daniel a chance to respond, the Earl quickly walked over to a small dresser next to his armoire, grabbed a bottle of wine and a small basket of fruit and immediately left the room.

While the Earl was quietly walking towards Nicolette's stateroom, he suddenly decided to turn around and go to Lady Elizabeth's stateroom first. He knocked softly on Lady Elizabeth's door and stood there waiting for her response. "Is that you, Daniel?" asked Lady Elizabeth. "No, my Lady, it is Lord Mayfield. Daniel is in a card game with Lord Atticus, and I have come to inquire about your safety, Lady Elizabeth." Lady Elizabeth slowly opened her door and smiled at the Earl. "I am fine, my lord. I thank you kindly for checking on me, my lord."

"It is my pleasure, my lady. I hope you sleep well."

Well, that was easy enough, Earl thought as he walked towards Nicolette's stateroom. *I'm not so sure it will be that simple with the lovely Nicolette.* When the Earl stepped in front of the door at Nicolette's stateroom, he heard a feminine voice talking out loud and meowing sounds. He strained his ears and stood there as quietly as he could before he gently knocked on the door. "Who's there? Is that you, Daniel?"

"It's Lord Mayfield, Miss Braxton; I have come here to check on your safety. Daniel is with Lord Atticus in the middle of a card game. I took Daniel's place, and I am here now. Would you please come and open the door, my dear? I have something to give you."

"What do you have, my lord? Why don't you just leave it at my door?"

"You know I can't do that, Miss Braxton; we have many thieves that wander these hallways. Please open the door?"

"Alright, if you insist, I shall open the door," replied Nicolette while she was shoving Biscuit into her armoire and quickly closing the door to the armoire without realizing the door did not shut all the way. She quickly glanced into the mirror, combed her fingers through a few blonde curls and walked over to open her door.

When she slowly opened her door, the Earl had to catch his breath. It was as if he was staring at a lovely sea goddess who had just emerged from the depths of the open sea. Her modest Mediterranean blue gown was clinging to the curves of her body since she was not wearing all those crinolines and petticoats underneath her gown. There was no way he could escape this vision, as his masculine body was on fire. Nicolette broke the spell when she suddenly spoke to him, "As you can see for yourself, Lord Mayfield, I am doing just fine, and what have you brought with you, my lord?" Before the Earl could reply, he heard a soft yowling and felt something rub against his leg. When he looked down, he saw Nicolette bending over and picking up Biscuit. "Why is Biscuit here, Nicolette," asked the Earl with a smirk on his handsome face. "You know that it's against the rules to have him here, and he looks rather hungry."

"Well, I did feed him some of my evening meal earlier, but he didn't much like it. I was planning on taking him back earlier today but I couldn't catch the right opportunity to sneak him back down to the lower deck, my lord. Every time that we have to be confined to our staterooms and I don't visit with him too often, he gets nervous and shaky every time. I wanted him to feel safe here with me."

"I can see how you feel, Miss Braxton, but we have to take him below deck now; I will help you."

Nicolette walked over to her armoire, grabbed her cloak and tucked Biscuit inside her cloak while the Earl placed the bottle of wine and basket of fruit inside the door to her room. "Please come quietly and follow me, Miss Braxton; it appears that most everyone on board is soundly sleeping in their rooms as we speak?"

Once the Earl and Nicolette arrived at the large wooden crate that was Biscuit's temporary home, they let out a sigh of relief. The Earl walked over to where the food was kept for the animals and found some for Biscuit. He brought the food to Biscuit, and then he decided to go check on the Dark Knight and Blubelle while he was there. When the Earl and Nicolette quietly tiptoed over to the horse stalls, they heard loud snoring. It was one of the animal caretakers sleeping on a cot a few stalls down. Nicolette couldn't help but giggle out loud when they walked by the stall. Suddenly, the Earl turned around, placed a finger over her pink lips, and whispered shush. All she could manage to do was quietly look at him with those big blue eyes of hers and not say a word. But her body trembled slightly from the touch of his finger on her lips. Unfortunately, there wasn't anything she could do about it; he happened to have this effect on her. The only thing she could do was to not be alone with him now; she must get back to her stateroom as soon as possible. When they arrived in front of the stall of the Dark Knight, The Earl heard footsteps coming towards them. He grabbed Nicolette's hand and ran to the bales of hay over towards the wall and hid behind them.

When he peeped around the corner of a bale of hay neatly stacked on top of several bales, he saw the fellow that was recently sleeping and snoring was now walking towards them. The fellow glanced around the room and looked into the stalls, but he did not see anyone, so he started walking back to his cot, where he was sleeping. Slowly, the Earl pulled Nicolette down on the hay to sit beside him and waited until it was safe for them to leave. Before she could reach the hay, her foot tripped over the Earl's foot, and she tumbled down on top of him. Suddenly, they were face to face and eye to eye. He could feel the warmth of her breath, and he parted her luscious lips with his mouth. He placed his hand around her neck, and his tongue delved into her mouth. Suddenly, she let out a loud gasp and yielded her mouth to his warm kisses. And in an abrupt volcanic explosion, her whole world changed. These were not George's kisses that still lurked in her memory. This was not those wet, sloppy kisses that made her feel helpless and ashamed, but this kiss was different. This was a kiss that she had never felt before. Again and again, he pressed his lips to hers and then retreated. He could feel her responding, and it made him moan with pleasure. *Oh, this is dangerous. Delicious but dangerous,* he thought. Then she drew his lower lip into her mouth to mirror the way he gently sucked her upper lip. Then she gave herself over to complete sensation. It was a blissful, consuming sensation that made her body shiver and ache. She wanted to feel his hands on her body somewhere other than her neck. So, she continued to lie on top of him, pressing her body into the warmth of his body, and her breasts met the welcome resistance of his hard chest. And he rewarded her by sliding his hands from her neck to the small of her back, over the swell of her hips and all the way down to her buttocks, which he cupped firmly in both hands.

The pleasure that was sharp and intense ran through her body. He moaned out loud, "Nicolette." Then, once again, his tongue delved into her mouth, and he kissed her over and over again until she pulled away. She stared into his dark blue eyes and smiled as she suddenly burst to her feet. "Sorry, my lord, I do not know what has come over me! You belong to my cousin and I will not allow you to kiss me ever again." Before he could utter a single word, she ran away from him as fast as she could.

The following morning, Nicolette woke up suddenly when she heard a soft knock on her door. She slowly got up from her bed and let her mother walk into her stateroom. "Why are you not getting ready to go to the dining room for breakfast, my dear?" asked Lady Elizabeth with a rather concerned look on her lovely face. "Do you not feel well? I thought maybe you would want to be like all the other passengers and be glad that we are no longer confined to our staterooms. I can see that the sun is out this morning, and I thought you, Daniel and I could join Lord Atticus and the Earl on the top deck for a stroll and some fresh air after breakfast."

"Yes, Mother, I am not feeling quite myself this morning. I am feeling rather queasy in my stomach. It could have been something I ate, I suppose."

"Or you could be feeling seasick, my dear. Either way, I hope you feel better soon. I will attend breakfast and bring you something back to eat. I want you to get some rest, and if you feel better when I return later, then you can join us on top deck. I truly believe the fresh air will do you good, my dear." Lady Elizabeth walked over to the bed, kissed Nicolette on the cheek, and quietly left the room.

Nicolette slid down into her soft bed and pulled the covers away from her body. Her body was still feeling the heat of the Earl's warm kisses. She touched her swollen lips, and her body shuddered with both the feeling of shame and desire. But this morning, her mind was occupied with the feeling of guilt and remorse. *I shouldn't have allowed the Earl to kiss me, but the truth is I wanted him to kiss me. It is just as much my fault as it is his fault. How am I going to face him now, but worst of all, how am I going to face Lady Anne? I suppose I shall worry about that later, but for now, I'm not going to lay here and waddle in self-pity and fear. Even though he is the Earl of Primrose and I do not have a title, I do have royal blood running through my veins as well. I am ever bit the lady that Lady Anne appears to be and I shall not fear the Earl, Lady Anne or no one.*

Quickly, she hopped out of bed, walked over to her armoire, and chose a rose-colored lightweight linen gown with white lace and a few white pearls sewn into the fabric. She suddenly remembered the hot summer day back in Charleston, working in her mother's seamstress shop. It was the first time that her mother had allowed her to design a gown on her own. She remembered sitting on that pink chaise lounge in the back room of the shop with charcoal pencils in her hand and creating this rose-colored linen gown she was now holding in her hand. The summers were so hot in Charleston and she designed and created a gown that would compensate for the Charleston heat. She remembered feeling so proud that day when she finished sewing the last stitch in this gown. From that day forward, her mother allowed her to keep creating her designs, so therefore Nicolette designed a bonnet that matched the gown, and it was in one of the trunks beside the armoire. She chose a corset that her mother had once designed that lace in the front so she could go ahead and dress herself. Once she got that on, it was much easier to slide on her chemise, drawers and stockings. She walked over to her vanity and selected a few hairpins to place in her hair. Once she finished pulling her hair up away from her shoulders, she noticed how pale she looked. She decided to put some pink rouge on her pale cheeks and a drop of rose oil on her swollen lips. Remembering her mother mentioning that the sun was out today, she reached inside her armoire for a matching parasol. Now, she would sit and wait for her mother to come back. She still had a slight queasy feeling in her stomach, but she was ready to face the Earl of Primrose.

When her mother came back to her room, she expressed to her that she was glad to see that she was feeling better. She even commented on how lovely she looked compared to earlier. Her mother noticed that her cheeks were rosy and her face was not pale. While they waited for Daniel to come and escort them to the top deck where Lord Atticus and the Earl would be waiting for their arrival, Lady Elizabeth handed Nicolette a fruit turnover and insisted on her eating it. Nicolette ate as much as she could of the fruit turnover when they heard Daniel knock on the door. They left with Daniel and walked to the top deck where Lord Atticus and the Earl were waiting. For a moment Nicolette couldn't help but hoped maybe the Earl would not be there. Maybe he found an excuse not to be there, just like she found an excuse not to be there for breakfast this morning. But in an instant, that thought was pushed aside when she looked up ahead and saw him standing near the side rail, staring out at the sea. And the closer she got to the Earl, the more she could feel her heart pounding in her chest.

"I am delighted to see that you are able to join us on top deck this morning, Nicolette," said Lord Atticus when Nicolette, her mother and Daniel stepped up beside Lord Atticus and the Earl. "Lady Elizabeth informed us that you were not feeling well earlier this morning, my dear."

"You are correct, my lord," replied Nicolette as she tried not to look at the Earl standing right beside Lord Atticus. "I was feeling rather queasy in my stomach this morning, my lord, but I'm feeling much better now."

"Well, we are certainly glad you are feeling much better, Miss Braxton," said the Earl with a smug look on his handsome face. Before Nicolette could reply, Lady Elizabeth suddenly commented, "I believe the fresh air will do her good, Lord Mayfield; as a matter of fact, I think that the fresh sea air will do us all good. I am most eager to stroll around the ship now. Please lead the way, my lord?"

The rest of the morning appeared to go smoothly. The weather was certainly cooperative, with the sun peeping out among the white clouds every now and then. The breeze coming from the sea air felt rather welcoming at times since it was starting to feel much warmer as the morning was slipping away. Lord Atticus seemed to have taken over much of the conversation among them while the Earl and Nicolette remained much quieter than usual. When the

Earl did join in the conversation, he mostly directed it toward Lady Elizabeth. Meanwhile, Nicolette practically hung on to Lord Atticus as they strolled side by side. It was obvious to her that the Earl was trying to avoid contact with her as much as she was with him, and she felt relieved. Just having him near her made her feel all warm and tingly inside, but she knew it was wrong to feel what she was feeling and she was determined to get rid of these feelings once and for all. But she couldn't help but notice the way he stared at her from time to time, and she could see a look of desire in his sapphire blue eyes. For God's sake, she was desperately hoping that he could not see that same look of desire in her big blue eyes.

"Please help me look for the curry comb I was using yesterday to brush the Dark Knight Lord Atticus," the Earl asked while he was busy looking around the stall. "I have one here in my hand, but the one I can't find is my favorite one, and it seems to do a better job."

"There it is, my lord, it is stuck in the hay over there near the door of the stall," said Lord Atticus as he reached down to grab the comb and handed it to the Earl. "I am more than thankful that this will be the last night that the Arabian horses will be spending on this ship, Lord Atticus. I feel certain that they will adapt to their new stalls at Primrose Estate rather quickly. I shall see to it that they have the best of everything. I hope to have the Dark Knight ready for racing as quickly as possible. As soon as the ship docks in London, Jackson will make sure the horses are safely on the train rail headed to Primrose Estate. Once they arrive on the train track on the edge of Primrose Estate, I arranged for my trainer and groom to make sure the horses arrive safely in the stables."

"It appears that you have everything perfectly arranged, my lord. Of course, I will be going straight home once we arrive in London. Of course, I must see that the Braxton family arrives safely at Old Wood Manor and hopefully settles in nicely in their new home. I'm sure everyone at Old Wood Manor is anxious about their arrival. It won't be long, my lord, that my family and I will be visiting Primrose Estate once everyone has settled in," said Lord Atticus as he walked towards the door of the stall. "I must go now. Daniel and I promised to meet up with the Devereux sisters for one last stroll around the top deck today."

"It seems as if you are doing a lot of strolling around the top deck lately, Lord Atticus," said the Earl with a slight grin on his face. "Dare I ask which sister has caught your eye, my lord?"

"Well, dare I say maybe they both have, my lord," replied Lord Atticus with a sly grin on his face. "I have been known to be a greedy man, my lord." A loud sound of masculine laughter echoed throughout the stall as Lord Atticus walked towards the stairs that led to the upper deck.

The Earl continued to brush the shiny black coat of the Dark Knight, but his thoughts kept coming back to Nicolette and what took place between them last evening. All he could think about were her warm kisses and her ample bosom pressing against his hard, masculine chest. And when his hands slowly slid over her curves and cupped her bottom, it set him on fire. But strangely enough, he thought to himself that her beauty wasn't the only thing that drew him to her. Now that he had gotten to know her better, he was safe to say that he was impressed with her intellect, charm and wit. He could see her thirst for knowledge and adventure, and it drew him to her like a magnet. There was no doubt that she was just as stubborn and strong-willed as he. After all, she had endured the devastation of war in her beloved Charleston and the tragic loss of her father. The thought of hurting her anyway was not what he wanted to happen. He knew that he had to honor his father and Lord Ashton's agreement, but how in the world was he going to marry Lady Anne, a woman he knew for sure by now he did not love? He knew that he was going to break someone's heart, and he's got a sneaky feeling that it just might be his own heart that will get sadly broken. He knew now that, somehow, he had to stop thinking of Nicolette all the time. This was their last night on the ship together, and he was quite certain that she would probably try to avoid him all evening. He stopped brushing the Dark Knight, left the stall and went to speak with the captain of the ship.

"Good day to you, captain," said the Earl as he entered the captain's quarters. "I'm glad to find you are off duty right now. I have a matter to discuss with you, captain, if I may have a moment of your time?"

"Please have a seat, Lord Mayfield," replied the captain in a deep seaman's tone of voice. "What is it that you have your mind, my lord?"

"I most certainly construed why you made the decision to cancel the orchestra from playing this evening during the evening meal, captain. I certainly understand why all the passengers on board are still somewhat skittish about the horrible murder that has recently taken place. It is such a terrible tragedy for that poor gentleman who lost his life trying to help a so-called friend. But we both know that it is tradition to have a captain's ball on the first night on board and a captain's gala on the last evening on board."

"So, what are you trying to say, Lord Mayfield?" asked the captain. "I am trying to say, captain, that I would like to at least have the orchestra perform this evening when we go to the evening meal and clear the dance floor for dancing afterward. Will that be possible, captain?"

"I suppose I can make that possible, Lord Mayfield. I will send my mate to inform the orchestra to prepare for the evening and send my third mate through the hallways of the passenger quarters to announce the new events that will be taking place this evening."

"I am much obliged, captain," said the Earl as he stood on his feet to shake the captain's hand. "Am I out of line to assume that there is a young lady that has caught your eye, my lord," said the captain with a slight chuckle in his voice. "She has caught my eye and my poor heart as well, captain," said the Earl as he slipped out the door and headed towards his stateroom.

Nicolette had just sat down on the chaise in her stateroom to stretch out her long legs when she heard a soft knock on her door. "That must be you, Mother; I recognize your knock by now."

"It is me, my dear, but you can never be too careful."

Nicolette pulled herself off the chaise and quickly walked to the door to allow her mother to enter the room. "I can see you have been busy all afternoon, my dear," said Lady Elizabeth out loud. "Yes, I have been busy, Mother. I have been busy going through my belongings and packing them since we will be leaving the ship tomorrow."

"I have been quite busy doing the exact thing, my dear," replied Lady Elizabeth while glancing around the room. "Have you heard the news, my dear?" asked Lady Elizabeth. "What news, Mother?" asked Nicolette as she sat back down on the velvet chaise and stretched out once again.

"There will be an orchestra and dancing taking place this evening, after all. I suppose the captain had a last-minute change of plans, so I come to help you pick out a lovely gown to wear, my dear."

"I already have a gown picked out for this evening, Mother. I left it hanging in the armoire beside the gown that I will be wearing tomorrow morning."

"Oh no, this gown will not due at all, my dear. After all, this is a captain's gala, not a day gown to stroll around in, Nicolette. I want you to look your very best, my dear."

"Mrs. Devereux has mentioned once or twice that her son James is quite smitten with you, my dear."

"I suppose he is, Mother. I have noticed on several trips to the dining room that he tries to sit as close as he can to where I am sitting, and he glances my way every chance he gets. He is rather handsome and can be ridiculously charming occasionally, but other than that, I haven't given him much attention."

"Well, maybe it's time you do, Nicolette; after all, you are not as young anymore, my dear."

"Why hush, Mother, you make me sound like an old maid, and we both know that is not going to happen, but I can't help but want to be in love with the man I marry. I want what you and papa had together. That's not too much to ask for, is it Mother?"

"No, my dear it is not too much to ask for because you deserve to know love just like me."

"Well, okay, Mother, you can go look in the trunk over there beside the dresser and take the gold satin gown with the citrine stones and the black lace trim and lay it on the bed. I remember when I helped you sew this gown. Papa had just brought home those citrine stones, and you fell in love with the yellow-gold color of the stones. You thought they looked so pretty with the gold satin and black lace that we stayed up all night creating this lovely gown. It so happened that a new shipment of fabric came into the shop the next day, and this gold fabric and a new bolt of black lace was just what we needed."

"We were rather excited about creating this lovely gown, my dear. So go wash up, my dear, and I will be back soon so we can help one another dress for the evening." Lady Elizabeth quickly went to the door and said out loud as she left the room, "Now I have to pick out what gown I shall wear this evening."

"There you are, my lord; I thought I might find you here," said Lord Atticus when he stepped beside the earl, who was standing on the top deck staring out to the open sea. "It is a rather pleasant evening, my lord, even though those dark clouds are starting to gather in the evening sky."

"It appears that we might have a bout of rainfall soon, Lord Atticus, but I thought I would breathe in some sea air before I head to the dining room."

"I could use a bit of sea air right about now as well, my lord. You are looking quite dapper in that black pinstripe suit with that white silk shirt and black silk tie, my lord," commented Lord Atticus as he straightened the long-tail ivory suit coat he was wearing this evening.

"I must say you will be turning a lot of pretty heads yourself this evening, Lord Atticus," commented the earl as he took his eyes away from Lord Atticus and continued to stare out to sea and think about the lovely Nicolette. Both gentlemen stood there for a while in silence, breathing in the sea air. The Earl was the first to break the silence and speak out loud, "I'm starting to feel famished; I believe it's time we go to the dining room, my lord."

Outside the dining room, inside the dining room, and the dance floor all the gas light lantern chandeliers lit up this evening.

Everything and everyone looked sparkling and shiny this evening. Even though there was still chatter about the tragic murder recently, most passengers were delighted to attend the evening events. The earl and Lord Atticus were already standing in the dining room with the orchestra softly playing a lovely tune when the French doors opened and allowed Nicolette, Lady Elizabeth, and Daniel to enter. When the Earl saw Nicolette, she looked so lovely that he could hardly breathe. She immediately took his breath away, and he couldn't keep his eyes off of her. He just stood there in one place as he watched James Devereux swiftly walk towards the Braxton family. That's when he decided to make his move and headed in that same direction. Once he arrived, James stepped aside and allowed the Earl to take the lovely ladies on each arm and lead them to the elegant dining table where they were seated for the evening meal. This is the first time that the Earl and she touched one another since what took place between them the other day. And that was all it took to make her tingle from head to toe.

Once they arrived at the large dining table, she was able to get a good look at him, and she couldn't help but notice how handsome he looked in his black pinstripe suit that evening. He smiled at her when he slid out of her chair, and she took her seat. She couldn't help but smile back at him and lower her gaze when she realized that she must be blushing because her cheeks were beginning to feel quite warm. Once her mother was seated beside her, she looked at her mother's beautiful face to see if she had noticed any of her reactions when the Earl kindly escorted them both to the dining table. She was doing her best to hide her feelings and emotions this evening in the presence of the Earl. It was obvious he was trying to do the same as she, so maybe she could relax now and enjoy the rest of the evening. This would be their last evening on the Royal Princess, and she planned on dancing the night away. So after she enjoyed a few dances with James Devereux, she noticed on several occasions that the Earl was enjoying himself in the arms of Charlotte Devereux, dancing around the dance floor. But Nicolette was the last one to end up in the arms of the Earl. He swirled her around the dance floor as if she was glued to him. It was magical between them, and neither one of them ever wanted to let go.

CHAPTER 6

May-June 1865

Even though she had danced the night away, she was extremely tired when she slipped into bed. But Nicolette still could not sleep well. All she could do was lay there and think about the Earl of Primrose and the fact that she would have to face Lady Anne soon. It was early morning and her last day on the Royal Princess Steam Ship. In a way, she felt relieved to leave this ship, but she was not looking forward to starting her new life in England. She knew that she had never been good at pretending or having secrets, but these feelings that she was having for the Earl were a secret that she would have to keep to herself. Suddenly, she realized that her thoughts had not been on George for a while now. She wondered if he was thinking about her or even missing her. She knew what she had to do once she was settled in her new home at Old Wood Manor. She will write George a letter and invite him to come to England. *This is an excellent idea, she said out loud. He will be the distraction I so desperately need. I will pretend to be so homesick that I need my friends here with me. Since George's Sister Caroline is my best friend, she must come with him. I will make them understand!* Just knowing that she had a plan up her sleeve, her spirits began to lift.

She threw the covers off and hopped out of bed to get dressed just in time to hear her mother's soft knock at her stateroom door.

"There you are, Jackson," said the Earl when he saw Jackson standing near the stall of the Dark Knight. "I just spoke to the captain's third mate earlier this morning, and he informed me that we will be sailing through the English Channel during breakfast and up the Thames River and fully docked in London by noon. I suppose when the Royal Princess docks in London, my grooms will be ready to help get the horses safely on the rail that will carry them to Primrose. I will need you, Jackson, to find the Mayfield carriage and load my trunks and other baggage into the carriage. My stomach is beginning to turn flips; I must go for breakfast now."

The Earl turned around and practically ran towards the staircase that led him to the dining room, where he saw Nicolette with her mother, Daniel and Lord Atticus seated at the dining table they all shared with the Devereux family. "Good morning, ladies and gentlemen," the Earl spoke breathlessly as he took his seat at the table. "Sorry I am late for breakfast, but I've had a lot of important matters to attend to on this lovely morning. And I say lovely morning because I'm sure all of you are just as anxious as I am to be leaving this ship, even though I am rather sad to be parting ways with each and every one of you. I am quite sure we will be crossing paths once again. After all, the summer gala will be held at Primrose Estate this season, and a cordial invitation will be extended to each and everyone."

"Indeed, my lord, there is no need to apologize. We are well aware of your urgency with those fine Arabian horses of yours, and I must say we feel extremely honored to receive an invite to your summer gala. Even though my family and I are looking forward to leaving the Royal Princess and settling in with Lord Chamberlain and his lovely family in London, we have tremendously enjoyed sharing this time with all of you," replied John Devereux as he held up his glass for a toast. "Until we meet again, my friends," exclaimed John Devereux as he held his wine glass up in the air. "Until we meet again," replied everyone at the table as they held up their drinking glasses in the air. Nicolette couldn't help but notice the Earl staring into her lovely blue eyes when he held up his glass. It was as if he could see deep down into her soul like no other man before him, and that was what scared her the most.

Most all the passengers were standing on top deck mingling amongst one another as they anxiously watched the Royal Princess glide into the London harbor. It was a much cooler day with gray clouds hanging over their heads. Nicolette was standing on top deck with Lord Atticus, her mother, and Daniel, who was holding the wooden crate that held Biscuit. The Earl had been below deck after breakfast all morning, making sure all his plans for the Arabian horses were going smoothly. Nicolette went with Daniel to retrieve the Biscuit after going to their staterooms first to check and make sure everything was packed and ready for Mobley to see to it that their belongings were delivered to the carriages that would be waiting for their arrival in London. That was when she decided to stop by to see Blubelle one last time. She remembered saying goodbye to Blubelle and being glad that she was carrying her embroidered handkerchief in her drawstring purse since she so desperately needed it to wipe a few tears from her eyes. There was no doubt in her mind that she had grown very fond of Blubelle, and she would miss her dearly. She was also grateful that she had a chance to quickly say goodbye to Blubelle without the company of the Earl. There was a part of her that was hoping that she wouldn't see him at all the rest of the day. They would be departing the Royal Princess Ship soon, and she knew that not seeing him would make it much easier for her to try to forget him, at least for now.

"It appears that we have safely arrived here, Lady Elizabeth," said Lord Atticus with a big smile on his handsome face as the Royal Princess safely glided into the London dock. "This has been quite the journey, but I am relieved to be home once again. I am very excited to have all of you here with me and the rest of our family. I sincerely hope you are looking forward to your new life here as much as I am looking forward to having you here." He completed. "I hope you know how truly grateful we are to be here, Lord Atticus," replied Lady Elizabeth with a lovely smile on her pretty face. "We are quite anxious to start our new life here in England, aren't we, my dear?"

"Why, of course we are, Mother," replied Nicolette, since she was the only one standing there with her mother and Lord Atticus. Daniel was only a few feet away, chatting with the lovely Emma Devereux. Nicolette could tell that Daniel was rather smitten with Miss Devereux. She did notice that Daniel had been spending a lot of time with Miss Devereux of late. Nicolette knew how gifted Daniel was with his craftsmanship. Their father had raised Daniel to be the best Tailor in Charleston. Who's not to say that once Daniel takes over Lord Gerald Ashton's brother's tailor shop in London, he might become the best in London? There was no doubt in her mind that the Devereux family seemed quite fond of Daniel, and it appeared that he would have no problem calling on Emma in the future. Oh, how Nicolette wished that things were that simple for her. *Why must I have these feelings for the Earl?* she asked herself over and over again. Only a fool will allow these feelings, and the last thing she wanted to be was a fool for the Earl or anyone.

"Will you please excuse me, ladies? I must go and find out when we can depart the ship now that it is safely docked," said Lord Atticus as he hurried away from them for the moment. "I will be back momentarily since I'm sure it will be any moment now." Daniel came over and joined Nicolette and his mother with somewhat of a sad look on his bronzed face. "I see that sad look on your face, Daniel," said Nicolette as she turned around and stared her brother in the eye. "Hopefully, you will be able to call on Miss Devereux sooner than you think, dear brother."

"I don't have the faintest idea what you are speaking of, Nicolette," replied Daniel with a grin on his face suddenly. "You know exactly what I mean, Daniel; you can't fool me." Daniel began to laugh out loud and raised his eyebrow at Nicolette when he replied, "And you can not fool me either, sister!" Nicolette decided not to say anything because all she could do was stand there and turn red in the face while holding her bonnet that was about to blow away from a gush of wind.

"I see Lord Atticus," anxiously said Lady Elizabeth as she saw Lord Atticus swiftly coming towards them. "Come follow me; we are ready to depart this ship," said Lord Atticus as he led the way. Mobley had already departed the ship and would be standing with the Ashton carriage that would take us to Old Wood Manor. Daniel grabbed the crate that was holding Biscuit, and they followed behind Lord Atticus as he led them off the ship. When they reached the Ashton carriage, Nicolette noticed Jackson standing next to the carriage that had pulled up behind their carriage. It must be the Earl's carriage, she thought to herself. And that thought was most certainly clear when she turned her head and looked at the Mayfield carriage and suddenly stared into the sapphire blue eyes of the Earl. She saw the look of desire in his eyes, and her body trembled slightly as Lord Atticus helped her inside the Ashton carriage that would carry her away from the man who was haunting her dreams.

There were only a few days left in the month of May, and as soon as Nicolette stepped outside the Ashton family carriage, she noticed a cool breeze in the air. If she was still in Charleston there would be a much warmer breeze in the air this time of year. She was already feeling homesick, and she had just arrived at Old Wood Manor. When Lord Atticus took Lady Elizabeth's arm to lead her up a few stairs where the Ashton family and a few servants were waiting for their arrival, Nicolette pulled her shawl around her body to cover her shoulders from the cool air as she and Daniel followed Lord Atticus and Lady Elizabeth up the stairs. The first to step forward to greet them was Lady Margaret Ashton, the sister of Lady Elizabeth. Lady Margaret and Lady Elizabeth embraced one another lovingly like two sisters would after being apart for a long period of time. After that, everyone else shared hugs and kisses on both cheeks.

"Welcome to Old Wood Manor," said Lord Gerald Ashton, the Earl of Old Wood Manor. "This will be your new home and I sincerely hope that you will find it to be a most pleasant one. We will do everything in our power to make that possible, my dear ones. So come inside and allow my staff to get you settled into your bed chamber and living quarters. My son Lord Atticus and Daniel, I shall see soon in the study. The ladies, I shall see when we all come together for the evening meal." After Lord Gerald Ashton finished greeting them, he turned around quickly and walked inside the manor. "Please come with me, Nicolette, and I will take you to your chamber. Your trunks and other baggage will be brought to you soon. I am sure you are anxious to get settled in after such a long journey to get here. I must say that I hardly recognize you, Nicolette; it has been a while since I last saw you. But I can see that your hair color is still as light and fair as the last time I saw you. I do remember that you and I are only a few months apart in age, and as I recall, you have a birthday coming up next month," said Lady Anne as she was climbing the stairs leading Nicolette to her bed chamber.

"Yes, it has been quite a while since ya'll come to visit us in Charleston. I can say the exact same thing about you, Lady Anne; I hardly recognize you as well. You have the same pretty shade of brown hair and you have grown much taller," softly replied Nicolette as she let out a sleepy yawn. "Oh my," replied Lady Anne. "You are the one who grew much taller, Nicolette. If I must say though, the height looks quite well on you."

"Why thank you kindly, Lady Anne," said Nicolette as she let another yawn slip out of her pretty mouth. Once they reached Nicolette's bed chamber, Lady Anne could see that Nicolette was rather exhausted from the trip, so she decided to leave and let Nicolette get some rest. Nicolette glanced around the room and could see that it was amazingly elegant and beautiful. It was a room fit for a princess with its shades of pink and deep scarlet reds. But at that very moment Nicolette didn't much feel like a princess. Instead, she felt more like a fool who had fallen for the looks and charm of an earl destined to break her heart.

Nicolette decided to get that thought out of her head and not think about the Earl of Primrose at all. Instead, she noticed the large canopy bed located in the center of the room. She took off her bonnet and gloves and placed them on the elegant velvet Queen Anne chair beside the large bed. Since the buttons were located on the front of her lovely gown, she managed to undo them and slip out of her gown, crinoline and petticoat. Without further hesitation, she pulled down the covers of her new bed and fell fast asleep, dreaming of a knight with black hair and blue eyes riding a dark horse through a field of yellow flowers.

"Nicolette! Wake up, Nicolette," exclaimed Lady Anne, leaning over the bed and staring at Nicolette's lovely face. "It is getting late, and you must get ready for the evening meal. I have brought Sally with me, Nicolette; she will be your new ladies' maid. Sally is the twin sister of Nora, who happens to be my lady's maid. Sally will help you dress and also help in many other ways when necessary."

"I do kindly thank you, Lady Anne," replied Nicolette in a low, soft voice, "but Mother and I were used to helping each other with our dressing and grooming needs since that terrible war that we had to endure back home in Charleston."

"Nonsense," replied Lady Anne. "There is no reason why Sally couldn't help you and Lady Elizabeth with your needs. You are part of the Ashton family now and we are most fortunate to have them both as a part of our staff at Old Wood Manor. Sally, please go inform the footman that Nicolette's belongings are ready to be brought to her room immediately and then return here to assist Miss Braxton with her needs. Now go, Sally, it is getting late."

Nicolette knew that it didn't do any good to argue with Lady Anne. She suddenly remembered how bossy Lady Anne could be at times.

"Well, if I must say so myself, Lady Anne, it will be rather nice for Mother and me to be pampered somewhat. We both have been through such hardships of late, especially with losing Papa. I miss him dearly, and I know Mother and Daniel do as well," said Nicolette with a look of sadness in her blue eyes. "I can't even imagine how sad you must be, Nicolette," said Lady Anne as she looked into Nicolette's face and noticed a tear that was sliding down her cheek. "I do know that your papa was a very brave man. He fought for a good cause. He fought for his beloved south and his family that he so adored. Your mother and my mother both had previously mentioned in one of the many letters that they exchanged over the years that you were a lot like your father, Nicolette. I am truly sorry that he had to leave us so soon!"

Suddenly, both ladies looked towards the bed chamber door, when they heard a loud knock at the door. Nicolette pulled the covers up over her body when Lady Anne answered the door and allowed the footman in with her belongings. Sally entered the room with a bucket of warm water for Nicolette's bath and Lady Anne left the chamber to go to her chamber to get ready for the evening meal. "Sally, if you open that small wooden trunk, you will find a box of bath oil. I prefer to bathe with the Jasmine oil; that happens to be my favorite," said Nicolette as she quickly got out of bed and grabbed a robe out of one of the larger trunks. When Sally returned with the last bucket of warm water and poured it into the large cast iron tub, Nicolette gladly stepped into the tub and slid her naked body into the fragrant water.

Her whole body began to relax, but unfortunately, her thoughts began to drift towards Lord Austin Mayfield. She couldn't help but wonder what he was doing right now, but she already knew the answer to that. There was no doubt it had something to do with those beautiful Arabian horses. But she couldn't help but wonder if he had thought of her at all.

After sharing an afternoon tea with his family, the Earl was quite eager to get to the rather large horse stables on Primrose Estate. "Let's go now, Lord Jared. I am very anxious to meet the new horse trainer and jockey you hired in my absence," eagerly said the Earl after he swallowed his last sip of tea.

"I truly believe you will be quite pleased with my selection, my Lord," said Lord Jared as they left the manor and jumped into the open carriage that would take them quickly to the stables. When they arrived, the Earl headed straight to the horse stall where the Dark Knight was beginning to settle in. The Earl couldn't help but notice a huge difference in the calmness of the Dark Knight. Evidently, it didn't take him long to get used to his surroundings. The Marquis had previously invested lots of money into building one of the finest horse stables around, and it was rather obvious to everyone who saw it. "So, what do you think of the Dark Knight, my brother," asked the Earl as he started to approach the Dark Knight. All Lord Jared could do was stand there in awe, admiring the beauty of this magnificent horse.

"You did well, my Lord; he is everything you wanted. He will make a magnificent racehorse. He is rather muscular with very strong legs. I can see that you already have a name for him. The name suits him well, my Lord since his coat is black and shiny.

But what is that I hear in the next stall brother? It sounds like the sounds of a mare that I'm not familiar with, my Lord?"

"Come with me, brother; I would like to introduce you to Blubelle," said the Earl with a large grin on his handsome face. When the Earl first glanced at Blubelle standing calmly in her new stall, he couldn't help but think about Nicolette. He knew how attached Nicolette and Blubelle had become these past few weeks. But the truth was that he became attached to Nicolette as well, and he was trying to deny these feelings. He was hoping that, in time, these feelings would fade away and this desire he had for her would vanish. "I had no idea you were bringing home another fine Arabian horse my Lord," exclaimed Lord Jared in a loud tone of voice. "I must say she is beautiful, brother. She will breed some mighty fine horses in the future. I could see that her coat was white all over and that she already had a name as well. I am rather curious to know how you came up with the name Blubelle, my Lord?"

"Daniel Braxton and his sister Nicolette came up with the name Blubelle," replied the Earl. "You must be speaking of the cousins of Lord Atticus," said Lord Jared as he turned around to greet the new trainer, who was walking towards the Earl and him. "Glad to see you here, Watson," said Lord Jared.

"The Earl and I were coming to see you in a moment. I want you to meet Lord Austin Mayfield, the Earl of Primrose Estate and my dear brother. This is Lord Watson Chamberlain, the younger son of Lord Chamberlain. He prefers to be called Lord Watson. He grew up as a young lad learning to train horses along with his older brothers at the Chamberlain Estate and he is quite experienced with the sport of horse racing."

"I am well aware of the reputation of your father, Lord Chamberlain, and the success he has endured over the years. It is rather obvious that our fathers and the Earl of Old Wood Manor have butted heads on a few occasions with one another over the years. Does your father know that you have an interest in working as a horse trainer for the Mayfield family Lord Watson? I do not want or need any conflict of interest now or in the future. Do I make myself clear, Lord Watson?"

Lord Jared was the first to answer the Earl, "I assure you, my Lord, there is no need to worry. I personally met with Lord Watson's father and brothers, and they are in agreement with Lord Watson becoming the Mayfield horse trainer. Lord Chamberlain knows that his youngest son, Lord Watson, is quite gifted with his training skills, and since he already has plenty of help with his own horses, he wants his son to put his skills to good use if that means going to work for the Mayfield family then so be it."

The Earl stood there for a moment, staring into the eyes of Lord Watson before he spoke, "Alright, I will take a chance with you, Lord Watson. You better not disappoint me!"

"I promise not to disappoint you, my Lord," replied Lord Watson with a smile on his handsome face. "This is the training routine I have in mind for the Dark Knight Lord Watson," said the Earl in a rather demanding tone. "I expect for the week an exercise regiment. There will be a fast gallop workout twice a week, steady trotting and cantering the rest of the week. Sunday will be a rest/quiet day depending on the schedule of races planned. Your focus will mainly center on the Dark Knight. You can pitch in and help the grooms with the other horses and chores when needed. Unfortunately, we had to miss two horse races already this season, but we should be able to attend the Epsom Derby coming up in June. Since the Dark Knight has already been trained as a racehorse in North America and has a few horse races under his belt, he should do just fine. But we do not know until we try, so let's have him ready, Lord Watson. I am counting on you."

Lord Watson shook the Earl's hand and quietly stepped into the stall of the Dark Knight with the Earl so he could get better acquainted with this magnificent beast of an animal.

CHAPTER 7

June 1865

"**P**lease come follow me, Lady Elizabeth and you too, Nicolette. We shall walk right through that large door on the other side of the Tailor shop. That door will lead us to a pair of large rooms that will be perfect for your seamstress shop. What makes it perfect is the fact that you can enter the rooms from the Tailor shop or enter from a door that opens to the front of the shop that takes you outside," said Lord Atticus as he led Lady Elizabeth and Nicolette through a large wooden door. Daniel remained in the Tailor shop with the Earl of Old Wood Manor. Lord Gerald Ashton continued to discuss with Daniel the take over of his brother's Tailor shop. As soon as both ladies stepped into the first room, they let out a loud gasp at the same time.

"You are absolutely correct about these rooms being perfect, my Lord. This will do just fine," replied Nicolette as she eagerly glanced around the room, envisioning in her head the shop of her dreams. "Even though you insist that the shop will be my own Mother, I do value your opinion."

"I agree with both you and Lord Atticus, my dear. It is absolutely perfect. You know that I will be helping you, Nicolette. I am not ready to quit yet. I am just handing the reins over to you, my dear," spoke Lady Elizabeth with pride in her voice. "When can we start setting up these rooms, Lord Atticus? I would love to start as soon as possible, my Lord," eagerly asked Nicolette.

"All you need to do, ladies, is write me a list of everything you need, and I shall see to it. I shall make sure you will have it as soon as possible. I can see that you are anxious to get started," said Lord Atticus as he led them outside the front door and back inside the front door of the Tailor shop where Daniel and his father were standing at the front counter. Lord Ashton was the first to speak in his somewhat loud, boisterous voice, "Greeting ladies! I assume you have already laid eyes on your soon-to-be seamstress shop. I certainly hope that you find it to your liking, dear."

"It is even better than I imagined, my Lord," replied Nicolette with a wide grin on her lovely face. "Mother is pleased as well, Lord Ashton." Lady Elizabeth softly spoke to Lord Ashton as she stared into his brown eyes. "We are so much looking forward to this new beginning. We are so excited about starting a new business here in London, and I promise we will do our best, my Lord. We are most grateful to all of you for giving us this opportunity, Lord Ashton."

"I have no doubt, Lady Elizabeth, that you, Nicolette and Daniel will always do your very best. Daniel, since the shop is already set up and ready for you to take over soon, you can start immediately.

You ladies can start working as soon as we can get the shop set up the way you like it. But first I would like to announce that we will be taking a trip to Primrose Estate in a few days. I understand that there are two new Arabian horses there that belong to Lord Austin, and I am most eager to see those beauties with my own eyes, as you all are well aware that I no longer race horses. I have had a few setbacks with my health in recent years, but that doesn't mean that I don't still get excited about the sport of horse racing. There will be time before we leave to get the shops ready to open for business when we get back from our trip to Primrose Estate. So now, where is Mobley with our carriage? I am most anxious to get home now since I seem to be rather famished."

Once they settled inside the carriage, all Nicolette could think about was the fact that she would be seeing the Earl a lot sooner than she imagined. All of a sudden, she started to feel slightly queasy, as if there were fluttering butterflies inside her tummy. Hopefully, it was because she suddenly realized that she could be famished just like Lord Ashton. After all, she only ate a couple bites of her food early this morning because she was too busy writing a letter to George and Caroline in Charleston, South Carolina. She made sure she gave it to the butler before they left this morning, and he gave it to a messenger to be sent to America. But who was she kidding; she knew exactly why she felt butterflies again. It was the thought of seeing the Earl and imagining his warm kisses on her soft lips.

It seemed as if the next few days passed by very quickly for Nicolette. The air was much warmer, and the days were longer. Progress was being made on the new tailor and seamstress shops in London. Nicolette and Daniel both agreed on a name for their new shops. Daniel decided to call his shop The Braxton Tailor's and Nicolette decided on the name Nicolette's Seamstress Shop.

"What do you think about this pink velvet chaise I chose for that far corner over there, Mother," Nicolette asked her mother when they stepped inside the seamstress shop. "I think it is lovely, my dear, and it seems to match quite well with those two Victorian chairs over there that are facing towards the front large windows of the shop. That is a very nice front counter with a glass display for your gloves and other accessories, my dear."

Once they stepped into the back of the shop, they noticed a very large rosewood work table that nearly stretched across the entire room. They also noticed several mannequins lined up against a wall that could be used to display their gowns and bonnets in the front windows and other areas in the shop. But what really caught their eye was all of the fine bolts of fabric stacked up on huge wooden shelves located on the back wall of the very large room. There was more fabric in that one room than both ladies had ever seen in their lifetime. "It appears as if Lord Ashton and Lady Margaret have been quite generous. Don't you agree, Mother," said Nicolette with a look of awe on her pretty face.

"I can hardly wait to get to work, my dear," replied Lady Elizabeth with a smile on her face. "This is like a dream come true, my dear."

"I agree with you, mother. As soon as we return from Primrose Estate, we shall start immediately making our gowns for the summer gala at Primrose Estate. And I already have my eye on that aquamarine blue silk bolt of fabric I just now noticed, Mother," said Nicolette as she quickly headed towards the bolt of fabric.

"What do you think, Mother," said Nicolette. "That color will bring out the blue in your eyes, my dear. It is perfect for you, Nicolette. You will be the belle of the ball, and maybe if we're lucky, you will find a suitor there as well, my dear," said Lady Elizabeth as she quickly glanced at Nicolette and noticed her face turning red. "Well, I do realize that since we are officially out of the mourning period for the passing of Father, it is time I get serious about finding a suitor and a possible husband. Maybe you are right Mother, I will find a suitor at the summer gala."

In that very moment, Nicolette thought about Lord Austin, and a stroke of sadness crossed her face. She knew very well that he couldn't be her suitor or husband since he belonged to Lady Anne. All she could do was hope that George and Caroline would come here soon enough. She needed her friends with her and all the strength that she could muster up to forget these feelings that had come over her since that day she saw the Earl spying on her and George back in Charleston. She loathed the idea of harboring secrets inside of her, but that was the only thing she could do in order not to hurt the people she loved. *I am ready now to go face the Earl and show him that we can only be friends.*

"I believe I hear the carriage pull up outside, Mother. It is time to go back to Old Wood Manor. I must help Sally pack for our trip to Primrose Estate since we shall be leaving first thing tomorrow morning."

The following morning, there were two of the Ashton family carriages strolling along the dusty roads leading to Primrose Estate, and you couldn't have asked for better weather this morning. The sky was blue with only a few white puffy clouds high in the sky. Nicolette couldn't help but be somewhat relieved that Lady Anne was riding in the other carriage with Lord Ashton, Lady Margaret and Lord Atticus. She was in the second carriage with her mother, Daniel and Nora, the ladies' maid. Nora had to come along on this trip since word got to Old Wood Manor from Primrose Estate that one of the Mayfield's ladies' maids had come down with a fever, so Nora came along to take her place while they were visiting the Mayfield family. Nicolette knew that she would be spending a lot of time with Lady Anne at Primrose, but it was good to have her distance for now. She tried not to think of the Earl at this very moment, but it seemed to be impossible. She caught herself thinking of him quite often, no matter how much she tried not to.

Nicolette woke up suddenly when the carriage wobbled back and forth over some rocky terrain on the dusty roads. When she glanced outside the carriage window, she could see wide open fields of wheat everywhere. She knew then that they were already on Mayfield land and were inching closer to the Mayfield Manor. That meant that she was inching closer to the Earl, and she could feel the butterflies fluttering in her stomach once again. She couldn't help but wonder how he was going to act around her now that he was home around his family and Lady Anne. Well, that thought left her rather quickly when the carriage came to a halt in front of the very large and lovely Mayfield Manor. Nicolette, her mother, Daniel and Nora waited inside their carriage for Lord Ashton and the others to exit their carriage first. And once they were all standing outside their carriages, Nicolette stared into the faces of the Mayfield family. The first to step forward to greet them was the Earl since he was the one to introduce them to his family. First, he shook hands with Lord Ashton, kissed Lady Margaret's hand, kissed Lady Anne's hand and hugged Lord Atticus. After he hugged Daniel and kissed her mother's hand, he was standing in front of her, staring into her big blue eyes. She slightly trembled when he lifted her hand, placed a kiss on top, and smiled his most charming smile as he continued to stare into her big blue eyes. There was no doubt in her mind that her cheeks were blushing because she could feel the heat from his gentle touch and the look of desire that was hidden in his sapphire blue eyes. When she pulled her hand back down by her side, he turned around and introduced his family to her family once again since it had been quite a few years since they last saw one another. Nicolette remembered visiting with the Mayfield family in the past. They were all young children at that time. That was why she didn't recognize the Earl when they first met in Charleston. Even her mother hardly remembered meeting the Mayfield family many years ago; she did not recognize the Earl that day in Charleston as well. But at last, they all were there together years later, and Nicolette didn't know whether to be relaxed or nervous about their visit here at Primrose Estate. But there was one thing she knew for sure, and that one thing was that she was looking forward to seeing Blubelle, and if she was lucky, the Earl would let her take Blubelle out for a ride. So, with that happy thought on her mind, she held her head up high, put a smile on her lovely face and walked inside the Primrose Manor alongside Lady Anne and Lady Miranda.

After everyone was shown to their sleeping quarters and bed-chambers, the Manor remained quiet until they all gathered for the evening meal. The Earl was seated next to Lady Anne and his sister, Lady Miranda. Nicolette was on the other side of the very large mahogany dining table across from the Earl, seated next to her mother and Daniel. The rest of the Mayfield family and the Ashton family members were seated in their usual places. The room was filled with loud chatter and delightful odors from the delicious food being served to each and everyone. Nicolette noticed Lady Anne continue to talk and laugh out loud with the Earl throughout the evening meal. There were a few curious questions and comments made to them about their journey to North America and back. Nicolette joined in the conversation and made a few comments of her own, but she did notice that the Earl would glance at her and smile quite often. She couldn't help but blush from head to toe and smile back at him occasionally. Lady Anne was so busy talking to the Earl non-stop that she didn't even notice him looking at her.

Nicolette was grateful that the evening meal was over, and everyone was finding their way to the parlor where the piano was located for their entertainment for the evening. Instead of Lady Miranda playing the piano this evening, the Mayfield family asked if Lady Anne would do them the honor of playing a lovely tune on the piano. Once Lady Anne finished playing a popular song and everyone applauded, Lady Margaret surprised everyone when she began to suddenly speak, "With all the letters exchanged between my sister Lady Elizabeth and me over the years, I am well informed of the lovely voice and piano playing of my beautiful niece Nicolette. Would you please do us the honor of sharing your lovely voice with us, my dear?" Before Nicolette could utter a single word, you could have heard a pin drop in the large parlor where everyone was seated. That was the last thing Nicolette expected to come out of Lady Margaret's mouth. Now that everyone was staring her way, she had to say something out loud, but she would prefer to run away. "I'm not at all certain that I can honor your request, Lady Margaret. I haven't done either one of those requests in quite a while. I do not want to disappoint anyone now, would I, my lady," replied Nicolette in a very soft, apologetic tone of voice.

Before Lady Margaret or anyone else could respond, the Earl stood up and walked over to the piano where Lady Anne was still seated. "Please take my hand, Lady Anne, and I will help you to your feet so we can make room for Miss Braxton." Lady Anne quickly glanced over at Nicolette with a slightly angry look in her eye and placed her hand inside the hand of the Earl as he gently pulled her to her feet. With a sweep of his hand, the Earl spoke out loud in a deep masculine voice, "Now it is your turn to entertain us, Miss Braxton. Please take your place?"

Nicolette knew at the moment she had no other choice but to take her seat at the piano. But the Earl better beware because she would pay him back for this somehow. But for now, she would play and sing one of her papa's favorite tunes, "When Johnny Comes Marching Home."

When she got about a third of the way into the song, Daniel and the Earl began to sing along with her. She was beginning to feel a lot more relaxed now since everyone there decided to join in on the singing. Once the song ended everyone was smiling while applauding her performance. Nicolette felt relieved and was anxious for the evening to come to an end. She was glad when Lady Constance Mayfield rose to her feet and announced that she was ready to retire to her bed chamber. She was even more relieved when she and the rest of the ladies announced that they were ready to retire to their bed chambers. Moments later, all the gentlemen in the room quickly left the parlor and headed to the study, where they would have their last brandy for the night. Lady Miranda and Lady Anne approach Nicolette and praise her for her performance. Nicolette kindly thanked them and gave praise to Lady Anne for her performance earlier.

"Ah, the Earl looks so handsome this evening, Lady Miranda," suddenly exclaimed Lady Anne. "It seems as if the trip to America made him even more charming and handsome than before. His skin is so bronzed, and his hair is sleek and shinier than ever. But my nerves are frazzled because I am so tired of waiting for his marriage proposal. If he insists on continuing to drag his feet, I may just have to look for another suitor, Lady Miranda. The summer gala taking place here at Primrose Estate this season will be here sooner than you think. Just maybe we will all get lucky and find a new suitor. Of course, there is no one as handsome and charming as the Earl, but I am getting older, and I have needs and desires like any other, and I am tired of waiting on your brother, my lady."

"I can very well see how you must feel, Lady Anne," replied Lady Miranda with a concerned look on her lovely face. "But I'm sure it will be soon that he will make you his bride."

"Well, what do you think, Miss Braxton?" asked Lady Miranda. "After being on the Royal Princess Steam ship recently with the Earl, did you ever hear the Earl mention to you or anyone about a possible marriage between the Earl and Lady Anne?"

"First of all, you may call me Nicolette, Lady Miranda, if you please. And as far as what I know about the Earl and Lady Anne, Daniel informed me that there was a marriage agreement between you and The Earl, Lady Anne, after we had boarded the Royal Princess on our way to England. It was common news to everyone who knew the Earl. You know how gossip spreads, especially among us nobles."

"I am well aware how charming the Earl can be; I'm sure he grabbed the attention of a few young ladies on your voyage here," said Lady Anne in a soft, condescending voice. Nicolette wasn't quite sure how to respond to Lady Anne, but she did know that this was the first time that they had spoken about this subject since she arrived in England. Nicolette was hoping to avoid any conversation with Lady Anne relating to Lord Austin, but she knew she was hoping for the impossible. So she decided to say as little as possible, "You are right, my lady; I did notice a few ladies vying for the Earl's attention. I would be telling a lie if I said that he was not handsome, Lady Anne since it is rather obvious. But as far as I noticed, he must have eyes only for you, my lady."

"Well, I must say I hope you are right, Nicolette," replied Lady Anne with a slight look of relief in her eyes. "I guess I still must be patient with the Earl, but my patience is running thin these days." Lady Miranda began to yawn out loud when she interrupted the conversation and said out loud, "It is time we retire for the evening; please follow me to our bed chambers, ladies."

Nicolette was relieved when she entered her bed chamber and quietly shut the door behind her. Suddenly, she heard a soft knock on the chamber door. It was Sally, and she told her to enter the room. After she undressed and put on her nightgown, she couldn't wait to slip into the covers on her bed. She couldn't go to sleep right away, so she lay there and thought about the Earl and everything that had taken place since her arrival at Primrose Estate. There was one thing for sure: she agreed with Lady Anne about how handsome the Earl looked since he got back from his trip to America. She did notice the Earl staring at her on several occasions with those sapphire-blue eyes of his. She tried not to stare back, but there were times that she could not help herself from staring into his eyes. She felt as if she spent the whole evening blushing from head to toe and there were times she felt like her cheeks were on fire. *Tiddlywinks!* She spoke out loud. *I can not keep allowing myself to be under the spell and charm of the Earl. I must find a way to resist his devilish charm. He will never have me as long as he is promised to another. I will look for another suitor at the summer gala. That will help me get over him for good.* She reached over and put out the candle burning beside her bed and fell fast asleep, dreaming of a knight on a dark horse with sapphire blue eyes.

The Earl was awake at the crack of dawn the following morning. He was feeling more anxious than usual but he probably could use a little more sleep since he was so restless in his sleep last night. He was exhausted when he slid into bed last night but thinking about the beautiful face and body of Nicolette kept him awake. *Damn her beauty!* He said out loud. *I can hardly contain my desire for her when she is near. I shall not allow myself to keep staring at her. I must keep my attention on Lady Anne, but how in the hell am I going to manage that with Nicolette in my presence?* Suddenly, Jackson knocked on the door and entered the Earl's bed chamber. The Earl was thankful for the distraction, and he immediately got dressed. He slipped downstairs quietly while everyone else was sleeping. He grabbed a few apples from the fruit bowl on the dining room buffet and headed out the door to find the coachman with the open carriage to take him to the horse stables on Primrose Estate. He glanced up at the sky and saw what looked like a few rain clouds. He was hoping that the rain would hold off long enough this morning so the ladies and gentlemen could enjoy a gallop across the fields of Primrose after breakfast this morning. He knew that the Ashton family was eager to see his new Arabian horses. Lord Atticus and the Braxton family were probably eager to see them once again, even though they were already familiar with them. That made him think of Nicolette once more, and he was certain she would be eager to see them again. He knew that she was especially attached to Blubelle, and she would be glad to see her once again.

The Earl continued to rub the shiny coat of the Dark Knight when he heard the wheels and horse hooves of more than one carriage pull up in front of the stable. They all must have come to the stables this morning, he thought to himself. He handed the curry comb to the groom and walked to the front of the stable. When he stepped outside, he saw that he had made the right assumption. Even his mother had accompanied his father, the Marquis, along with Lord Gerald Ashton and Lady Margaret, followed by everyone else. He knew the ladies would be the first to want to ride the mares, so he would get the grooms to bring them out in front of the stables right now. But first, he would lead those who had yet to see the Arabian horses to their stalls while everyone else who wanted to ride this morning could get ready for their ride. Everyone was in awe after seeing the Dark Knight and Blubelle. Lord Ashton couldn't refrain from talking about how magnificent of a horse he was.

When the Earl stepped back outside, where the ladies were standing admiring Blubelle, he heard Lady Anne mention that she would like to ride Blubelle this morning. He immediately glanced over at Nicolette and noticed a slightly sad look on her lovely face. There was no doubt in his mind that she desperately wanted to be the first to ride Blubelle. But he knew at this very moment that there was nothing Nicolette or he could say. Lady Anne was his bride-to-be, and of course, she would be the first to ride Blubelle. The groom slowly brought her over to Lady Anne while Lady Miranda got ready to saddle her own horse named Rose. Rose was the mother of Penelope the horse that Lady Anne took out for a ride on all her visits to Primrose Estate ever since she first rode Penelope. Nicolette was to ride Penelope since Lady Anne wanted to ride Blubelle. But when Lady Anne began to rub the shiny white coat of Blubelle, she started to stir around, somewhat shaking her head back and forth. After waiting a moment for Blubelle to be still, Lady Anne decided to place her foot inside the stirrup and mount Blubelle slowly, but Blubelle did not allow Lady Anne to mount her.

Blubelle began to rear up on her hind legs, and Lady Anne quickly moved away from her. Once Lady Anne moved away, Blubelle began to calm down. By now, Lady Anne and Blubelle had everyone's attention. Lady Anne decided to try to mount Blubelle once more but Blubelle was not cooperating at all. This time, Blubelle was so stirred up that Nicolette, who was the closest to Blubelle, took her by the reins and calmed her down. Nicolette continued to rub Blubelle to calm her down. Lady Miranda was the first to speak, "Maybe you should stick to riding Penelope Lady Anne since Blubelle is not allowing you to mount her without a fuss. There are a few other horses that Nicolette can choose from to take out for a ride."

That's when the Earl decided to speak up, "I am most curious to see if Blubelle will allow Miss Braxton to mount and ride her. After all, Blubelle got familiar with Miss Braxton on the Royal Princess Steam Ship on the trip home. Please try to mount Blubelle, Miss Braxton," kindly said the Earl while everyone was watching and waiting for Nicolette to mount Blubelle. Nicolette placed her foot inside the stirrup and pulled herself up on top of the mare. Blubelle slightly moved around a couple of times and began to settle down. "How does it feel, Miss Braxton? Do you feel comfortable enough to ride Blubelle?" asked the Earl with a slight grin on his handsome face.

"I do feel comfortable, Lord Mayfield," replied Nicolette with a slight grin on her lovely face. "I believe Blubelle and I are ready to take that ride, my lord." Lady Anne was mounted on top of Penelope beside Lady Miranda, who was mounted on top of Rose. When the Earl glanced over at Lady Anne and saw that her bright red cheeks were flushed, he also saw a look of anger in her light brown eyes. But what just happened was not his fault or Nicolette's fault. Blubelle had made her choice, and she didn't have anything to do with Lady Anne. The Earl almost wanted to laugh out loud, but he knew better than that. Instead, he kindly said, "Be safe, Ladies; I hope you have a lovely ride. It looks as if the clouds moved away, and the rain will hold off for now." He stood there and watched as Nicolette rode away on Blubelle as if she had been riding her all her life.

Lady Miranda tried to stay clear of riding into the woodlands where all the beautiful yellow primrose flowers were blooming this time of year. Even though that was the path, she usually rode her horse, Rose, when Lady Anne wasn't with her. So this morning, she led Lady Anne and Nicolette into an open meadow of lush green grass and other wildflowers that hopefully do not make Lady Anne sneeze as the primrose flowers do. Nicolette was having somewhat of a challenge with Blubelle following behind Lady Anne. Blubelle wanted to run much faster than the other horses, so she had to hold her back the best she could. Lady Miranda began to slow Rose down when she saw the pond up ahead. When they got to the lovely pond, all three ladies dismounted their horses. Lady Miranda brought a blanket, some delicious cheesecakes, a bottle of wine and three wine goblets inside a basket along with her. All three ladies took their places on the blanket beside the pond and gladly shared a goblet of wine. Lady Anne couldn't help but remember the last time she visited this pond. She and the Earl had a lovely picnic here on her last visit to Primrose Estate. But she also remembered that it ended in disappointment for her. She thought the Earl had invited her here for a marriage proposal that day since this would have been the perfect place and time for such a thing. But all she got that day were a few kisses and some of them rather passionate kisses as she recalled. But there were no promises of marriage from the Earl. She had to leave the Earl once more carrying a sad heart with her.

"I can see that Blubelle feels comfortable around you, Nicolette," said Lady Miranda as all three ladies stared at the lovely mallard ducks swimming near the edge of the pond where they were seated. "I was most fortunate to get very acquainted with Blubelle on my trip to England, Lady Miranda. Since Lord Atticus and Lord Mayfield were close companions on the trip, I had the privilege of visiting Blubelle in her horse stalls on the ship." Nicolette glanced over at Lady Anne and noticed a sad look in her eyes. She was being rather quiet and that was not normal for her. Lady Anne was always the most talkative of all the ladies, but she noticed how quiet she had been ever since they arrived here at the pond. Something was troubling Lady Anne right now and she had a feeling that it had something to do with the Earl. All three ladies moved to spread their blankets under a large oak tree to get away from the bright, beaming sun. Nicolette and Lady Miranda mostly did all the talking since they wanted to learn more about each other. Nicolette talked about her new seamstress shop in London and how excited she and her mother were to get started on making some new gowns for the upcoming summer gala. "I would love to visit your shop as soon as you open it, Nicolette. I will mention that to Mother, and we will be delighted to make a trip to London soon," said Lady Miranda with a kind voice. "Mother and I will be delighted to have you and Lady Constance visit our shop, my lady," replied Nicolette.

"Lady Anne and Lady Margaret have already visited the shop a couple of times and helped us with some of the decorating. We are most grateful for your help, Lady Anne," said Nicolette while staring up at the dark clouds that all of a sudden decided to make an appearance, hiding the bright sun in the sky. A moment later, all three ladies stood on their feet when they heard the sound of thunder. "We must leave now and hurry back before it pours down rain." They mounted their horses quickly and swiftly rode across the meadow, where they almost made it back to the horse stables when the rain came pouring down on top of them. They were soaking wet when they led their horses inside the stables, where the Earl and his grooms came quickly to help them with their horses.

Lady Anne mentioned that she wasn't feeling well because she had a slight headache. Lady Miranda was in such a hurry to get out of her wet clothes, and Nicolette wanted to visit Biscuit, who was staying out in the stables while they were visiting the Mayfield family. They had brought Biscuit with them from Old Wood Manor. So a closed carriage pulled up in front of the stables to escort Lady Miranda and Lady Anne back to the Mayfield Manor, and Nicolette walked over to where Biscuit was located. She was feeling a slight cold chill come over her as she reached into the large wooden cage to grab Biscuit into her arms. She missed

Biscuit being able to come to her bed chamber since she came to Primrose Estate. Lady Margaret allowed Biscuit to come to visit her in the chamber and also allowed him to roam freely outside from time to time. When Nicolette took a stroll with Biscuit in the gardens at Old Wood Manor, she spent most of her time trying to keep Biscuit out of the flowers but he was beginning to learn to behave himself.

When Nicolette turned around and started to walk with Biscuit in her arms, she was surprised to see the Earl standing there holding a small warm blanket. "I saw you standing there holding Biscuit earlier, and I couldn't help but notice that you were shivering from your wet clothes, Miss Braxton. So I thought you could use this warm blanket to wrap around your shoulders," said the Earl in a deep masculine voice. Nicolette just stood there for a moment and couldn't yet speak. The Earl noticed her hesitation, so he quickly said, "I assure you, Miss Braxton, that this warm blanket does not belong to any of the horses. This is a clean blanket from the stack of clean blankets left on the bed cots that I have been known to sleep on out here in the stables from time to time. Please allow me to help you, Miss Braxton?" The Earl walked over to Nicolette and wrapped the warm blanket around her shivering body. When his warm, masculine hand touched her arm and shoulders, her body immediately began to warm from the mere touch of his hands. She was overwhelmed by his presence, and all she wanted to do at that moment was to reach out and touch him. The Earl was somewhat reluctant at first to go and get the warm blanket to offer her; he couldn't help but notice how her bosom and hard nipples were visible through her wet riding gown. He got so aroused from the sight of her, and he still was from the touch and smell of her skin. Oh, how he wanted to kiss her warm lips and touch her soft body under this warm blanket now wrapped around her shoulders. But they were not alone like they were before when they were on the ship and he had to control himself. "Thank you, Lord Mayfield; I feel much warmer now that you have offered me your blanket. I want to see Biscuit before I go back to the manor, my lord," said Nicolette as she stared into the handsome face of the Earl. "Before you leave, Miss Braxton, may I inquire about your ride today on Blubelle? How did she do with you as a rider? I am rather curious since you were the only one of the ladies she would allow to ride her," the Earl asked with laughter in his voice.

"You ought to be ashamed, my lord," said Nicolette with a wide grin on her pretty face. You know as well as I do that riding Blubelle this morning was my deepest desire, and you also know perfectly well that she did just fine."

"I have a feeling that the chances of Lady Anne ever riding Blubelle are rather slim," said the Earl while staring into Nicolette's big blue eyes, "Especially if you happen to be around Blubelle when Lady Anne is here, Miss Braxton." Before Nicolette realized what she was saying, she blurted out, "What will Lady Anne do about riding Blubelle when you make her your bride, my lord?" All that Nicolette could do at that very moment was to stand there with a total look of astonishment on her pretty face. She continued to stare into Earl's dark blue eyes when he touched her forehead with his hand and moved a strand of wet blonde hair from her eyes. "Do not worry, Miss Braxton; Blubelle will never belong to Lady Anne," tenderly said the Earl. "Well, how about you? Will you ever belong to Lady Anne, my lord?" asked Nicolette as she quickly handed Biscuit to the Earl and ran as fast as she could out the barn door of the horse stables.

When Nicolette got outside, she could see that the rain had completely ended, and the sun was shining through the clouds. She stood there for a moment, trying to catch her breath. When she looked up ahead, she saw a carriage heading towards the carriage house, so she decided to put her hands up in the air and signal the carriage to come towards her instead. She needed desperately to get back to the manor and get out of her wet gown and undergarments. The coachmen saw her waving at him, so he turned the carriage in her direction. Once she was seated comfortably inside the carriage, she let out a huge sigh of relief. Not only was she on her way to the manor, but she was getting far away from the Earl. At that moment all she could think of was that she must be out of her mind and why did she say that to Lord Mayfield. He could have easily told her that it wasn't any of her business if he belonged to Lady Anne. And then she could have easily reminded him that he made it her business when he so passionately kissed her on the Royal Princess Steam Ship. Maybe the kiss meant nothing to him and he has already forgotten that it ever happened. Who was she kidding? There was no doubt in her pretty little head that the Earl would have kissed her moments ago if they had been alone. And the real question was, would she have resisted his kiss?

Before she could give that another thought, the carriage pulled up in front of the west wing of the manor where her sleeping quarters were located.

She stepped out of the carriage and walked as quickly as she could to the door leading inside the manor. She decided to take the back stairway to her bed chamber and avoid contact with anyone if she could help it. When she reached her bed chamber, she immediately slid out of her wet gown. Sally must have heard her, and she came knocking softly on her door. When Sally entered the chamber, she quickly helped Nicolette out of her wet undergarments and went to fetch a bucket of water for a nice warm bath. Nicolette wasn't at all thrilled about joining the others for the afternoon tea. But it was their last day at Primrose Estate, and she knew that there was no way that she could avoid it. The only hope she had right now was that the Earl would not show up for the afternoon tea. After all he was awful busy getting ready to leave for London. He would be heading to Surrey for the Epsom Derby with the Dark Knight. If there was one thing for sure that she had come to learn about the Earl these past few weeks, it was the fact that he likes to be sure that everyone who works for him does an excellent job performing their duties as well as he does. But for now, she would forget about the Earl and lay across this big mahogany bed while she waited for Sally to pour her a warm bath.

When Nicolette stepped into the front parlor, she saw Lord Jared seated across from his father, the Marquis. Both Gentlemen stood to their feet when she entered the room. "Good afternoon,

Miss Braxton," said Lord Jared as he walked over to place a kiss on the top of her lace-gloved hand. Before she could say anything, she heard the sound of laughter behind her. When she turned around to look, she saw her mother, Lady Margaret, Lady Constance, Lady Katherine and Daniel enter the parlor. Lady Constance was the first to speak, "Lady Miranda and Lady Anne will be joining us soon." Daniel cleared his throat and announced, "The Earl and Lord Atticus will not be joining us for tea. But they want you to know that they will be joining everyone for the evening meal." Nicolette took her seat next to Lord Jared and he immediately captured her attention when he started inquiring about her new seamstress shop and Daniel's new tailor shop. Suddenly, Lord Jared stopped talking and stood to his feet when Lady Anne and Lady Miranda quietly entered the parlor. She couldn't help but notice the look in his eyes when he kept staring at Lady Anne. If she wasn't mistaken, it appeared to be the same look she saw when the Earl looked at her. It was as if he looked at her with desire in his eyes. *Oh my, please don't tell me that Lord Jared has his eye on Lady Anne.* Well, she did think that they would be better suited for one another. She never thought Lady Anne and the Earl were suited for one another, and the more she was around both of them, the more obvious it became. But there was one thing for certain she was going to do, and that was to keep a keen eye on Lord Jared and Lady Anne and possibly find ways to encourage whatever it was she saw in Lord Jared's eyes when he stared at Lady Anne.

When the afternoon tea in the parlor came to an end, most everyone went outside for some fresh air. Nicolette enjoyed participating in a game of crochet and archery. She was rather good at both, and she discovered that her biggest competition was Lord Jared. But eventually that all changed when the Earl and Lord Atticus suddenly showed up and joined the rest of them in the games. That was when they decided to pair off into teams. Lady Miranda and Lord Atticus were a team. Lady Anne and the Earl were a team; Nicolette and Lord Jared were a team, and Daniel and Lady Katherine were a team. The winner of the game of crochet happened to be Lady Miranda and Lord Atticus. Lady Anne and the Earl were in a tied game with Nicolette and Lord Jared in the game of archery and both Nicolette and Lady Anne were left to break the tie.

"It appears now that we are depending on one of you ladies to break the tie and win the game. So who will it be? I believe it's your turn, Miss Braxton," said the Earl with a sly grin on his handsome face. When Nicolette stepped up to take her position to break the tie, she glanced over at the Earl with a smug look on her face. When she held up her bow and was ready, she released her arrow straight into the bull's eye. Everyone remained quiet while Lady Anne took her place. When she released her arrow, it landed on the very edge of the bull's eye but didn't quite make it. Therefore, Nicolette and Lord Jared were declared the winners.

At that point, everyone was ready to retire from the games and go find cold refreshments. Nicolette watched as Lady Anne took her place beside the Earl and placed her arm inside his arm to walk towards the refreshment stand. Nicolette and everyone else followed behind the Earl and Lady Anne to get their refreshments. After Nicolette got her refreshment from the outside table, she saw her mother sitting under a canopy with her sister and Lady Constance. When she started walking over to where they were seated, she noticed that the Earl and Lady Anne got their refreshments and went walking into the lovely Mayfield gardens. Then she started to think about what she had promised herself. She promised that she would not be under the spell of the Earl any longer. And she knew that there was only one way to do that, and it was to find her a new beau. After all, the summer gala was right around the corner, but in the meantime, she would go find Lord Jared. Nicolette knew that she was rather skilled at using her charm to catch the eye of any gentleman, and Lord Jared happened to be available at this very moment.

CHAPTER 8

June-July 1865

"**P**lease come and take your seat next to mine, Miss Braxton," politely asked Lord Jared when Nicolette and Lady Elizabeth made their entrance into the Mayfield dining room this evening. The Earl, who was standing near Lord Jared and speaking to Lord Atticus at that moment, turned to gaze at Nicolette when he heard Lord Jared ask Nicolette to sit next to him. The Earl could hardly catch his breath when he saw her walk towards Lord Jared. He didn't exactly know how to name the color of the silk gown she was wearing that evening. All he knew was that it resembled the color of the red wine that was now being poured into their crystal wine glasses at this very moment, and it looked so darn lovely on her. He knew in an instant that he wasn't going to be able to keep his eyes off of her the rest of the evening. "Why I do, thank you, my Lord. I will be honored to take my seat next to yours," replied Nicolette in her soft, sweet southern voice.

Daniel, Lady Miranda, Lady Anne and Lady Katherine were next entering the dining room. Nicolette noticed that Lady Anne was wearing a much brighter shade of red than what she was wearing, but she thought it looked lovely on her. Lady Miranda and Lady Katherine also looked lovely in their soft ivory silk gowns with yellow pearls. At last, the Marquis and the lovely lady Constance came into the dining room, and everyone took their seats at the large dining table. Nicolette took her seat next to Lord Jared as promised, while Lady Anne took her seat next to the Earl directly across the table from Nicolette and Lord Jared. The Earl knew in his mind that he was going to keep as close as he could to Lord Jared and Nicolette this evening. He could tell that something was brewing between his brother and Nicolette, and he could tell that, more than likely, it was something Nicolette had up her sleeve. But for the moment his attention turned to Lady Anne when she brought up the incident that took place earlier this morning with her attempt to ride Blubelle. "After what happened this morning with Blubelle, my lord," said Lady Anne with determination in her soft voice. "I have decided that I need to visit Primrose Estate more often and get better acquainted with Blubelle. I can spend more time with her before I try to ride her again. She is such a magnificent horse, and I would love to ride her when I come for visits if that is alright with you, my lord."

Even though Nicolette was in conversation with Lord Jared, she couldn't help but hear every word that Lady Anne had just said to the Earl. All of a sudden, before the Earl could even speak, he suddenly dropped his dinner fork on top of his dinner plate, and when his hand went to grab it, he accidentally knocked over his wine glass. All at once, the room became silent, and everyone was staring in the Earl's direction. The Earl glanced over at Nicolette while the servants were cleaning up the spilled wine. He noticed that her cheeks were a bright red, and her eyes were filled with fire. The Earl knew that he had to think of something quick to say, so he began saying, "Ladies and gentlemen, I most graciously apologize for my clumsiness. I shall be more careful from now on. Please continue with your meal and conversation."

"I am waiting for you to give me your opinion on this matter, Lord Austin," said Lady Anne. "I sincerely hope you and I agree on this matter, my lord."

"It does make perfect sense that getting better acquainted with Blubelle will certainly help her feel more comfortable around you, my lady. But right now, all my attention is mostly on the Dark Knight and preparing for all the horse races we will be attending quite often. You are always welcomed here at Primrose Estate, Lady Anne, but if you would be so kind as to have a little patience, my lady, we can try to make what you are suggesting come true."

"I can see that you have your hands full with racing the Dark Knight my lord. Unfortunately, this is not the only thing I've learned to have patience with lately, my lord," said Lady Anne with slight sarcasm in her voice. But before the Earl had a chance to reply to Lady Anne, Lord Jared interrupted by asking what the Earl thought about the chances of the Dark Knight winning the Epsom Derby this weekend.

The Earl felt relieved that Lord Jared quickly changed the subject because he already knew what Lady Anne was trying to imply, and he didn't want any part of that. Before he answered

Lord Jared, he quickly glanced over at Nicolette and stared into her big blue eyes, and she watched as his eyes moved toward the top of her bosom. Before he could turn his eyes away from her, she could see the deep, dark desire that lay beneath those sapphire-blue eyes of his. Suddenly, she felt a warm tingle between her legs and a yearning to feel the Earl touching her in places she had never been touched before. Suddenly, she came back to reality when the Earl began to speak, "Well, to answer your question, brother, I believe the chances for the Dark Knight to win the derby are quite favorable. You and Lord Atticus both have seen the Dark Knight train and run often around the track here at Primrose. What do you and Lord Atticus think his chances are of winning?"

"I agree with you, brother," said Lord Jared. "But I guess we will know more once we get to Surrey and see him run around the track."

"You are right about that, Lord Jared," replied Lord Atticus. "Tomorrow will be here soon enough, so I think I will skip this evening's brandy and retire early to my chamber, gentlemen. The rest of my family, including Lady Elizabeth and Nicolette, will be heading back to Old Wood Manor tomorrow morning, so I would like to wish them a safe trip home. The Earl, Lord Jared, Daniel and I will be leaving at the crack of dawn in the morning, and I shall see the rest of you on the day of the race. So, therefore, will you please excuse me, everyone."

After the departure of Lord Atticus, the Marquis, Lord Gerald and Lord Austin departed to the gentlemen's study upon the request of the Marquis. Everyone else decided to retire to their bed chambers for the evening. The Earl immediately followed his father and Lord Gerald into the study and took his seat in the leather upholstered chair across from his father and Lord Gerald. After taking a rather large sip of his brandy and a puff off his large cigar, Lord Austin sat quietly, waiting for his father to be the first to speak.

"I am very well aware of how busy and preoccupied you have been, my Lord," spoke the Marquis to his son in a deep masculine voice. "It appears you have made an excellent choice when you sailed to North America and brought back those fine Arabian horses. I have no doubt that those beauties will reap you great rewards, my lord. But there is one other beauty I would like to mention to you, and that is Lord Gerald's only daughter, the lovely Lady Anne."

"May I say something, my lord," said Lord Gerald suddenly as he took his attention away from the Marquis and glanced over at the Earl. "I am most curious, Lord Austin, of what your future intentions are with my lovely daughter. Do you plan on honoring the marriage arrangement that was made between us long ago, and if so, how long do you plan on keeping her waiting?"

The Earl sat there in silence for a moment, trying to gather the right words to speak out loud to his father and Lord Gerald. "My intentions towards your daughter have been most honorable Lord Ashton. I shall plan on making her my wife if that is what she wishes as well but I am graciously asking for all of you to give me more time. I would like to be able to focus all of my attention on the Dark Knight and successfully make my way back into the sport of horse racing this season. I will enjoy her company as often as the opportunity allows. I will say towards the end of this year, before the Christmas season is upon us, I will be honored to ask Lady Anne for her hand in marriage if she still so wishes that as well, my lord."

Before Lord Gerald answered the Earl, he glanced over at the Marquis and said, "If anyone understands the attention and hard work that goes into horse racing, that would be you and I, Lord Mayfield; we have been truly blessed to have had that opportunity. But I do wonder if you will ever come to love my daughter, Lord Austin," Lord Gerald continued to say with a somewhat curious look on his aging, handsome face. "She is quite smitten with you, Lord Austin, as you probably already know. I suppose a proposal by the end of this year will be rather sufficient with me, Lord Austin. Do you agree, Lord Mayfield?"

"I suppose that will be fine with me, gentlemen, so if you please excuse me, I shall retire for the evening," replied the Marquis as he rose from his chair and immediately left the room. The Earl decided to stay in the study for a while now that his father and Lord Ashton both retired to their chambers for the evening. He knew that he had to wake up very early the next morning, but he was feeling rather restless at the moment. He poured himself another glass of brandy and thought about what had just taken place between his father, Lord Ashton and himself. He was relieved to know that he could keep delaying this marriage proposal between him and Lady Anne, but he also knew that the day would come when he wouldn't be able to delay it any longer. But right now, he was hoping for a miracle because he couldn't keep his mind off a lovely sea goddess with big blue eyes.

Once Nicolette returned to her bed chamber after leaving a rather eventful evening meal earlier, she quickly undressed with Sally's help and slid into bed. She felt rather tired after having such an eventful day, but unfortunately, she wasn't able to fall asleep. Suddenly, she remembered the one thing that had always helped her fall asleep, and that was reading a book. But she immediately realized that she did not bring any books of her own with her. But then it dawned on her that she knew exactly where the Mayfield library was located in the manor, and she would put on her robe and slippers and quietly head to the library on her own. She knew that she had to be very quiet when she shut her chamber door and walked out into the hallway leading downstairs to the room where the library was located. Immediately, she let out a sigh of relief when she made it to the library without anyone seeing her there.

The Earl was still in the study, sitting in his leather chair when he heard what sounded like light footsteps in the library adjacent to the gentlemen's study. So, he picked up one of the oil lanterns on a nearby table and walked as quietly as he could towards the library door. He slowly opened the door, peeped inside and saw Nicolette standing in front of one of the bookshelves with her back towards him. He didn't want to scare the wits out of her, so he decided to say her name quietly so that she could still hear him while standing just inside the doorway where she could know who was calling her name. But when she turned around to see who was calling her name, she was still startled seeing him standing there.

Nicolette gasped out loud before she began to speak, "Lord Mayfield! What are you doing here? I thought I was the only one here. I came here to get a book to read, my lord. I found myself rather restless this evening, and reading always helps me fall asleep. I suppose that is the reason you are here as well, my lord."

"That is not my reason, Miss Braxton," replied the Earl while staring at her beautiful face and body. "I happened to be alone in the gentlemen's study next to the library, and I heard a noise, and I came to see what the noise was all about, my dear. I will be glad to help you find a book, Miss Braxton. Do you have a particular book you're looking for?" said the Earl as he walked over to Nicolette and stood in front of her.

He was standing so close to her that he could smell her womanly scent mixed with a slight fragrance of Jasmine, and it was intoxicating. At that very moment, he wanted to reach out to her and gently sweep her into his masculine arms and carry her to his bed. But he knew that there was no way that was happening, so instead, he stared into her big blue eyes, and his face leaned into hers as if he wanted to kiss her. Before he had the chance to kiss her, she suddenly spoke out loud, "Lately I have been reading the novel "Emma," Lord Mayfield. It is one of Jane Austen's romance novels from her collection."

"I do know her books, and it appears that Mother has obtained the entire collection of Miss Braxton. I believe that we shall find it located on the shelf just above your head. Please allow me to get it down for you, Miss Braxton, since I can reach it much easier," But when the Earl suddenly reached over her to grab the book off the shelf, he found himself reaching for her lovely chin instead. He stared into her big blue eyes, placed his warm lips on her pink lips, delved his tongue inside her mouth and kissed her with a passion that he had never felt before. When he released her lips, he began to nibble the underside of her jawline, and his breath warmed the curve of her neck. He dipped one of his masculine fingers into the tender valley of her cleavage and quickly drew his finger out. Then he grasped her by the shoulders and found her lips once again. Once he delved his tongue into her mouth, he gave her kiss after kiss that grew increasingly hungry and fierce. Labored was her breathing now, and she felt faint with warm desire.

Once more, the Earl dipped down inside the tender valley of her cleavage and slid farther down in order to cup her firm breast. Then she felt his finger drawing a wide circle around the areola of her breast, and his thumb brushed her hardened nipple. Nicolette thought she would explode with pleasure. While continuing to brush her nipple, he removed her nightgown away from her shoulders with his other hand. His finger covered the small freckle on top of her left breast. "God, yes," he said as he pushed her breasts together.

He leaned forward and buried his face in them, nuzzling teasing licks back and forth to either side of her breast. Then he pulled back and drew her left nipple into his mouth. She couldn't hold back any longer, so she began to moan out loud, and so did he. She brought one hand to the back of his head, teasing her fingers through his dark silky hair as he sucked and licked.

Without even realizing what she was doing, she began to rock her hips against his, grinding against the hard ridge of his arousal. "Nicolette," he passionately spoke her name out loud. "Lord Austin," she whispered in his ear.

"Enough! That's enough," he suddenly exclaimed while pushing back and releasing her. "What just happened is my fault. I must go now!" Quickly, he reached for the book she wanted, placed it on a nearby table, reached for his oil lantern and swiftly left the room. Nicolette stood silently and still while the glow of her oil lantern cast a shadow of her on a wall nearby. She could see where he had slid her nightgown down her shoulders and exposed her now swollen breast and hardened nipples. She was still in shock, but she knew why he left so suddenly. It was for the same reason why she ran away from him earlier when he offered her the warm blanket when they were together in the stables. They both knew that what was going on between them was wrong, and the Earl went as far as to say that it was his fault. But she knew what the truth was, and the truth was that this was her fault as well. She had made a promise to herself that the next time he tried to kiss her, she would resist, but instead, she allowed him to not only kiss her but to leave her standing there, a frustrated, trembling mass of desire and unfulfilled need. But a moment later, a feeling of guilt and shame spread throughout her body as she reached for her oil lantern, grabbed the book off the table, and headed quickly and quietly to her bed chamber.

Alone in his chamber, the Earl unscrewed the top of his bottle of whiskey with trembling fingers. He tossed back a huge scorching swallow and placed it back down on the small wooden table. He was feeling overly excited and agitated at the same time when he stripped himself of his waistcoat. He put out the lantern and strode over to the table to light a fresh candle. He suddenly started to swear quietly into the candle-lit room while he tugged at the buttons of his breeches and undone them. He placed his aching erection in his hand and felt that he was still hard and primed for release.

"Damn," he said out loud as he thought about her breasts, her hips, her mouth on his and the softness of her skin. He thought about the moans of her pleasure and the sound of his name on her lips. The taste of her skin and those nipples….God, she had the most luscious nipples he had ever laid eyes on or thumbs or lips upon. Holding on to the table with his other hand, he knew that he had to release himself, and when he did, he discarded his soiled shirt and slid into bed. Relief for now, yes, but there will be no relief for wanting Nicolette, and now he was determined more than ever to find a way to make her his now and forever.

Nicolette realized the following morning that it wasn't the dark clouds hanging low in the sky that were making her feel slightly gloomy; it was leaving Primrose Estate with a horrible feeling of shame and disgrace. After what took place between the Earl and her last evening, she was relieved that she didn't have to face him this morning. He had left Primrose Estate much earlier this morning with his Arabian horses and all the others that had accompanied him to Surrey for the Epsom Derby. The Ashton family, her mother, and she would be attending the race day after tomorrow on the day of the horse race. Until then, hopefully, she could find a little solitude. She certainly would like to avoid Lady Anne as much as possible. After they returned from the horse race in Surrey, her mother, Daniel, and she was supposed to take a visit to Lord Gerald Ashton's brother's cottage in London near Daniel's tailor shop and her seamstress shop. Their plan was to live in the cottage during the weekdays while working in their shops and return to Old Wood Manor on the days when the shops were closed.

"You appear to be rather quieter than usual this morning, Nicolette," Suddenly said Lady Anne, sitting directly across from her in the Ashton family carriage as it headed home to Old Wood Manor. "Are you feeling well this morning, Nicolette?"

Nicolette hesitated a brief moment before she answered Lady Anne, "I am well, Lady Anne; I am thinking about my new seamstress shop and the new gowns to be made for the upcoming summer gala."

"Well, you don't have to worry about Mother and me. We have already purchased our new gowns for the summer gala. Although I am rather sure they will not be quite as lovely as the ones that you and your mother will create. As a matter of fact, when we arrive at Old Wood Manor, I would love to show the gowns to you and Lady Elizabeth. As you both are well aware, the colors of the summer season are lilac, pale blues and pale greens, and we have chosen those colors for our summer gowns."

"You have made an excellent choice, my lady," replied Nicolette with a slight smile on her lovely face. "Your mother and you shall look quite lovely in those colors."

"Why, thank you, Nicolette; I am rather looking forward to this season's summer gala, and I'm sure you are as well since this will be your first. This will be like a coming out into noble society event for you and your family now that you have made England your new home."

"Yes, I suppose it will be," replied Nicolette in her soft southern voice. For a moment she couldn't help but think about the summer gala being an opportunity to help bring Lord Jared and Lady Anne closer together. And she was not only doing this because she didn't want the Earl and Lady Anne to marry, it was because she knew that those two were not right for each other and they would not be happy together even if she wasn't here. Even if she had never met the Earl and met only Lord Jared, she could tell that he adored

Lady Anne, and they were so much more suited for one another, and she would do everything in her power to help make that happen. But most of all, she could tell that the Earl did not want to marry Lady Anne even though he did not want to disappoint his father and Lord Ashton. Until then, she needed to learn to control herself around the Earl, but she knew very well she was almost asking for the impossible. And at that very moment, when she closed her eyes, all she could vision was a dark-haired Earl with sapphire blue eyes and warm, passionate kisses.

It was the last day of June, and it was also the day of the Epsom Derby. The Earl, Lord Atticus, Lord Jared, Daniel, Lord Watson, the horse trainer, the Earl's horse jockey, Teddy Pendleton, and the Earl's grooms all arrived at the race a couple of days ago. The Earl had been so busy making sure everyone and everything was in perfect order for today. But he still couldn't stop thinking about what had taken place between Nicolette and him the other night when he found her inside the Mayfield library at Primrose Estate. Her sweet voice, her soft skin, her warm lips, her beautiful body, her quick wit and intellect were among the things that he adored about her. But right now, all those magnificent qualities of hers were forbidden to him, and wanting all of her made him feel selfish. He knew deep down that if he kept his promise to his father and Lord Ashton and asked Lady Anne to be his wife, Nicolette would belong to another man one day, and just the thought of that made his blood boil with rage. But right now, he'd got a horse race to win, so he cleared his head off the thoughts and stared ahead as he watched the Mayfield family carriage heading towards the Mayfield tent.

"Good morning, Mother, Father, Lady Miranda and Lady Katherine," said the Earl as he took his mother's hand and gently helped her step outside the carriage. "It is quite a lovely day for the race, isn't it dear," kindly spoke Lady Constance to her son, the Earl. "Indeed, it is Mother as long as the rain holds off. And it will be an even lovelier day if the Dark Knight is fortunate to be the winner today."

"Well, I'm feeling rather lucky today, my lord, and we shall see," replied Lady Constance while she watched Daniel help Lady Miranda and Lady Katherine step out of the carriage. Once everyone was out of the carriage and escorted to their seats, the Earl started walking towards the horse stables when he suddenly saw the Ashton family carriage strolling towards him, heading for the Mayfield tent. As the carriage slowly passed by him, he couldn't help but notice the beautiful blue eyes of Nicolette underneath her lovely blue derby hat peeping out the small window of the Ashton carriage. He suddenly stopped walking and looked inside the carriage window at Nicolette and Lady Anne. And in a manly manner, he took off his hat and smiled his most charming smile as he waved at everyone inside the carriage. Since he needed to hurry back to the horse stable where the Dark Knight was getting ready for the race, he turned around and continued to walk to the stables.

Now that the crowds were all gathering, there was a lot of noise and excitement in the air. The sky was still as blue as before and the sun was shining its warm rays on the large crowd that was eagerly waiting for the race. There was a lot of chatter in the air about "Gladiateur," the horse that was the most favored to win today. But at this point in time, the Earl was feeling rather confident about the "Dark Knight's" chances to win. Word had gotten around the track about the "Dark Knight," but this was his first race, and it was up in the air whether he had a chance to win. The "Gladiateur" has already won the 2,000 Guineas so far this season, and it was one of the most prestigious races of the year. The "Gladiateur" and the "Dark Knight" both were three years old. All the horses that entered the race were that age. The "Dark Knight was American-born, and the "Gladiateur" was a French-born thoroughbred horse. "Gladiateur" was sent to England to be trained by Tom Jennings at New Market Racecourse and didn't begin racing until the fall of last year. And, of course, the "Dark Knight" began his training in North America and continued training in England now that he belonged to the Earl.

Now, it was time for the Earl's horse jockey, Teddy Pendleton, to bring the "Dark Knight" to the starting line while the Earl found his seat with his family and friends. Nicolette was seated nearby with the rest of the ladies, and she was close enough that he could see her lovely smile. The race began and everyone was standing on their feet by now. At first, it didn't look so good for the "Dark Knight," but the "Gladiateur" was maintaining a slight lead with another horse bearing down on him to take the lead. When they almost crossed the finish line, the "Dark Knight" pulled ahead of the other horse but could never catch up with the "Gladiateur" who won the race. But the "Dark Knight" finished second out of 30 runners. The "Gladiateur" won by 2 lengths in 2 minutes 46 seconds with a ½ length between second and third place. Of course, the Earl was slightly disappointed that he didn't win, but he was not disappointed with the "Dark Knight" taking second place. As a matter of fact, he felt rather proud of his horse and the results he had today. And so was everyone else proud to shake his hand and congratulate him on his second-place victory. When Nicolette made her way towards him, she made a slight curtsy as she spoke to him, "Well done, Lord Austin; I know that the "Dark Knight" has it in him; he will be a winner soon. But a second-place finish is honorable, my lord." The Earl gently lifted Nicolette's lovely hand and placed a warm kiss on the top of it as he stared into her big blue eyes. "I agree, Nicolette; there is no doubt in my mind that the "Dark Knight" will be a winner in the future."

Lady Anne happened to be standing close by and saw what just took place between the Earl and Nicolette. This was the first time she had witnessed both the Earl and Nicolette suddenly speaking to one another on a first-name basis. The Earl had always called her Miss Braxton, and she had always addressed the Earl by saying, Lord Mayfield. Lady Anne couldn't help but wonder when and why that had suddenly changed. *Oh, that's the last thing I need to be doing right now, and that is to allow my imagination to get the best of me.* Lady Anne thought to herself while watching the Earl shake so many hands of those who were congratulating him for his second-place finish. *It's probably the fact that they have known each other long enough to be friends now, and therefore, it is appropriate to address one another on a first-name basis. After all,* she thought to herself. *I am the one who will become his bride, and the sooner, the better. As a matter of fact, I have noticed Nicolette paying much attention to Lord Jared lately.*

Lady Anne knew that Lord Jared was quite the catch, and if she hadn't already promised to the Earl, she would have her eye on Lord Jared. *I have noticed that Lord Jared has given me a lot more attention than his brother lately and I do so enjoy his company.* Suddenly, she thought of something that she could do that might make the Earl notice the next time they were all together. Maybe if the Earl saw that she was paying more attention to Lord Jared than him, he would feel a slight jealousy and would try harder to get her attention. That was an excellent idea, she thought. *I wonder why I never thought of that idea before.* Now, it was time to bid farewell to the Earl and approach him once again before he headed back to the stables with the "Dark Knight." The Earl smiled at Lady Anne while bending over to kiss the top of her lovely hand, "I shall see you in a couple of weeks at the summer gala my lady. I am very much looking forward to it. Please have a safe trip home my dear."

When Lady Anne walked towards the Ashton family carriage where Nicolette was standing, the Earl tried not to look at Nicolette, but he couldn't help himself. He had to get one last look at the lovely goddess who had aroused his desire like no other before her.

CHAPTER 9
England Summer 1865

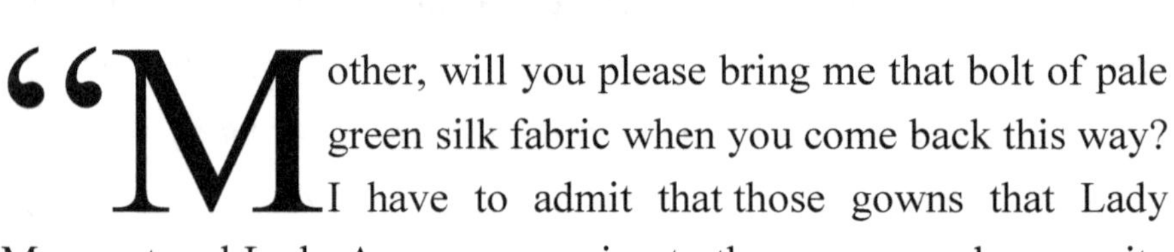

" "Mother, will you please bring me that bolt of pale green silk fabric when you come back this way? I have to admit that those gowns that Lady Margaret and Lady Anne are wearing to the summer gala are quite lovely. Don't you agree, Mother?" said Nicolette while she was cutting a piece of lilac silk fabric to be a part of the gowns that her mother and she were wearing to the summer gala.

"Yes, I do agree, dear," replied Lady Elizabeth as she carefully took the bolt of lilac silk fabric off the spindle. The colors were quite lovely for this season. *I find them to be light and airy. As a matter of fact, they will be perfect for the Charleston summer season; you well know how hot it gets there during the summer season.* Nicolette put her scissors down on the table, glanced over at her mother for a moment, and saw a rather sad look in her mother's eyes. Her mother must be thinking about papa and how much she missed him and her home in Charleston with him. Nicolette missed her papa and her home in Charleston and thought of them both quite often. Suddenly, it made her think of George and Caroline. She had been so busy with her new life in England that she had completely forgotten that she had written a letter to George and Caroline asking them to please come to England. *The letter should be arriving any day now, and hopefully, I will be fortunate enough to receive a response from them. I do miss them terribly,* she thought. *I would love to see them both.*

"Mother, I believe the Ellington family carriage has arrived. I think I hear it pull up outside. I remembered you have a fitting with the Duchess of Ellington today," said Nicolette as she stood up to walk towards the front window of her seamstress shop. "Are you sure you will be fine while I'm gone to the Ellington estate? The Duchess insisted on me coming there instead of coming here to the shop," said Lady Elizabeth as she grabbed her bonnet off the sewing table and headed to the front door. "Hopefully, I won't be gone too long, dear."

"Relax, Mother, Daniel is right next door, and you do not have to worry. So go, Mother, you do not need to keep the Duchess of Ellington waiting." Nicolette turned away from the window and sat back down at the sewing table. Recently, she had been going back and forth in her head about whether she would use the aquamarine blue fabric with lilac and ivory lace for trim or the lilac silk fabric with an aquamarine top bodice with lilac trim. Her mother had already reminded her that either one would look lovely on her to wear to the summer gala. But for the moment, she was thankful that it was quiet in the shop. Even though she needed customers, the word hadn't yet gotten around London about her new shop quite yet. Nicolette and her mother were hoping that showing off their new gowns at the summer gala would grab the attention of the elite. She knew for certain that the Duchess of Ellington showing up to the summer gala with one of her gowns would be a huge influence. Suddenly without wanting to, her thoughts were on the Earl once again. She thought about how the Earl had mentioned to her that he liked the color blue of her eyes. She almost giggled out loud when she remembered that he described them as being the color of the Mediterranean Sea. Well, then, that thought helped her make up her mind that she would choose aquamarine silk as the main color of her gown for the summer gala.

"I can see that you have turned Lord Gerald Ashton's brother's shop into your own, Daniel," said Lord Austin while standing still inside Braxton Tailors. "I am truly impressed with what you have done to the shop." Daniel continued to take the measurements of the Earl when he replied, "I am honored that you are impressed with the shop, my lord. I do hope you are just as much impressed with the suit I will be making you for the summer gala."

"Well, I have to admit I am taking a risk, but I do have faith in you, Mr. Braxton," replied the Earl as he slightly chuckled out loud. "Please do not let me down, but so far, I am pleased with what we chose." Once Daniel finished taking the measurements for his suit, the Earl walked towards the front door. He said his goodbye to Daniel, grabbed his hat off the hat rack and left the shop.

When the Earl stepped outside the shop, he looked up at the sky and saw that some dark clouds were starting to appear. He was hoping that the rain would hold off since he had a few more places to go while he was in the city. But first, he wanted to go inside Nicolette's Seamstress Shop. He knew that this was probably not the best idea, but his curiosity had got the best of him. Plus, he wanted to see her again. He couldn't get her off of his mind. So, he decided to step inside, but no one was in the front room. He walked over to the counter, picked up the bluebell, and started ringing it. A moment later, he looked up and saw Nicolette entering the front room. He was speechless for a moment. He thought she looked so lovely standing there in her modest green and white striped day gown with her blonde hair braided down her back. But the look on her face made him wonder if he had made the right choice by coming there. She didn't look very pleased, or maybe it was the fact that he had surprised her.

"Hello Nicolette," softly spoke the Earl in his deep masculine voice. "I truly hope you don't mind me paying a visit to your lovely shop, my dear. Since I was next door receiving a fitting in your brother's Tailor shop, I thought I could see your shop as well. I hope you don't mind me stopping by while I'm here in London today. I must say that I'm even more impressed with your shop than I am with Daniel's shop. It is lovely just like the lady that the shop is named after. Lady Elizabeth must be in the back room working; I would love to say hello to her." The Earl suddenly took a few steps towards the back room when Nicolette quickly burst out loud, "Mother is not here right now, Lord Mayfield; she happens to be doing a fitting for the Duchess of Ellington today."

"Ah, The Duchess of Ellington," replied the Earl with a half grin on his face. "I wish Lady Elizabeth well since everyone in England knows by now that the Duchess can be quite the handful. But I must say, if this fitting is for a new gown for the Duchess to wear to the summer gala, then you have done rather well for yourself. From what I hear, the Duchess of Ellington has quite the influence on ladies' fashion."

"Then I am truly fortunate that the Duchess has chosen my shop, my lord," replied Nicolette as she stood there staring at the Earl, her heart pounding in her chest.

"But your shop will succeed even without the Duchess's influence. You have a gift, Nicolette. You shall do quite well on your own. I want you to know that I adore you, and I can't get you out of my mind," said the Earl with a voice full of deep desire and admiration. As he stepped closer to Nicolette, her body began to tremble slightly. "What is it, my love?" said the Earl as he stared into her big blue eyes and gently lifted her chin. "You should know by now that you don't have to be frightened of me."

"It isn't that I'm frightened of you, my lord," replied Nicolette. "You know as well as I do that we cannot continue to do what we did that night in the library. We have to put an end to this," said Nicolette as she couldn't help but stare into the handsome face of the Earl. "Is that what you really want to do, my love?" replied the Earl as he dropped her chin and stepped away from her. "No, my lord, it is not what I want to do, but it is what I have to do," sadly replied Nicolette as she stood there watching the Earl grab his hat off the counter and walk towards the front door of the shop. Before he walked out the door, he turned and looked at Nicolette and said, "I will never take Lady Anne as my bride in the present or the future. Good day to you, Nicolette," said the Earl as he stepped outside the shop and felt rain drops on his handsome face.

Now, she was even more confused about what to do about her feelings for the Earl. *How dare he to say such a thing,* she spoke out loud. *What sort of nonsense or mind games is he playing with me now? Does he take me as a fool? But if there was any chance that he truly meant what he said about not asking Lady Anne to be his wife, then it's time I share with him what I have discovered. I'm certain the Earl will be interested to hear that his younger brother, Lord Jared, has his eye on Lady Anne. With that thought deep in her mind, Nicolette hurried over to the sewing table, determined to make her the finest gown she ever made.*

"It certainly is busy around Primrose Estate these days, my Lord," said Lord Watson as he walked the Dark Knight onto the horse track near the Mayfield horse stables. "Yes, it has been rather noisy around here lately, Lord Watson," replied the Earl, who was walking on the other side of the Dark Knight inside the track.

"Mother has been on edge lately as well. As you well know, Lord Watson, we are getting ready for the summer gala that is taking place here at Primrose in a couple of days, and a message has arrived to inform us that Queen Victoria's half-sister Fedora, Princess of Langenburg and Queen Victoria's daughter, Princess

Victoria and her son Bertie, Prince of Wales will be attending the gala. And Mother and staff are in a frenzy making sure everything is perfect."

"Well with the looks of things around here, I am most certain that it will be, my lord," replied Lord Watson as he was instructing the Dark Knight to run around the track. "It is probably out of place to say this, but you know by now that word has gotten around that you and Lady Anne will be married. I'm rather curious about whether or not there will be a big announcement of your marriage at this gala Lord Mayfield." The Earl just stood there leaning against the wooden fence, frozen for a moment before he could speak, "I suppose everyone attending the gala is suspecting to hear that I have proposed marriage to Lady Anne and what I am about to tell you, Lord Watson stays between you and me. I have already spoken to Father and Lord Ashton and told them I want to postpone the proposal until the end of the horse racing season. I want to divert all of my attention on the Dark knight this season." Lord Watson had a slight notion of what the real reason for the delay was and it probably had something to do with the lovely Nicolette. He couldn't help that he was nearby the day she rode Blubelle and came into the stables wet from the rain. He saw a glimpse of what was taking place between the two, and it looked as if there was a lot more than friendship between those two. He could tell that the Earl would think of Nicolette when he was around Blubelle, or if Lady Miranda mentioned Nicolette's name, his face would light up.

There was definitely something brewing between those two, and he was afraid that things were not going to end well for everyone involved. But right now he had a secret of his own. He couldn't keep his eye off the lovely Lady Miranda, and he knew that the Earl would send him packing if he got the slightest inkling of that. "I shall never betray you, my lord. What you have told me about the delay of your marriage is safe with me, my lord."

"It looks as if the Dark Knight is performing better than I even imagined, Lord Watson. The slightly strained muscle in his right leg appears to be completely healed. Too bad we had to miss the Grand Prix de Paris race held in France back in June and now we will not be able to attend the Grand Prix de Prince Imperial since it also takes place in France. Now that I have postponed the marriage proposal, I know that Mother and Father will be disappointed if I don't come here for the summer gala," said the Earl as he continued to watch the Dark Knight run around the track.

"Well, I do have to admit that I am rather fond of the idea that this season's summer gala is held here at Primrose Estate, and it is quite the honor, as you well know, Lord Watson."

"Indeed, my lord, I will be obliged to agree with you. It is quite an honor that the summer gala will be here at Primrose. My family and I are very much looking forward to attending the gala Lord Mayfield. Too bad Mother is not here to attend with us; she would be thrilled," said Lord Watson before he started to walk toward the Dark Knight.

"I am truly sorry for your loss, Lord Watson; your mother was a kind and gentle soul who is truly missed by us all," replied the Earl as he watched Lord Watson walk towards the Dark Knight to rein him in and lead him back to the horse stables. "The Dark Knight's leg seems to be back to normal," the Earl loudly spoke before he turned around and headed towards the horse stables.

When the Earl got back to the horse stables, he summoned a coachman to take him to the manor. It had turned out to be a much warmer day than he anticipated earlier. As he glanced around the lovely grassy lawns around the manor, he noticed several large tents that were waiting to be set up very soon. For some reason, they made him think of the lovely Nicolette. Ah, he thought to himself, *I know why these tents make me think of her because last time she was here, she was standing under one of these tents looking so beautiful, trying to charm the daylights out of my brother. And it was rather obvious that she had succeeded since Lord Jared could not keep his eyes and attention off of her at dinner that evening.* But suddenly that made him also remember a few times in the past when Lady Anne would be visiting Primrose Estate; he noticed on several occasions that Lord Jared would stare at Lady Anne with a much more intense look. It was as if he was looking at her with desire in his eyes. There was no doubt that he knew that look because he was certain that he probably had that same look in his eyes when he gazed at Nicolette. *Well, there was one thing for certain, and that was both of the ladies are quite lovely in their own way, but no one will have Nicolette; she belongs to me.*

When the coachman pulled the carriage to the side entrance to the manor, the Earl heard voices as he stepped down from the carriage. So, instead of walking into the side door of the east wing of the manor, he decided to walk around towards the front of the manor so he could see who was there. Once he arrived there, he saw two carriages and realized that they were Mayfield carriages. Lord Richard Mayfield, the brother of the Marquis and the uncle of the Earl, has just arrived with his family. He watched as his uncle, Lord Richard, and his Scottish wife, Lady Olivia, stepped down from their carriage along with their oldest son, Lord Alistair, and the oldest daughter, Luisa, of Lady Olivia's late sister and brother-in-law. Lord Richard and Lady Olivia raised Luisa from a baby after the tragic accident of both her parents. Lady Olivia's Scottish sister had married a Spanish Count, and they were both killed in a robbery by river pirates. Luisa survived the tragedy and soon after was brought to Scotland by the midwife to live with Lord Richard and Lady Olivia. The Earl continued to watch as a second carriage suddenly pulled up behind the first carriage. He watched as the second oldest son descended from the carriage along with two other children and a lady's maid. Immediately, his eyes wandered back to the lovely Luisa with her dark copper curls. It had been a long while since he had seen her, and she had now blossomed even more into this lovely vision.

Suddenly, a memory from the past came to mind, Lord Atticus and the Ashton family were visiting at the same time that his uncle and family were visiting Primrose Estate. He recalled Lord Atticus spending a lot of time in the presence of the lovely Luisa. It was obvious Lord Atticus was quite fond of her. The Earl couldn't help but think about how Lord Atticus would feel the moment his eyes would land on her in a couple of days at the summer gala. There was no doubt in his mind that she would sweep Lord Atticus right off his feet. Suddenly, it dawned on him that a marriage between Lord Atticus and Luisa would be another means to bringing bloodlines between the Mayfield family and the Ashton family. And with that cheerful thought in his mind, the Earl turned around quickly and ran towards the door that led inside the manor, where he would quickly head to his chamber to freshen up for the afternoon tea in the Mayfield parlor. As the Earl was practically running up the stairs, he couldn't help but think about Nicolette and how much he was looking forward to seeing her again, and he suddenly said out loud, *If she thinks that I'm going to stay away from her for good. She better think again because that will never happen as long as I am breathing.*

It was a lovely day to be hosting a summer gala at the Primrose Estate. The sky was a lovely shade of blue, and there wasn't a cloud hanging anywhere in sight. It was mid-morning, and the Ashton family carriages had just arrived at Primrose Estate. The Earl was in the horse stables checking on a mare and her colt when he heard carriage wheels and horse hooves far off in the distance. The Earl hurried out the door of the stables and motioned for the coachmen to take him to the front of the manor so he would be there to greet the Ashton family and the Braxton family upon their arrival. When he arrived there, Nicolette was standing outside the Ashton carriage about to take the arm of Lord Jared. The Earl noticed Lady Anne standing there looking off in the distance. When his carriage came to a sudden halt, the Earl jumped down from the carriage and walked over to greet everyone. Lord Atticus was the first to greet the Earl, and they both walked over to where Daniel, Lord Atticus, Lady Anne, Lord Jared and Nicolette were waiting. Lady Anne quickly stepped forward and spoke in her softest, sweetest voice, "Good Morning, Lord Austin! I have been much looking forward to this day my lord. I hope you are planning on attending today's festivities, and if so, I will also look forward to saving several dances with you on my dance card this evening, my lord."

"Yes, my lady, I will be attending today's festivities, and I am quite honored that you will make plenty of room for me on your dance card. I am also looking forward to this day, Lady Anne." The Earl quickly glanced over at Nicolette, but she was gazing into the eyes of Lord Jared and smiling as he took her by the arm and led her up the large steps to the front door of the manor.

Nicolette was relieved to throw her bonnet down on the bed in her chamber and stretch her long legs across the bed. She loathed these long carriage rides with Lady Anne. Even though the time seemed to pass by rather quickly since Lady Anne couldn't seem to quit talking during the entire trip there, it did raise her nerves and made her wonder how the Earl would ever be able to endure it. But she was quite sure Lord Jared wouldn't have any problem listening to Lady Anne's constant chatter because he appeared to adore every word that came from her endless chatter. She couldn't help but chuckle out loud but stopped when she heard a soft knock on her door. It was her lady's maid.

"Good morning, Miss Braxton," the lady's maid spoke in her soft, timid voice. "Will you soon be joining everyone outside on the lawn for lunch, my dear? I'm quite sure you will like to freshen up from your trip first. I brought you some fresh water to pour in the basin over there. I will be glad to help you braid your hair if that is what you so wish, my dear. It is getting much warmer outside, and the sun is very bright today."

"That will be lovely, but on second thought, bring me my riding gown. I feel like taking Blubelle out for a ride. I'm not very hungry right now, so have a carriage ready to carry me over to the horse stables. So, hurry over here and help me out of these clothes so you can braid my hair and help me into my riding gown. Then go tell the footman to have my carriage waiting outside the west wing door. I will be there soon after."

It didn't take Nicolette long to be ready to crawl into the carriage. Once she got to the horse stables, she went inside and found Lord Watson. Nicolette knew that riding Blubelle without the Earl's permission was probably not a good idea, but she knew that a horse ride across these lovely grassy meadows and woodlands was just what she needed at this moment. Now that she was living in the city of London most of the week, working in her seamstress shop and enjoying every moment of it, she still felt somewhat confined. So, taking Blubelle out for a long ride would be invigorating for her well-being. The Earl would just have to oblige. "Oh, there you are, Lord Watson," kindly said Nicolette when she approached him. "I would like to take Blubelle out for a ride, Lord Watson. Will you please get her ready for me, my lord? I will be waiting outside when the groom brings her out."

"I will be glad to tell the groom to get her ready for you to ride Miss Braxton. But I can't help but wonder if the Earl knows that you are about to take Blubelle out for a ride," said Lord Watson with a puzzled look on his handsome face. "No, he does not know that I want to take Blubelle out for a ride, Lord Watson. I thought he might be here at the stables, and I would be able to ask him Lord Watson, but I can see that he is not here."

"I honestly don't think the Earl would mind if you take Blubelle for a ride, Miss Braxton. It is the idea of you riding alone that might make him apprehensive, my dear."

"Well, I shall take that chance, Lord Watson, and if he is displeased with me, I shall take full responsibility for my actions. I will tell him that you tried to talk me out of it, Lord Watson. So, I will be waiting on Blubelle outside. Good day to you, my lord."

Moments after Nicolette mounted Blubelle and took off on her ride, the

Earl showed up at the horse stables. The Earl stood there staring at what appeared to be the back of Blubelle and a rider off in the distance. He immediately entered the stables and looked for Lord Watson inside the stables. "Was that Blubelle I saw leaving the stables, Lord Watson?" asked the Earl when he swiftly walked up to him. "That is Blubelle, my lord, and Miss Braxton is taking her out for a ride," replied Lord Watson. "I do not like the fact that Miss Braxton is riding out alone," said the Earl as he was looking for his groom to saddle up his horse. It didn't take long for the Earl to mount his horse and swiftly hurry after the lovely Nicolette.

The Earl rode so fast that it didn't take him long to enter the woodlands where the vibrant yellow Primrose flowers were still spreading across the landscape. When he rode a little farther into the woodlands, he suddenly heard a loud feminine scream. As he got closer to where the scream was coming from, he heard the sound of a horse rearing up on his hind legs. Once he got to the scene of what was taking place, he saw the culprit of the tragedy taking place. A wild Boar was running through the woods towards Nicolette and Blubelle. Once the Boar was in plain sight, the Earl immediately fired his rifle and shot the boar. Quickly and carefully, the Earl rode over to where the Boar was lying on the ground to make sure it was dead. Now that they were safe from the Boar, The Earl rode over to Blubelle and Nicolette and dismounted his horse. When he walked over to Nicolette, he helped her dismount Blubelle and held her safe in his arms. "You are safe now, my love," said the Earl in his most tender voice.

"I have never been so thankful to see you, my lord," softly spoke Nicolette while gazing into the sapphire blue eyes of the Earl.

"I am truly sorry that I did not listen to Lord Watson. I do not know what I was thinking, my lord. You have every right to scold me."

"I will not scold you, Nicolette; you are not a child." Immediately, he leaned towards her face and placed his lips on her warm lips, opened her mouth with his tongue and kissed her with a passion that set his body on fire. Then her hands slid over his shoulder to the back of his neck, and she pushed her body even closer to him. Her soft breasts flattened against his hard chest. Excitement rushed over him, and every inch of him enjoyed the exquisite sensation of her kiss. When he released her from the kiss, Nicolette kept her hands clasped behind his neck and lifted her head. She went absolutely still in his arms. She seemed to have ceased to breathe, and he was standing there catching his breath. "We must go now, my love; we do not want to encounter another wild Boar today," said the Earl in a slightly hesitant tone of voice.

"Even though I feel quite safe here with you, my lord, I prefer not to encounter another wild Boar today as well," replied Nicolette as she placed her foot in the stirrup of Blubelle and climbed into her saddle. "Please lead the way, Nicolette; I am right behind you, my sea goddess."

Once the Earl and Nicolette arrived back at the horse stables, Nicolette quickly dismounted Blubelle and handed her reins over to the Earl. "I must go now and prepare myself for today's festivities. I am quite sure Mother is wondering where I am by now, and I happen to be rather famished at this moment," said Nicolette while staring into the handsome face of the Earl with a sense of longing in her big blue eyes. The Earl smiled at her with a look of love and desire in his eyes but remained silent. He raised his hand towards the carriage house and motioned for the coachman to come and take Nicolette back to the manor.

Nicolette's nerves were finally starting to unravel as she slid even farther down into the fragrant water of her bath basin. The smell of Jasmine was consuming her, and it smelled divine, along with a faint smell of musk and leather still on her face. Naturally, her thoughts were on the Earl and the events that had taken place earlier today. The forbidden ride on Blubelle into the woodlands, the afternoon games and festivities they shared with everyone in the afternoon, but most of all, she thought about the passionate kiss that she shared with the Earl when he rescued her from the wild Boar. At this moment, she did not know whether to be happy or furious at herself for allowing the Earl to kiss her once again. Then she thought about Lady Anne and how tight she was clinging on to the Earl during today's festivities. But at the end of the day, she noticed it was Lord Jared who was making Lady Anne smile and giggle while giving her all of his attention. The only time she was receiving attention from the Earl was when they had to partner up for the outdoor games. When it came to playing horseshoes, the Earl practically had to teach Lady Anne how to play the game, and Nicolette could tell that Lady Anne was savoring every moment that the Earl had to touch her to show her the technique of how to throw the horseshoe. But Nicolette couldn't help but realize that Lady Anne must know by now that the Earl did not love her and that his only intention was to honor his father and Lord Ashton's agreement. So now she was determined more than ever to help bring Lady Anne and Lord Jared together. *This evening will be the perfect time to tell the Earl, and perhaps he will agree to help.* With that thought in mind, Nicolette slid down into her bath to wash her beautiful golden hair.

When the Earl and Lord Atticus entered the large ballroom at the Mayfield manor, they were struck with awe at how lovely the room appeared. There was a shimmer of light that sparkled everywhere from the oil lantern chandeliers hanging from the high ceilings. They could smell the aroma of fresh-cut flowers in the vases scattered around the room, but what caught their attention most of all were two ladies in particular. Lord Atticus couldn't help but stare at the lovely Lady Luisa with her dark copper hair, and the Earl couldn't take another step once his eyes gazed into the big blue eyes of the lovely Nicolette. "Good evening, gentlemen," said Daniel as he and Lord Jared approached the Earl and Lord Atticus. "Who might the lady with the red hair and lovely green gown be, my lord?" asked Daniel to the Earl as he suddenly turned around and noticed her standing with her mother nearby. "That is my cousin Lady Luisa from Scotland, Daniel."

"Yes, indeed, it is your cousin Lord Austin, and perhaps it is time I ask her to dance," suddenly said Lord Atticus as he handed his champagne glass over to the servant while heading straight towards the lovely Lady Luisa.

Moments later, the Earl's attention was back to staring at Nicolette when he saw Lord Chamberlain's eldest son, Lord Justin, approach her and take her by the hand to lead her to the dance floor. He knew that the evening was still young yet, and he must look for Lady Anne. When he turned around to grab another glass of champagne, he noticed Lady Anne and Lady Ashton walking towards him. He quickly gulped down the champagne and headed their way. "Good evening, ladies," politely spoke the Earl as he nodded his head their way. "You look so lovely this evening, Lady Anne, and so do you, Lady Ashton. May I have this dance, Lady Anne?"

"Yes, you may, my lord," replied Lady Anne as she slightly curtsied and placed her hand inside the Earl's hand. When they walked onto the dance floor, they couldn't help but notice that all eyes were on them. The Earl realized that everyone was probably thinking that there may be an announcement made tonight. They were wondering if there would be an announcement of a marriage proposal to Lady Anne from the Earl of Primrose. But when Lady Anne raised her head and gazed into his eyes, he did not see the lovely big blue eyes of Nicolette staring back at him. Instead, he saw the dark brown eyes of a lady he was quite fond of and loathed the idea of causing her any pain. One time, he thought that he might learn to love her, but he knows for sure now that he did not love her, and he always wanted to marry for love. But how in God's name was he going to wiggle his way out of this? He was determined more than ever now to find a way.

After downing a couple of glasses of champagne and a few suitors twirling her around the dance floor, Nicolette stood still next to a burning candle that glowed against her beautiful skin. As the Earl was slowly walking her way, he noticed how beautiful she looked tonight in the lovely silk aquamarine-colored gown that she made herself. *It is the most beautiful gown there, and she is the loveliest lady there,* thought the Earl.

"Good evening, Nicolette," kindly spoke the Earl as he nodded his head towards Nicolette. "Good evening to you as well, my lord," replied Nicolette in her soft sweet voice. "I have come to ask you to dance with me," said the Earl as he reached his hand out to Nicolette. "I'm not quite certain that dancing with you is a good idea, Lord Austin, but there is a matter that I must discuss with you, my lord," replied Nicolette as she placed her hand inside the Earl's hand, and he led her to the dance floor. Now, all eyes were on the Earl and Nicolette when their feet touched the dance floor, and the orchestra began to play a favorite waltz. The Earl took a deep breath and slowly breathed in the lovely fragrance of Jasmine as he began to twirl her around the dance floor. "What is it you want to discuss with me, Nicolette?" asked the Earl as he gazed into her big blue eyes and pulled her closer to him. "I can not discuss it with you as I first thought, my lord; it appears as if all eyes and ears are upon us now, my lord."

"I can see what you mean," the Earl whispered in her ear. "So why don't you meet me outside in the garden after waiting a few moments once our dance is over? I will be meeting you there soon after."

Nicolette hesitated for a brief moment before she replied to the Earl, "I suppose I can, my lord, but you do know that it is rather risky."

Nicolette quickly walked over to where her mother was standing and began to tell her mother that she was stepping out onto the terrace for some fresh air when Lord Douglas Chamberlain approached her and her mother. "May I have this dance, Lady Braxton," asked Lord Chamberlain in a deep masculine voice. Lady Elizabeth stood there completely quiet for a moment before she could answer Lord Chamberlain. "Please go right ahead and dance with Lord Chamberlain, Mother," said Nicolette in a very anxious tone of voice. "I need some fresh air now. May I be excused, mother? I shall return soon." Lady Braxton took the hand of Lord Chamberlain, and they walked to the dance floor while Nicolette found her way outside, walking towards the lovely Mayfield gardens. Nicolette found a lovely spot inside the gardens that was just enough light from the outside burning lanterns to see her surroundings. It is rather peaceful here, she thought for a moment until she heard the soft, deep voice of the ever so handsome Earl, and then her heart began to pound against her lovely chest.

"Ah, there you are, Nicolette," said the Earl as he walked into the garden. "I see that you have chosen my favorite nighttime place in the garden. The stars in the sky appear to shine a little brighter from the way the light flickers off the oil lanterns. Don't you agree, Nicolette?"

Nicolette quickly glanced up into the sky and saw that the stars were brighter than she had ever seen them before. "You are right, my lord; I have never seen the stars so bright in the sky as of now." The Earl took another few steps towards Nicolette and stood there for a moment admiring her beauty. "I never had a chance tonight to tell you how beautiful you look. Your gown is as lovely as the lady that is wearing it," said the Earl with admiration in his voice. "I do thank you, my lord, but I did not come here for your flattery. I have a matter I want to discuss with you, my lord," replied Nicolette while staring into the handsome face of the Earl.

"I do not know how you will take what I have to say, but I have discovered that your brother Lord Jared has his eye on Lady Anne. When I first noticed how he looked at Lady Anne, I wasn't sure about what I saw, my lord since Lady Anne is quite the beauty, and I can see why any gentleman would look at her in a certain way. But since I wasn't sure what I saw, I started observing both of them every time I was in their company. I could most definitely see that the way he looks at her is the same way that you have looked at me, my lord. He is the main one who is always around her, and it seems as if they clearly enjoy each other's company. It is as if they are like moths; they are drawn to a flame. Lady Anne may not know it yet, but I think she feels the same way about Lord Jared. I hope I have not offended you in any way, my lord. Now that you have told me that you do not plan to take Lady Anne as your bride, I thought you should know what I now know, my lord."

The Earl continued to stare into the eyes of Nicolette as he took a few more steps towards her until he was close enough to touch her. "You have not offended me, Nicolette. I have on occasion observed that very same thing as you have observed my dear. But I was like you, Nicolette; I wasn't quite sure what was actually brewing between those two, but now that you are rather sure that there is something brewing between Lord Jared and Lady Anne, I have to agree. I believe my brother and Lady Anne will be a perfect match for one another, and if they marry, my father, the Marquis and Lord Ashton will have their bloodline after all." The Earl leaned his head over towards Nicolette and placed his arm around her back to pull her closer to him when they suddenly heard the sound of a gentleman's voice say out loud, "Nicolette!"

"Oh, my gracious, is that you, George?" exclaimed Nicolette out loud. "For God's sake, what are you doing here?" shouted Nicolette with a look of shock on her lovely face.

"As I recall, you wrote me a letter asking my sister and me to please come to England as soon as possible. You said that you were lonely here and homesick and that you needed us to be here with you. But from the looks of things, you don't look too lonely at the moment. Who is this gentleman, Nicolette? He looks like the same gentleman who was spying on us in your Uncle's garden back in Charleston," spoke George as he clenched his fist tight, ready to take a punch at the Earl's face.

"Please settle down, George," said Nicolette in a much calmer voice than before. "George and Caroline, I would like to introduce you to Lord Austin Mayfield of Primrose. Lord Austin is the eldest son of the Marquis of Primrose. "But before George and Caroline could utter a single word, the Earl suddenly spoke out loud, "It is lovely to make your acquaintance. I must leave now." The Earl quickly stepped away from Nicolette, abruptly left the garden and walked back inside the manor.

"What did we interrupt, Nicolette?" asked George once he managed to calm down and release his hand from a rather tight fist. "Why are you and Lord Mayfield alone here in the garden?" Nicolette gazed into the familiar dark brown eyes of George as she quickly began to speak, "Lord Mayfield and I met here in the garden so we could discuss a private matter that we both are aware of between Lady Anne and the Earl's younger brother Lord Jared. It is a long story and a rather complicated matter, and I will be glad to discuss it with you later, but for now, I would love to give my best friend, Caroline, a warm embrace. I am so happy to have both of you here in England." Nicolette immediately stepped forward and hugged Caroline and George as she told them that she was ready to go back inside the manor and introduce them to her family and friends. "You must tell me where you are staying and how long you plan to be here?" asked Nicolette as she led George and Caroline back inside the ballroom.

"We are staying in London at The Langham London Hotel," replied George as he turned to face the lovely Nicolette. "Well, how in name's sake can you afford to stay at such an expensive hotel, George!" exclaimed Nicolette. "Did you and Caroline have to rob the Bank of Charleston to afford such luxuries?" George and Caroline couldn't help but giggle out loud at Nicolette's remark before Caroline suddenly replied, "As you are well aware, Nicolette, George receives a pension from the Government for the wound he obtained during the war. He has been saving a lot of his money for a while now. Even though the war ended the thriving of our cotton industry, it has begun to thrive once again. Since the end of this horrible war recently, papa's cotton fields are growing and we are selling our cotton once more. Papa had enough money to help with our trip to England. Therefore, George and I feel most fortunate to be here in England with you, Nicolette; we have missed you desperately." Nicolette smiled and gazed into her best friend Caroline's eyes as she softly and kindly replied, "I have dearly missed you both; I am thrilled to have you both here with me. Now, George, let's go dance to this lovely waltz they are playing at this moment; we shall show them how well those of us from our beloved Charleston can dance the night away."

CHAPTER 10

Summer~Autumn 1865

It was quiet as a mouse the following morning at Primrose Manor. Even the servants were quieter than usual as they were going about their daily chores. It was such a contrast from the previous evening where everything and everyone was so alive from the events of the summer gala. Truth be known, there were a few who were hunkered down inside their chambers, feeling exhausted from staying up most of the night or overindulging in too much of the champagne. In Nicolette's case, it was quite a bit of both. She was still lying in bed thinking about the Earl and all the events that had taken place last evening at the summer gala. When she first woke up, she thought that George and Caroline showing up at the gala last evening was nothing but a dream. But after being awake for a while now, she came to her senses and realized the hard, cold facts of the matter. George and Caroline were most definitely here in England, and she was most grateful, but she would never forget the look on the Earl's face when he first saw George in the garden last evening. She wasn't quite sure what to make of it because after the Earl left the garden so abruptly and found his way back to the ballroom, he chose to ignore her the rest of the evening. He did take to the dance floor on several occasions with a few debutantes and the lovely Lady Anne when she was not dancing with Lord Jared. Nicolette couldn't help but notice how the Earl would keep glancing her way every time she and George would take to the dance floor.

Perhaps she was imagining things, but that look on the Earl's face last evening when he saw George tell her that the Earl was not too happy about him being here in England. *Well, fiddly do, she suddenly said out loud. The Earl will just have to accept the idea of me wanting my dear friends here. Surely, he must know by now that he has stolen my heart forever.* Nicolette quickly slung the covers away and hopped out of bed when she heard Sally softly knock on her chamber door. When Sally entered the room, she quickly helped Nicolette dress in one of her most recent designs: a modest, soft satin day gown of pale blue with caramel and ivory lace trim. "Please don't forget your new bonnet, miss," exclaimed Sally. "The morning sun is already bright in the sky, and it appears that it will be a rather hot day, my dear. I will make sure you are all packed for the trip back to Old Wood Manor, and then, from there, you will continue into the city. As I recall, the Ashton family and you, your mother, and your brother will be taking your leave from Primrose Estate soon after the mid-day meal."

"Thank you, Sally," politely spoke Nicolette. "You certainly do take good care of me, and I am most grateful. But for now, I believe I shall take my breakfast in the dining room and catch a carriage ride to the horse stables. I must check on Biscuit and say goodbye to Blubelle before my trip home."

Nicolette quietly made her way to the dining room, where she immediately saw her mother, Lady Constance, Lady Margaret, Lady Miranda, Lady Katherine, Lady Anne and all the ladies who were members of the Mayfield family from Scotland. It was as if the gentlemen had fallen off the face of the earth. They were nowhere in sight. "Good Morning, Mother and ladies," softly spoke Nicolette as she found her seat at the large dining table. "From the looks of things, I assume this is a ladies-only breakfast, Lady Constance," said Nicolette with a somewhat puzzled look on her pretty face. "You are correct, my dear," kindly replied Lady Constance.

"There were a few gentlemen who decided to leave earlier this morning on a hunting trip into the woodlands, and there were a few gentlemen who decided to stay close to their chambers for their morning meal. And as far as our guest from last evening, their carriages were able to escort them safely to their destinations. Over all, I do believe that the summer gala held here at Primrose Estate was quite a success. I sincerely hope that everyone attending feels the same as I do." Lady Margaret was the first to reply to Lady Constance, "Indeed, my lady, the gala was such a success. There were quite a few potential matches made amongst the debutants attending the gala. We shall be looking forward to quite a few weddings to attend in the near future. But there was one wedding announcement that we surely hoped we would embark on last evening, but it appeared to have been overlooked." Lady Constance cleared her throat and fanned her warm cheeks before she began to speak, "If you are speaking of the Earl, my lady, I do not know what he is thinking nowadays. Ever since he brought those horses home from America, he has been so consumed with them that he spends all of his time with them."

"Maybe we should ask Lady Anne; she would be the one to know why the Earl hasn't proposed marriage." The room got so quiet that you could hear a pin drop on the marble floor. Lady Anne's face turned as red as the silk curtains hanging from the large windows overlooking a small area of the Mayfield gardens, and Nicolette nearly choked on her hot tea as she loudly and clumsily placed the teacup down on the saucer. Lady Anne immediately stood up from her chair and announced to everyone in the room, "The Earl proposed last evening, and there will be a wedding coming December. Now, if you will excuse me, I must go lie down. I have not fully recovered from last evening's events." Lady Anne lifted her soft yellow gown and swiftly left the room while everyone else was still seated at the dining table with a look of utter shock on their lovely faces.

"Well, ladies, I don't know what to say since this is the first time I have heard about this proposal. I can't help but wonder why my daughter would have kept such wonderful news from me until now," said Lady Margaret as she stood up from the table with a look of shock still on her face. "Please excuse me, ladies; I must go see my daughter; she does not look quite well. We shall discuss this matter another time." Lady Margaret left the room, and Nicolette continued to sit quietly. Immediately, the room became loud and noisy when everyone started to talk at once until Lady

Constance spoke out loud to Lady Miranda, "Did you know about this proposal, my dear?"

"No, Mother, I did not know about the proposal. This is the first I've heard of it, Mother, and I am utterly shocked like everyone else."

Nicolette continued to sit quietly at the table, trying not to show any emotion, but she was dying on the inside. She felt faint and sick to her stomach. She could hardly breathe, and she knew she must leave this room immediately. Her mother must have noticed her, and she suddenly asked, "Are you well, my dear?"

"No, Mother, I am not well; I must go lie down and rest a bit. I'm sure I will feel better soon," replied Nicolette in a low, soft voice. "I will come check on you soon, my dear," replied Lady Elizabeth with concern in her sweet voice. Nicolette left the room so quickly that she nearly tripped over her own feet.

The morning sun was already blazing hot in the light blue sky above. The Earl and all the gentlemen who attended the hunting trip early this morning were glad to be dismounting their horses in front of the Mayfield horse stables. Even though the hunting trip was a successful trip for some, others would have been better off just staying at the manor. When the Earl entered the stables, he was sort of hoping he would find Nicolette there checking on Biscuit before her carriage left Primrose Estate later today. *Maybe she came earlier this morning,* he thought to himself, *or maybe she will come soon.* He did not know why he wanted to see her so desperately, but the truth was that he looked forward to seeing her every chance he got. Now that George and his sister Caroline were here in London, he wondered if she would forget him and spend all of her time with them instead. *Well, perhaps I will have to do something about that,* he told himself. *I will be making a lot more trips into the city in the coming days because if Nicolette thinks that just having George here will keep me away from her, well, she's got another thinking coming.* "There you are, my lord," said Lord Atticus when he approached the Earl. "I am ready to head back to the manor now, my lord. The events of the previous evening and this morning's hunt have left me rather worn."

"Ah, speaking of last evening, Lord Austin, I can't help but notice that you spent most of the evening in the company of my cousin, the lovely Lady Luisa. Is there something you would like to say about the two of you, my lord?" asked the Earl with a half grin on his handsome face. "The most important thing I can possibly think to say at the moment, my lord, is that I hope that Lady Luisa will be able to extend her stay here at Primrose Estate. I could find myself in the coming days spending a lot more time in her company. What do you say about the idea, my lord?" asked Lord Atticus with a look of complete determination on his handsome face.

"I say that is the best idea I have heard so far today, Lord Austin, and I will be honored to help make that happen. Go find us a carriage back to the manor; I'll be there soon."

When the Earl returned to the manor, he immediately headed to his chamber, where he stepped into a much-needed bath to relax his sore muscles and his tense masculine body. He could hardly remember a time when he felt so much tension, and he knew that most of it was centered on his beautiful goddess Nicolette. His desire to be near her, hold her in his arms, and never let her go was almost more than he could endure. He could feel his muscles begin to relax as he continued to soak in the warm bath, but his manhood continued to swell every time he thought of Nicolette's warm kisses and soft body against his. And now he was left wanting more of her. When he slid further down into the water, he rested the back of his head on the back of the large copper tub, closed his eyes and thought about the events that took place last evening. The evening had really not gone as planned. Well, at first, it did, but then there was George. He knew that it made sense that she would want her friends here with her, and he couldn't blame her for that. But he was a man, and he knew that George had other intentions in mind. And that was where those intentions would stay; he will never allow George to have Nicolette, *she belongs to me. Now let me get out of this bath and go find my lovely sea goddess who has put a spell on me.*

Once the Earl was fully dressed, he stepped out of his chamber into the hallway. Immediately, he heard his mother's sweet voice as she came hurrying towards him, "What is this I hear, my lord? Is it true what Lady Anne announced out loud this morning while the ladies were all gathered in the dining room enjoying our morning meal?"

"Is what true, Mother?" asked the Earl with a startled look on his face. I know of no such announcement, Mother."

"I am talking about your marriage proposal to Lady Anne last evening," replied Lady Constance with a look of uncertainty on her lovely face. There was no way the Earl could open his mouth and speak a single word. Instead, he just stood there frozen, resembling one of the statues that graced the hallways of the manor. Lady Constance took a few steps away from her son when she witnessed his handsome face go from pale white to a raging red. He balled his hand into a fist as if he wanted to hit something, but instead, he blurted out in a loud, deep voice, "Lady Anne is imagining things, Mother! I did not propose marriage to Lady Anne last evening or any other time. My plan is to wait till the horse racing season has ended, and then I am considering a proposal by the Christmas season. I thought Father, whom I have already informed of my plans, would have already told you by now. I made a point to speak with Father and Lord Ashton about my plans, and they both agreed. But now I'm not sure if I want to propose marriage at all. If anyone should marry Lady Anne, it should be Lord Jared. He has loved her for a long time, and they are perfect together. How dare she to make such an announcement without my knowledge. Where is Lady Anne, Mother? I must go to her now."

"She is in her bed chamber with her mother as we speak," said Lady Constance with deep concern in her eyes. Perhaps you need to inform her to meet me immediately downstairs in the drawing room, and I will not take no for an answer," said the Earl as he excused himself and headed straight for the drawing room.

Instead of Lady Constance calling on her footman to send Lady Anne's ladies maid to inform her that the Earl was expecting to meet with her immediately in the drawing room, she decided to take a walk across the long hallway to the guest quarters where Lady Anne's bed chamber was located. When she knocked on the door, Lady Margaret opened the door and invited her inside the room. Lady Anne was sitting in a Queen Anne upholstered chair next to the window, sobbing out loud, holding a lace handkerchief in her trembling hand. "Now," exclaimed Lady Constance as she walked over to Lady Anne. "We shall have none of this sobbing. This is nothing that can't be fixed, my dear. I do somewhat understand your dilemma. I can see that the Earl has kept you waiting longer than he certainly should, and you are growing rather weary of all the inquiries about a wedding announcement coming your way. But hopefully, when you suddenly blurted out that there was a marriage proposal between you and the Earl last evening, no one but us ladies that were present heard the news. Therefore, I will inform them immediately that the news should go no further than this manor. Now dry your pretty eyes, dear, and please make haste because the Earl has requested your presence immediately in the drawing room, and he will not take no for an answer."

When Lady Anne entered the drawing room, she saw the Earl standing with his back turned to her, staring out the large picture window. Lady Anne was the first to speak, "I heard that you want to speak with me, my lord." The Earl slowly turned around to face Lady Anne and spoke out loud in a very deep masculine voice, "I am furious with you at the moment, my lady. How could you say such a thing this morning to the other ladies when you know that no marriage proposal took place between you and me last evening? Why would you say that?"

"I do owe you an apology, my lord. The only answer I can give you is that I blurted out those words before I realized what I was saying. I have grown so weary of this long wait from you, my lord, and also weary from all the gossip and speculation. That is probably no excuse, but what are your intentions, my lord," replied Lady Anne with a slight quiver in her soft voice. "Do you or do you not plan on marrying me, my lord?"

"Ah, my lady, I always knew that you were quite bold and very outspoken, but that so happens to be a quality that I admire in you, Lady Anne," said the Earl with a much calmer tone in his voice. "Perhaps it's time I become bolder and outspoken with you, my lady. Even though I have known you for a long time now and I am quite fond of you, I have come to the realization that I do not love you the way you deserve to be loved. I do not believe that I am the man that you belong with. I have recently become aware that my younger brother, Lord Jared, is deeply and sincerely quite fond of you. It will surprise me if you tell me that you aren't already aware of this. Surely, you must know by now."

"I always knew that Lord Jared and I got along well as friends, but I do not love him, my lord. It is you who I love and want to marry someday."

"Is it really me you say you love my lady, or is it my title that you seek above everything else? You have always been more pampered and spoiled than most of the debutantes, so therefore, it seems as if money and titles are more important to you than feelings. I am not saying that is a bad thing, my dear, but I want to marry for love. For now, I will go along with the fact that the marriage proposal is out in the open now. We will tell everyone that we will be having a wedding this coming December before Christmas, but in the meantime, I want you to spend more time with Lord Jared, and I promise you will come to realize that you and he belong together. I believe you have feelings for Lord Jared that exceed the boundaries of friendship. Therefore, in December, there will be a wedding, but it will not be our wedding, my lady. It shall be a wedding between you and my brother, Lord Jared. I am truly sorry, but this is the way it shall be, my dear, because I do not want to marry you. In the meantime, we shall continue to honor our father's wishes, but they will not be disappointed come December because they will get their wish after all. There will be a bloodline between the Mayfield and Ashton family. But it will be with you and my brother, and we both know that we do not want to have a worse scandal than we probably will have, or most of all, we do not want to disappoint our fathers. Are we in agreement, my lady? I hear voices at the door."

"I suppose I will agree, my lord. I will go along with our plan. I see that you do not love me, my lord, and I am not whom you want. I suppose I can see myself with Lord Jared even though he does not have your title, but we will have to be discreet, my lord. No one must know our intentions. But what are you going to do about a wife one day, my lord? Who or what will make you happy? Is there someone you already have your eye on, my lord?"

"Don't you worry about me, Lady Anne," said the Earl with a look of relief on his handsome face. "I'm going to be just fine, my dear."

This was not how Nicolette planned on spending her last few hours here at Primrose Estate. She was confined to her bed chamber, wearing out the carpets by pacing back and forth nonstop. She was having a hard time believing what came out of Lady Anne's mouth earlier at breakfast. She thought there was no way that the Earl proposed to Lady Anne last evening. *When I spoke to the Earl in the garden last evening, we both agreed that Lord Jared and Lady Anne were a match and that they belonged together. So why would he betray me and go behind my back and ask for Lady Anne's hand in marriage? It does not make any sense to me, so therefore, I have every reason to believe she is not being truthful. But why would she say such a thing,* she wondered. *Well, there is only one thing left to do and that is get to the bottom of this and find out what is the real truth.*

Nicolette immediately glanced up at the clock and saw that she had enough time left before they would be leaving Primrose Estate today. So, she grabbed her blue bonnet and her brise fan off the vanity and ran swiftly down the stairway to look for a carriage to take her down to the Mayfield horse stables, where she hoped to see the Earl of Primrose.

Nicolette immediately used her brise fan to cool the dampness off her soft skin when she stepped down from the open carriage that carried her to the horse stables. Sally was certainly right about needing a bonnet more than ever today. The sun was beaming so bright in the clear blue sky, and it was already warmer than usual today. Once she entered the stables, she decided to go check on Biscuit first and then go see Blubelle. And then maybe, if she was lucky, she would happen to see the Earl. When she got to the side of the stables where they kept Biscuit, it didn't take him long to come to her and start rubbing against her legs, purring for her to pick him up. Biscuit was so used to his surroundings here at the Mayfield stables by now that the grooms let Biscuit roam free most of his time here.

"Good morning, Nicolette," said Daniel when he walked up behind Nicolette.

"Oh, you startled me, Daniel. Good morning to you as well, or should I say mid-day? It is probably close to the noon meal by now, and I must say I am quite famished. Due to usual circumstances earlier this morning, I did not get to eat my breakfast," replied Nicolette in a slightly sarcastic tone of voice. "And why is that, Nicolette? Are you not feeling well, sister?"

"No, Daniel, that is not the reason. I guess you have not heard the latest news this morning. Perhaps you were on the hunting trip with the other gentlemen this morning?"

"No, I did not attend the hunting trip this morning; I took my breakfast in my room and came straight here to the stables. So what news are you talking about, Nicolette?"

"Lady Anne announced or should I say blurted out that the Earl proposed to her last evening at the summer gala."

"Well, that is quite a surprise," said Daniel with a look of surprise on his handsome face. "I wonder why there was a marriage proposal from the Earl last evening, but they chose not to make an announcement. That does seem rather odd, Nicolette."

"But what appears to be even odder is that she just blurted the news out at breakfast but she or the Earl never told their families," said Nicolette as she tensed from the sound of very loud thunder in the far distance. "Have you seen the Earl or Lord Atticus this morning, Daniel? Surely, the Earl would have informed Lord Atticus of the news by now."

"No, I have not seen or spoken to the Earl or Lord Atticus since last evening. When I got to the stables earlier, Lord Watson informed me that the Earl had recently left Primrose Estate for a trip into London for a couple of days, and I suppose Lord Atticus is still at the manor."

"I suppose we should hurry back to the manor as well, Daniel. It appears that a rainstorm may be approaching soon." Daniel couldn't help but notice a somewhat worried look on Nicolette's face as they both hurried out the stable door to motion for a carriage to take them back to the manor.

As Nicolette was hurrying up the large flight of stairs to her chamber, she began to hear the sound of rain pounding hard against the large window panes of the manor. She was most certainly relieved that the rain held off until she was safely inside the manor. But most of all, she hoped that the storm would be gone when it was time to leave Primrose Estate because the thought of the rain and the company of Lady Anne on the carriage ride home was more than she wanted to endure. When she got inside her chamber, she noticed her gown was slightly damp from her perspiring due to the hot morning sun. She was quite used to hot summer days in Charleston, South Carolina, but it seemed to be rather unusual warm temperatures for England. After choosing a different gown to wear at home and freshening up at the small water basin on the far side of the room, Nicolette hurried down to the dining room to join the others for the noon meal. She thought about George and Caroline and how excited she would be to see them once she got back to London. No matter how sad and confused she was feeling at this time, she would be grateful to get back into her seamstress shop and also have a chance to spend time with her dear friends. Then she thought about the Earl and how he suddenly left Primrose Estate. It did seem rather unusual that the very morning after the Earl asked for Lady Anne's hand in marriage, he would run off and leave her so soon.

You would think that he would want to be here to say his goodbyes to his bride-to-be before she heads home to Old Wood Manor. None of this makes any sense to me and the Earl better have a doggone good explanation if and when I shall choose to see him again. When she first entered the dining room, she saw that almost everyone was present for the noon meal except for the Earl. The second thing she noticed was the sad look on Lord Jared's face and the red swollen eyes on the slightly pale face of Lady Anne. Nicolette quietly took her seat at the large dining table and pretended that she did not hear all the chatter about the Earl and Lady Anne's upcoming December wedding.

Even though the rain had stopped before they left Primrose Estate, and the sun was shining as bright as before, the rain clouds were still hanging around. But for now, the rain was holding off but Nicolette's nerves were getting the best of her. It took all her effort to sit there, pretending to listen as Lady Margaret asked her and Lady Anne for their opinions on her wedding ideas. What made it even stranger was that Lady Anne seemed just as uninterested in her mother's plans as she was.

When the Ashton carriages pulled up in front of Old Wood Manor, Nicolette felt a tremendous sigh of relief. She knew that she would be even more relieved when she stepped inside the carriage that would be escorting her, her mother and Daniel back to the Ashton cottage where they were staying in London. But before they left for the city, they had a short time to spend at Old Wood Manor.

When she stepped out of the carriage, she started to swiftly walk towards the entrance of the manor when Lady Anne caught up with her. "Are you well, Nicolette?" asked Lady Anne, trying to catch her breath. "I am well, my lady, considering I'm still slightly recovering from last evening," replied Nicolette. "Why do you ask Lady Anne?"

"I just happen to notice that you have been much quieter than usual today, but you have reassured me that you are recovering like the rest of us from last evening."

"Oh, by the way, my lady, I have not personally congratulated you on your upcoming marriage to the Earl. We knew it was coming, but the announcement this morning at breakfast was quite a shock to everyone. I was rather surprised that your mother had not heard the news until then. I suppose you had your reason for that, so all I can say is that I hope you and the Earl have a happy life together. Now, if you will excuse me, I must hurry to my chamber to freshen up in order to continue my carriage ride to London."

CHAPTER 11

Late Summer-Autumn 1865

"Yes, Mrs. Devereux, I also happen to agree that you and your daughters have made excellent choices on your fabric for the new gowns for the October Regency Ball that will be held at the Duke and Duchess Estate in York. I will send a messenger to the Chamberlain Estate, where you, Mr. Devereux and the rest of your family are residing, to let you know when we are ready for your fitting," said Nicolette as she stood behind the counter in her seamstress shop receiving a down payment from Mrs. Devereux. "My daughters and I are very much looking forward to hearing from you, Miss Braxton," replied Mrs. Devereux as they stepped outside the shop. Nicolette and Lady Elizabeth had only been back in their seamstress shop for a few days, and they could hardly catch their breath from all the business that was coming their way. The Earl was right, thought Nicolette, when he said that the summer gala would bring her lots of business. She had not wanted to think about the Earl since she had gotten back to the city working in her shop and staying busy, but here she was thinking about him anyhow. Sadly, she hadn't spent as much time with George and Caroline as she would like. They have all met for lunch and dinner on several occasions and

George had called on her on a couple occasions without the lovely Caroline. Fortunately, Caroline and James Devereux met at the summer gala, and Mr. Devereux had called on Caroline on several occasions. There was no doubt in Caroline's mind that George wanted to spend more time with Nicolette, but time was not something that Nicolette was able to spare lately. But George did mention to her that he did have a chance to meet with the Earl, Lord Jared and Lord Atticus at the Ashton-Mayfield Cotton Industry on the outskirts of London.

He went on to tell her that their cotton fields back home in Charleston were thriving once again since the war between the North and the South ended, and the Ashton-Mayfield cotton mill was planning on doing more business with his father and him in the near future. Nicolette told George she was happy to hear such good news and that he and his father would not be disappointed doing business with the Ashton and the Mayfields.

"Perhaps you should go on home, dear," said Lady Elizabeth to Nicolette while standing at the large sewing table unfolding a bolt of silk fabric. "You do look rather tired, and a short nap before you go to dinner at the Rainbow Restaurant is just what you need, Nicolette."

"Are you certain you can spare me right now, Mother?" asked Nicolette between yawns. "I can manage just fine here on my own, dear. You just do what I say since I just saw Lord Gerald's brother's coachmen outside Daniel's shop moments ago. He will be glad to escort you to the cottage."

"You are right, Mother; I could very well take a nap before my dinner with George. I will go see Daniel now to inform the coachmen to take me home."

The Earl was about to pull his dark, shiny hair out, trying to get some alone time with the lovely Nicolette, but lately, he found it to be rather impossible. He had taken several short trips into London recently for business with the cotton mill and occasional trips to London's gentlemen's club. But soon he will not be able to make as many trips to London since he is planning on entering the Dark Knight in the upcoming horse race, the Derby Trial Stakes in England at Lingfield Park. The Earl was hoping to visit Nicolette at her shop, but every time he got near the shop, he could see that she was very busy with customers, just like he predicted she would be after the summer gala. And then the next time he was in London, he decided to go to the shop and ask her if she would like to join him for the mid-day meal at a Piccadilly near her shop, but when he got there, he noticed George and her leaving the shop arm in arm laughing out loud together.

There was no doubt in his mind that telling her the truth about what was really going on between him and Lady Anne was absolutely the right thing to do. *By now, she is probably furious with me, and if she does have any feelings at all about me, she probably loathes me by now. But what I will regret the most will be that I've hurt her, and she will forget that I ever existed. Then she will fall into the arms of George and return to her beloved home in Charleston, South Carolina.*

"Please come help me pick out a suit for this evening, brother," asked the Earl, standing in his small bed chamber at the Mayfield cottage in London, where Lord Jared resided most of the time. "I need your help because I am in such a hurry to meet Lady Anne, Lord Atticus and the lovely Lady Luisa for dinner at the Rainbow Restaurant this evening. I can't wait for one of the groomsmen to get here, so I desperately need your help, brother."

"Well, my lord, what in the world would you do without me?" asked Lord Jared with a grin on his handsome face. "There is no doubt that I would be lost at sea without you, dear brother," replied the Earl with a kind and tender tone in his voice.

While Lord Jared was helping the Earl get dressed, the Earl couldn't help but think about his agreement with Lady Anne. The Earl so much wanted to tell his brother about the plan that he had made with Lady Anne. He wanted to say that he already knew that Lord Jared had feelings for Lady Anne and that he did not have those same feelings for her. He wanted to tell him that this was all a hoax and he did not want or would not marry Lady Anne.

There will be a wedding come December, and it will be Lord Jared's and Lady Anne's wedding was what he was most anxious to say to Lord Jared at the moment. However, he knew it was not the right moment to say anything. Still, he knew he would have to tell him very soon because Lady Anne, Lord Atticus, and Nicolette were coming for another visit to Primrose Estate, and he was busy preparing for the upcoming horse race.

Lady Anne will give most of her attention to Lady Miranda and Lord Jared and allow his brother to fall even more madly in love with her. The Earl knew that there was no easy solution to the mess he'd got himself into, but he was determined more than ever to follow through because the final goal was to see his brother and Lady Anne happy and to have his lovely sea goddess in his arms and by his side forever.

"Have I told you how lovely you look this evening Nicolette," said George while helping Nicolette to her seat at the small dining table at the Rainbow Restaurant.

"Yes, George you have mentioned that more than once so far this evening and I am much obliged," replied Nicolette in a soft feminine voice. "Well, you do not have to flatter me, George; after all, we have been friends for a long time now, and you have seen me at my best and my worst by now."

"And must I say, Nicolette, you look even more beautiful every time I am fortunate enough to be in your presence, my dear?" Nicolette stared at George for a brief moment while he now diverted his attention to this evening's menu. She couldn't help but admit that he was a rather handsome lad, but that was just it; he was only a lad, whereas the Earl was a man like none other. The Earl was strong, muscular, clever, determined, arrogant and much too handsome for his own good. But yet, he could be rather gentle, kind, loyal and quite funny at times.

"Nicolette! Nicolette," said George out loud as he was trying to get Nicolette's attention. "Oh, sorry, George, I am thinking about how busy Mother and I are at the shop and how busy we will be in the near future. Especially how busy we will be now that we have started making new gowns for the up coming October Regency Ball. I suppose you will not be attending the ball, George, since you will be going back to your home in Charleston to help your father with the cotton industry."

"Now that my leg has completely healed from the wound I obtained in the war, I do feel obligated to go back home and help Papa with the business, but I do have two younger brothers, as you well know by now, and they are very active in helping papa when I'm not able to be there. When I met with Lord Atticus, the Earl and Lord Jared recently, they mentioned that there is an opening for a new supervisor for the cotton mill here in London. The salary is more than generous, and there is also room for my father and me to become part owners of the mill in the near future. They told me to give their offer some consideration and let them know soon."

"Well, I must say that is quite the offer, George," replied Nicolette while raising her eyebrows upward. "So, have you given the offer any thought, George?"

"I must say I have thought of nothing else but that lately, but it has a lot to do with you and Papa, my dear Nicolette."

"What do I have to do with your decision, George?" curiously, she asked. "It depends on whether your answer is a yes or a no." Suddenly, George got up from his chair and kneeled down on one knee, pulled a ring out of his pocket, stared into the big, beautiful blue eyes of Nicolette and said, "Will you marry me, Nicolette?"

Before Nicolette could utter a single word, she suddenly heard familiar voices coming towards a table that was very near to her and George's table. When she glanced up and looked, she saw the Earl, Lady Anne, Lord Atticus and Lady Luisa. They all stopped walking suddenly when they noticed Nicolette and George, who was on one knee, proposing to Nicolette at that exact moment. Nicolette's blue eyes locked with the Earl's blue eyes, and she felt as if she couldn't breathe. Quickly, she turned her attention back to George, and she knew that he was eagerly waiting for her to answer, but it appeared that he was not the only one waiting for her answer. Even though the Earl was helping Lady Anne to her seat, he didn't completely take his eyes off her. Once Lady Anne was in her seat, she saw Lady Anne look up at the Earl and smile before they all diverted their attention back to her and George. Suddenly, Nicolette blurted out loud, "Yes!"

"Did you say yes, Nicolette?" anxiously said George as he was rising to his feet. "You will marry me, Nicolette? I must say I am probably the happiest man alive at this very moment!" George leaned over to place a kiss on Nicolette's slender hand and brought her hand to his lips in order to place a warm kiss on her lovely hand. When George released her hand, she glanced over to the table where the Earl was seated and saw smiles on everyone's faces except for the Earl's face. His typical bronzed face looked as pale as the Victorian lace tablecloths gracing the dining tables in the large dining room. Nicolette noticed that he made sure that his eyes did not look into her eyes, and he raised the hand of Lady Anne and placed a warm kiss on top of her hand.

"But George, don't you think that we should postpone our wedding until you return from your trip to America? You did mention that you need to let your papa know about the job offer from the Earl and Lord Atticus and to make sure that everything back home in Charleston with your papa and his cotton fields is in order," said Nicolette with a slight trembling sound to her voice. Nicolette quickly glanced over at the Earl's table when she heard female laughter coming from there. The Earl was busy talking, and he did not notice her gazing at him. Nicolette couldn't help but notice how extraordinarily handsome he looked this evening. Suddenly, she realized that just now she accepted a marriage proposal from someone she truly cared about, but yet here she was admiring the man she truly wanted, and he was to be married to another. At that very moment, she truly knew that the Earl was the gentleman who had stolen her heart forever and what was a seamstress from Charleston, South Carolina, going to do about it.

"George, don't you think we should keep our engagement a secret for now?" asked Nicolette as she gazed across the table and stared into the dark brown eyes of George. "After all, we will be apart for a while when you journey back home to Charleston and in the meantime, I will be very busy working at the shop making new gowns. Once you return to England, we can make our announcement known to everyone. Don't you agree, George?"

"I do see what you are saying, Nicolette," replied George with a slightly confused look on his handsome face. "But first of all, my dear, I never said that I would be taking the job offer from Lord

Atticus and Lord Austin. I believe I mentioned that I would consider the offer and give them an answer soon. Secondly, I was kind of hoping that if you did agree to be my wife, you would consider moving back home to Charleston as my wife."

"Oh, George, you do give me a lot to think about. After all, I do miss my home and the friends I left behind. But Mother, Daniel and I have made a new life here in England thanks to the Ashton family, and we love our new seamstress and tailor shops. We are truly blessed, and if you accept the job at the cotton mill, you will feel the same way." In that very instant, Nicolette knew that she never wanted to hurt George in any way. She knew that she had no right to agree to be his wife, but right now, she knew that she had plenty of time to decide if a life with George could substitute for the life she truly dreamed of having with the Earl of Primrose.

It was early autumn now, and the leaves on the trees were beginning to display their vibrant autumn colors. There was a slightly cooler breeze in the air and a welcome relief from an unusually hot summer. The past few weeks passed by quickly since the Earl devoted most of his time preparing for the Derby Trial Stakes at Lingfield Park. There were only two days left before the Earl would be leaving Primrose Estate for the upcoming Derby Trial Stakes horse race and the Dark Knight seemed to be favoring the sore muscle in his right front leg. His timing was off, and the Earl and Lord Watson were in a frenzy trying to decide whether to pull out of the race. They needed to make a decision quickly to take a chance on the Dark Knight, find a substitute or pull out of the race completely.

The Earl was well aware that Nicolette, Lady Anne and Lord Atticus had arrived at Primrose Estate last evening. He was rather surprised to see that Nicolette had joined the others on their visit to Primrose. Perhaps spending her spare time with her husband-to-be would have been what he thought she would be most likely to do, but now that George had left England and was on his way back to his home in Charleston, she chose to visit Primrose Estate. But he did remember her telling him once that when she felt tired and exhausted from her work and she needed a break, she loved to come to Primrose Estate and take Blubelle out for rides across this beautiful English countryside. Or perhaps he was thinking that maybe she was hoping to see him as much as he was hoping to see her.

He couldn't help but think back on the evening he saw George down on his knee proposing marriage to Nicolette, and what was obvious to the Earl and the rest of them was that Nicolette agreed to be George's wife. He had never seen a happier look on a man's face than that of George that evening. So, they all assumed that she must have said yes. But they had not heard anything from anyone on that matter until the arrival of Lady Anne and the others last evening. Even though the Earl had not taken any of his meals with the family or his guests since their arrival, he decided to speak with Lady Anne privately in the parlor after she had had her breakfast in the dining room with the others.

"Oh, there you are, my lord," quickly spoke Lady Anne as she entered the parlor at Primrose Manor. "Good morning, my lady," replied the Earl to Lady Anne while suddenly hearing loud voices walking towards the parlor. "Perhaps we need to remove ourselves from the parlor into my study. Please come follow me to my study, my lady; we need to talk privately."

"Please lead the way, my lord. I am right behind you," replied Lady Anne as she lifted her lovely taupe-colored gown and hurried towards the Earl's study. "As you can see, I am very busy with making preparations for the upcoming horse race. Lord Watson and I are in a dilemma with having to make a last-minute decision whether or not to pull out of the race due to a sore muscle on the right leg of the Dark Knight."

"I am truly sorry to hear that you have to make that choice, my lord, but knowing you, I am sure you will make the right choice," said Lady Anne with a concerned look on her pretty face. "This will be your opportunity to spend more time with Lord Jared. He will be coming to the horse stables soon, and I will ask him if he would be willing to take the horses out for a ride with you and Lady Miranda this afternoon. So if that is okay with you, Lady Anne, I suggest you be ready to come quickly to the stables later on today."

"You know how much I love to ride across your land here at Primrose Estate, and I don't have to worry about me sneezing every time I come upon those lovely Primrose flowers since they are starting to fade away, my lord," replied Lady Anne with a slight grin on her face. "I must excuse myself and hurry to the stables," said the Earl as he walked towards the door of the study. "But before I leave, I want to ask if you heard any news about what we saw at the Rainbow Restaurant that evening?"

"Are you asking about the marriage proposal we saw take place between Nicolette and George, my lord," asked Lady Anne as she walked past the Earl to leave the study.

"The last time Mother and I were in the city, we went to Nicolette's shop to look at some new bolts of fabric that had just arrived at the shop. I happened to notice that her mother, Nicolette or no one else had said a single word about George's marriage proposal, so I assumed that no one knew about it yet. Obviously, they have not told anyone else the news. When our mothers were deep in conversation in the front room of the shop, Nicolette and I sneaked off to the back room and spoke privately. Nicolette informed me that she did not give George an answer yet. She said that she told George to wait for an answer since he had to make a trip home to America."

"So obviously, it is still up in the air whether there will be more than one wedding to take place in our families this coming season," said the Earl with a look of relief on his face as he watched Lady Anne leave his study.

Nicolette was struck by the beauty of the land and the autumn leaves on the trees as she glanced outside the window of the carriage that was escorting her down to the horse stables on Primrose Estate. It had been a while since she last saw Blubelle, and she was desperately hoping to take her out for a ride this morning with Lord Atticus and the lovely Lady Luisa. When she entered the stables, she quickly headed over to the stall where Blubelle was located. She immediately reached out her hand and fed Blubelle a few carrots she had in her cloak pocket. When she started to rub the shiny white coat of Blubelle, she heard a familiar voice coming towards them. When she looked up, she stared into the sapphire blue eyes of the Earl.

"I can see how glad Blubelle is to have you in her presence, Nicolette," said the Earl in his most pleasant tone of voice. He wanted to say that not only was Blubelle happy to see her, but he was happy to see Nicolette as well. But he knew it would probably be better to keep that thought to himself for now. Nicolette kept rubbing Blubelle while replying to the Earl. "Blubelle can't be any happier than I am, Lord Austin. I am happy to be here with her also my lord. I would love to take her out for a ride if that is okay with you, my lord. Lord Atticus and Lady Luisa will be accompanying me on my ride."

"You will always have my permission, Nicolette, as long as you are not alone, my dear." Suddenly, Nicolette remembered the last time she rode Blubelle alone, and the Earl suddenly appeared and saved her from that horrible wild boar in the woods coming towards her. Then she began to blush from her head to her toes when she remembered the passionate kiss between them when he held her safely in his warm embrace. When she gazed into the face of the Earl, she saw that look of desire in his eyes and knew that he was remembering what took place between them that day in the woods. She knew deep down in her very soul that the Earl did not want to marry Lady Anne. He made it very clear to her when they last talked inside the garden on the evening of the summer gala. *Why is he pretending otherwise,* she kept asking herself. The Earl and she had a plan, and what happened to their plan of Lady Anne and Lord Jared coming together? *He very much agreed with everything I mentioned to him that evening. So, he is either lying to me, or there is some other secret I am not aware of, but he will soon find out that I will not stand by and let him treat me this way. One way or another, I will get to the bottom of this*, but before she could speak another word to the Earl, Lord Atticus, Lady Luisa walked up to the open door of Blubelle's horse stall.

"Lord Watson informed us that we will find you here with Blubelle Nicolette, and we can see that he is correct, my dear. You are welcome to join us if you want to take Blubelle for a ride this morning since Daniel did not join us on this trip to Primrose Estate and he is the one who usually joins you when no one else is riding."

"That is very kind of you, Lord Atticus and Lady Luisa; I will be delighted to join you," replied Nicolette. Suddenly, the Earl blurted out loud, "I will be joining all of you as well; I shall inform the grooms to have the horses ready to ride. Going for a ride right now will probably help me clear my head since we all know that I have to make a decision this morning about whether to keep the Dark Knight in the horse race that takes place in a few days. The grooms will bring the horses out in front of the stables, and I shall see you soon."

When Nicolette stuck her foot into the stirrup of Blubelle and mounted on top of her, she still couldn't believe that the Earl was mounting his horse and joining them for the morning ride. She had to admit that part of her was thrilled to be in his company, but there was another part of her that was slightly furious with him for not being honest with her. But right now, her heart was pounding, and she longed to be near him. She could smell his manly scent and still imagine his warm kisses on her rosy lips. She was beginning to tingle all over when he rode up beside her, and they both rode quickly away.

Lord Atticus and Lady Luisa didn't try very hard to catch up with the Earl and Nicolette. Lord Atticus was more than glad to have some alone time with Lady Luisa. Just by the look on Lady Luisa's lovely face, he could tell she felt the same way, too. Therefore, Lord Atticus decided to turn around and take the lovely Luisa to the small pond by the large oak tree, and Nicolette and the Earl continued to ride through the woodlands towards the beautiful waterfalls. When the Earl and Nicolette reached the largest waterfall on the land, they dismounted their horses and tied them to a tree in the woods. There was still a slight breeze in the morning air, and Nicolette was glad that she wore her cloak. They found a small grassy spot to sit near the waterfall, and the Earl took her by the hand and helped her to the ground. "Are you comfortable here, Nicolette?" asked the Earl with a tender, kind voice.

"I am comfortable sitting on the grass gazing at the most beautiful waterfall I have ever seen, but if you are asking me if I am comfortable being here with you at this moment, knowing that you will be marrying Lady Anne in the near future. Then my answer is no, my lord, I am not comfortable knowing that." The Earl moved closer to Nicolette, lifted her chin with his masculine hand and turned her face towards him where he could stare into her big blue eyes and said with a firm tone in his masculine voice, "I do not want you to marry George Nicolette; he is not the man that will make you happy."

"How do you know that, my lord?" asked Nicolette with a slight tear in the corner of her eye. "I know that Nicolette, because I am the man that can make you happy."

"You have no right to say these things to me no longer my lord. Not now or ever since you plan on marrying Lady Anne. You are not truthful with me, Lord Austin, when you tell me that you will never marry Lady Anne. If you are having a difficult time making up your mind, my lord, then I will help you by telling you that I will not wait around for you to make up your mind. I will marry George when he gets back from Charleston,"

When she started to stand to her feet, the Earl pulled her up into his arms and kissed her with such passion as if he would never let her go. When he released her mouth from his, he could feel her trembling body next to his loins, and he was on fire. She immediately pulled away and lowered her head as she quietly and softly told him that it was time to go. They mounted their horses in silence and rode back to the stables without uttering a single word to each other. When they dismounted the horses and handed them over to the groom, she immediately signaled for a carriage to come and take her back to the manor. She would not look his way any longer, so the Earl turned towards the door of the stables and realized at that very moment that he wanted Nicolette more than he had ever wanted anyone or anything in his entire life and being an Earl all his life it had pretty much got him everything or any woman he could ever want but right at that very moment he felt helpless and he could feel her slipping away from him for good.

When Nicolette returned to the manor, she instructed the coachman to pull up to the side door of the visitor's quarters and let her out of the carriage. She was hoping to make it to her bed chamber without running into anyone else. Right now, all she wanted was to be alone after what had just taken place between her and the Earl. She practically ran through the hallway leading to her chamber, and she arrived safely without seeing anyone. When she entered her chamber, she threw her cloak and her bonnet on the chair and fell across the big poster bed, sobbing warm tears into her soft feather pillow. When she fell asleep, she dreamt of Blubelle racing around a horse track and the Earl standing off in the distance with the Dark Knight and his horse jockey by his side.

When she woke up from a short nap, she remembered her dream. Then suddenly she wondered about the dream and started to ask herself if the horse jockey was standing beside the Earl and the Dark Knight in her dream, then who was riding Blubelle when she was racing around the horse track? Then it came to her that it was she who was on the back of Blubelle. She was the horse jockey who was racing Blubelle in the Derby Trial Stakes. *I must go now and tell the Earl that I might have the answer to his dilemma.*

Therefore, she quickly headed over to the basin and washed her lovely face. She ran the comb through the curls of her hair, straightened a few pins in her golden hair and pinched her rosy cheeks. She was almost out the door of her chamber when she remembered to grab her bonnet and cloak. When she got to the bottom of the stairs, she asked the footman to get her a carriage to take her to the stables. But when she arrived at the stables, she did not see the Earl, so she asked one of the grooms if he knew where the Earl might be. The groom informed her that the Earl was at the horse track with the Dark knight. Since the horse track was only a short distance from the stables, she lifted her gown and ran as fast as she could to the horse track.

"Lord Austin! Lord Austin," exclaimed Nicolette as she approached the Earl, Lord Watson and the horse jockey; all three were standing near the wooden gate of the fence surrounding the horse track. "What are you doing here, Nicolette?" asked the Earl while staring at Nicolette, trying hard to catch her breath.

"Has something terrible happened?" asked the Earl with a devastated look on his face. "No, my lord, nothing happened; I have something important to tell you," exclaimed Nicolette after finally catching her breath. "Can you tell me now, Nicolette?" asked the Earl.

"Yes, I will tell you that I believe I have the answer to whether or not you need to pull the Dark Knight out of the race, my lord," replied Nicolette. "And how would that be possible, Nicolette?" asked the Earl as he stared deep into her big blue eyes. "Why don't you enter Blubelle in place of the Dark Knight, my lord? We all know that Blubelle can run as fast as the Dark Knight and she has run around this track here on your land quite often. She is even more disciplined and compliant than the Dark Knight, my lord, and I'm sure you agree with me, my lord?" asked Nicolette while staring into the sapphire blue eyes of the Earl.

"I do see what you are saying, my dear, but there is only one problem, Nicolette," said the Earl. "And what problem might that be, my lord?" asked Nicolette with raised eyebrows. "Blubelle will hardly allow anyone to ride her except for you, Nicolette. You seem to be the one she is the most comfortable with, my dear, and that will make it impossible to let her take the place of the Dark Knight," replied the Earl with a slight look of admiration for Nicolette on his handsome face.

"Well, since we are extremely short on time, I suggest that we could at least bring her out to the track and let the jockey take her around the track for a few practice runs and then we will know what to do, my lord," said Nicolette with a determined look on her lovely face.

Suddenly everyone got quiet for a moment while the Earl stood there staring off into the distance as if he was trying to make a decision. "Go find the groom, Lord Watson, and saddle up Blubelle. Bring her to the track and Teddy will ride Blubelle around the track. Hurry up, Lord Watson! I have to make a decision as soon as possible because you know the rules as well as I do, my lord," said the Earl with a lot more hope in his tone of voice. Nicolette slowly turned away from the Earl and started walking towards the stables when she heard the Earl call her name out loud, "Where are you going, Nicolette?" asked the Earl. "I am finding a carriage back to the manor, my lord," replied Nicolette as she turned to face the Earl with her warm cheeks and slightly swollen lips. "I need you to stay here, Nicolette since this is your idea. Your idea might just be the solution to our problem. I really don't want to take a chance on racing the Dark Knight if he is still favoring his leg. He probably needs a little more time to recover completely. So please tell me that you will stay, Nicolette?"

Nicolette took a deep breath and started walking towards the Earl and stopped beside him. She looked into his eyes and softly replied, "I shall stay if that is what you wish me to do, my lord. I have to admit I am rather anxious to see what Blubelle shall do." The Earl smiled at Nicolette and turned his head to look at his jockey standing against the wooden fence. "Please come over here, Teddy," suddenly asked the Earl. "You do remember that it is Nicolette whom Blubelle feels the most comfortable with, but maybe Blubelle will feel that way with you, Teddy. All we can do is give it a try, and it looks as if Lord Watson is already here with Blubelle."

Teddy mounted Blubelle and ran her around the track a couple of times at a normal pace. The third time around the track, Teddy picked up his speed and ran her as fast as she would allow. Lord Watson was timing her speed, but it was clear to Nicolette that Bluebelle wasn't performing at her full potential. With a slight look of disappointment and a few shakes of their head, Nicolette was the first to speak, "Perhaps you should allow me to ride Blubelle around the track, my lord?"

"And why would I do that, Nicolette?" replied the Earl. "As you well know, that would be a waste of time, my dear; they do not allow ladies to enter the race."

"I am well aware of that, my lord, but just allow me to ride her around the track, and I will show you how fast she really is, my lord," asked Nicolette with utter determination in her sweet, soft voice. "Please, my lord, I promise to be safe?"

Lord Watson, Teddy and Nicolette all three stood quietly waiting on the Earl to answer Nicolette, "I suppose you can give it a try, Nicolette. I am as anxious as the rest of you to see how fast Blubelle will run. But you have to promise me you will be careful, my dear; I shall die if anything happens to you." Immediately, everyone glanced up at the Earl when he finished speaking. Nicolette could tell by the startled look on Lord Watson and Teddy's faces that they were surprised by what the Earl said. But somehow, she knew that the Earl meant what he said and he would probably die if something happened to her, and at that very moment, she knew that the Earl really did care deeply for her. Nicolette mounted Blubelle and gracefully ran her around the track, increasing her speed on each run. This was her last run, and she could feel that this was the fastest speed she had ever experienced riding on the back of Blubelle. Even her hair pins had come loose from her hair, and the wind was blowing her golden hair everywhere. When she finished the run and headed back to where they were waiting, Lord Watson announced that Blubelle's speed with Nicolette on top was even faster than the speed of the Dark Knight.

When Nicolette dismounted Blubelle after hearing that, the Earl lifted her up in his arms, swirled her around in a circle and gently let her go. "That is magnificent, Nicolette; it is a shame that they don't allow ladies to race. We would have a winner with Blubelle. Don't you agree, Lord Watson?" After clearing his throat, Lord Watson replied to the Earl, "You are right, my lord. It is unfortunate that Miss Braxton can not race Blubelle in the Derby Trial Stakes. She will have to disguise herself as a male jockey in order to qualify for the race, and we all know that will be impossible to do, my lord." Suddenly, they all burst out into laughter at what Lord Watson had just implied. "I realize that you think that idea is rather funny, and I have to agree, gentlemen. But maybe the idea is not as impossible as you think, my lord," said Nicolette in her most convincing tone of voice. "I could disguise myself as a male horse jockey. If Teddy has the clothing and accessories that I can borrow, I will hide them inside my cloak and quickly go to my chamber and put them on and see what I look like. If I think that my idea will work, I will sneak back down to the stables wearing the clothing so you can see for yourself, my lord."

"Have you gone mad, Nicolette?" said the Earl with a half grin on his face. "You can't be serious, my dear. What in God's sake makes you think we can get away with such a thing?"

"I do not have that answer right now my lord, so if you allow Teddy to go to the stables and get all the items that are necessary to pull this off, we shall know if my idea is worth a try."

Everyone stood quietly, waiting for the Earl to make his decision. The Earl locked eyes with Nicolette and then he noticed how beautiful she looked at that very moment with her golden hair all in disarray. Her cheeks were rosy, and her lips looked warm and inviting. Her bosom appeared to be swollen and suddenly emerged out of the top bodice of her green plaid riding gown. At this very moment all he wanted was to lift her up in his arms and carry her over to the spot where they met before in the Mayfield garden and make her his lady forever. But damn, what was he thinking; he knew he couldn't do that now. Nicolette was the first one to break the silence, "My lord! What do you say?"

"I say that I think this idea is insane yet brilliant, my dear," replied the Earl. "I do have a lot riding on this race, as you well know, Lord Watson. Derby horse races always allow the owners to throw in their wagers or bets on the horses. That is one of the reasons I do not want to have to pull out of the race completely. I have big plans to throw in a large wager on the Dark Knight, but now that Blubelle may be taking his place, we still have a good chance to come out of this race as a winner."

"Alright, Nicolette, I shall agree but you have to follow all instructions and be as discreet as humanly possible. No one can know about this except your mother, Daniel, Lord Watson, Teddy and me, of course. Do I have your word, my dear?" Nicolette gazed into the eyes of the Earl once more and softly and sweetly replied, "You have my word, my lord."

"Now go get the items that Nicolette needs to take to her chamber, Teddy, and I will send you and one of my grooms to the shop where he can purchase some new jockey clothing, boots and all accessories we need. We will meet you in front of the stables shortly."

Once Nicolette received the items she needed, she quickly took a carriage back to the manor. She was fortunate once more to be able to make it to her chamber without seeing anyone except her lady's maid. Nicolette told Sally that she did not need anything except to rest for a while. At that moment, she felt famished once she realized that she had hardly eaten anything all morning, and now it was way past the mid-day meal. But now was not the time to eat; she knew she must hurry to try on the jockey items. Nicolette was glad that she and her mother had designed a few corsets that were laced in the front instead of the back of the corset, and at this very moment, she was wearing one of them. It made it a lot easier to undress herself, but when she glanced into the mirror, she suddenly realized that she was going to have to make something to help disguise her full bosom. She scurried around, looking in her armoire, and found one of her older cotton nightgowns and began to rip it into large strips of fabric so she could wrap the pieces of fabric tightly around her bosom so they could lie flat against her chest. She walked over to her sewing kit and grabbed a few pins that could hold the fabric together. She was rather tall in stature for a lady, so it seemed as if the trousers, shirt, suspenders and jacket were almost a perfect fit. When she sat down to try on the boots, she found them to be a good fit as well. But when she walked over to the floor-length mirror, she saw her long golden curls cascading over her shoulders and down her back. So, she grabbed a handful of hairpins out of the box on her vanity, pulled her hair up on top of her head and pinned it as close to her scalp as she could. Then she placed a gentleman's British Empire Pith Helmet on top of her head. When she stared into her mirror, she saw a horse jockey by the name of Nicolas Pendleton, cousin of Teddy Pendleton, staring back at her. She couldn't help but giggle out loud for a moment. She was hoping that the Earl wouldn't laugh at her when he saw her in this get-up. When she turned away from the mirror, she glanced over at the clock and realized that she must hurry and run down the stairs and out the door so she could head back to the stables without being noticed. She must not keep the Earl waiting too long, she thought; he might change his mind.

CHAPTER 12

England Autumn 1865

Once Nicolette ran outside the side door of the manor, she immediately recognized Lord Watson and Teddy sitting in the seat of the carriage waiting to escort her to the stables. She hurried inside the carriage and quickly took her seat. Lord Watson and Teddy stared at Nicolette with a look of awe on their stunned faces. Teddy was the first to break the silence, "Good afternoon, cousin Nicolas. It is indeed a pleasure to have you here at Primrose Estate." Nicolette tried very hard to deepen the tone of her voice to a more masculine tone of voice. She was finding that not only deepening her voice was rather difficult to do, but dropping her southern drawl was even much harder. "Maybe it would be much better to stay as quiet as you can when other people are around Nicolas unless you are speaking to the Earl or one of us," said Lord Watson as he desperately tried not to laugh out loud.

"Go ahead and laugh, Lord Watson, and you too, Teddy; I know that you can't hold it in much longer."

"But I do admit Nicolette, you certainly do look the part, and you shouldn't have any problem convincing the Earl."

The carriage was almost to the stables when suddenly, sounds of loud laughter filled the autumn air.

"It's about time you get here," said the Earl as he stood up from his desk that was located in his private study near the back of the horse stables. "Lord Mayfield, I would like to introduce you to my cousin Nicolas Pendleton from East London," said Teddy as he stepped behind Nicolette with a grin on his face. "It is a pleasure to meet the cousin of Teddy," replied the Earl with a look of total amazement on his handsome face. "Well, what do you think about my disguise, my lord?" asked Nicolette. "If you want to know the truth, Nicolette, I must admit I am very impressed. I do believe we can pull this off. I must leave for London immediately so I can do the necessary paperwork that is required to enter Blubelle into the race instead of the Dark Knight, but first, I want you to listen carefully to my instructions. You need to go pack your belongings and prepare to leave Primrose Estate immediately. Perhaps you can tell the others that you have endured plenty of rest, and it is time to get back to making gowns."

"I do believe Mother and everyone else will understand that."

"Therefore, I will have one of the Mayfield carriages escort you back to the city. When you get back there, you are not allowed to tell anyone except your mother and Daniel about our plan. They must keep this news to themselves as well. They must not speak a word to anyone. As far as anyone knows you are busy as can be making new gowns for the upcoming ball. In a couple of days, I will have a carriage pick you up at the crack of dawn, and that will be the day before the race begins. You have to be at the track in your disguise, ready to have some trial runs around the track with Blubelle. Lord Watson will bring extra horse jockey apparel, which includes undergarments and necessary accessories, along with him. I suggest you leave the Ashton cottage that morning wearing one of your lovely gowns. The carriage that arrives there to pick you up will first escort you to the Mayfield cottage located in London. No one will be occupying the cottage since Lord Jared will be at the race track with the rest of us. When you arrive at the cottage, you must immediately change into the horse jockey apparel and leave your gown and other belongings at the Mayfield cottage. Then, you will quickly get back into the carriage that will be waiting to escort you directly to the hotel at Lingfield Park. You can have my hotel suite, which is located on the premises near the track, and I will have a cot set up so I can sleep inside the Mayfield tent. I will make sure that you will have everything you need inside the suite so you won't have anyone come to your room to offer service. No one but us should know that you will be occupying that room. Now, have I made myself clear to everyone? Please don't let me down; I have a lot at stake here. Even though this idea appears to be utterly insane, I don't believe I have told you, Nicolette, how grateful I am that you have taken it upon yourself to take such a risk to help me. I am forever in your debt, my dear, but we shouldn't get ahead of ourselves. We must be on our toes because the task ahead will not be an easy one."

When the carriage that left Primrose Estate earlier escorting Nicolette pulled up in front of the Ashton cottage, Nicolette noticed that the rain had suddenly stopped. Nicolette also realized that it was around the time that her mother and Daniel would be eating their evening meal. And her stomach had begun to turn flips from the lack of food. Once she stepped inside the cottage, the coachmen delivered her belongings over to the butler, and Nicolette hurried to the dining room, where she saw her mother and Daniel sitting at a medium-sized oak dining table where they regularly took their meals. "Well, I must say this is quite a surprise to see you here, my dear," said Lady Elizabeth with a surprise look on her lovely face. "Yes, Mother, I suppose you are rather surprised. I had to leave a day earlier than what was planned because there's something I have to do and the fact that both you and Daniel are here will be a good time to tell you. But first, please inform the cook to set another place for me; I am famished," replied Nicolette as she took her seat at the table.

"You have our attention, Nicolette, so what is it you need to tell us," asked Daniel suddenly. "Once I tell you what I am going to be doing the next couple of days, you are going to think I have gone completely mad," said Nicolette in between shoveling down her throat the delicious food on her plate. "Lord Austin's Arabian horse, the Dark Knight, has to be pulled out of the Derby Trial Stakes here at the last minute before the deadline is up, and I helped the Earl come up with a solution."

"And what solution is that Nicolette?" asked Lady Elizabeth. "I suggested that the Earl enters Blubelle into the race to take the place of the Dark Knight," replied Nicolette. "So what is it that you will have to do, Nicolette?" asked Daniel with curiosity in his voice. "I will have to disguise myself as a male horse jockey so I can be the one who races Blubelle in the Derby Trial Stakes," replied Nicolette while staring into the pale white startled faces of her mother and Daniel.

"I must say, my dear, you have gone completely mad," exclaimed her mother in an unusually loud tone of voice. "Why would you suggest doing such a thing, Nicolette, and why would the Earl allow such a thing? Has he gone mad as well?"

"The Earl has placed a rather large wager on this race, and he will lose all his money if he pulls out completely," replied Nicolette. "But if he enters Blubelle in the place of the Dark Knight, he still could lose some of the wagers, but he will not lose most of it. Plus, who says that we don't have a chance to win? Blubelle rides just as fast around the track as the Dark Knight, but only if I am the rider."

"What I am anxious to know is why you would go as far as to risk your reputation and possibly your safety for Lord Austin, Nicolette," asked Daniel with a suspicious look in his eyes. Nicolette could feel that she was beginning to turn red in the face; she could feel the warmth of her cheeks when she touched her face. "I have suspected all along that there may be something brewing between you and Lord Austin. I even noticed how he looked at you and how you looked at him on the ship when we were on our way to England. But I could also tell that you were trying your best to deny what was happening between you and the Earl. But the morning at the Mayfield horse stables when you asked me if I had heard the news about the Earl's proposal to Lady Anne, I could see the sad look in your eyes and a small tear develop in the corner of your eye," said Daniel with tenderness in his voice.

"Is any of what Daniel is implying true, my dear? Please don't hold back, my dear; you can tell us the truth," said Lady Elizabeth as she got up out of her chair to place her hand on Nicolette's shoulder. Suddenly, Nicolette stood up, placed her arms around her mother and began to sob a river of tears as she buried her face into her mother's shoulder. Moments later, Nicolette raised her head and dried her tears with the handkerchief Daniel kindly placed into her trembling hand. "Yes, Mother, what Daniel is implying is true, but believe me, Mother, this was never my intention. I don't know why I have these feelings for the Earl, and I realize that I have no right to feel this way."

"Does he know that you have feelings for him, my dear, and does he have these same feelings for you?" anxiously asked Lady Elizabeth with concern in her voice.

"No, Mother, I have never told the Earl of my feelings, but I do not have to say the words out loud since my behavior when I am around the Earl is quite revealing of how I must feel," sadly replied Nicolette. "What behavior are you referring to, sister?" exclaimed Daniel. "The Earl better not have taken advantage of you in any way, Nicolette? If so, I will go find him now, and he will not like what I shall do."

"No, Daniel, he has not taken advantage of me in the way you are implying. There has only been a kiss or two that has taken place between me and Lord Austin, and I should have known better than to allow even that to happen." At that moment, Nicolette decided that she would not reveal any more of her feelings or actions that had taken place between her and the Earl. She felt as if she would be better off not sharing all of her secrets. But keeping all of these secrets inside her these past few months had been rather unbearable at times. She was already starting to feel somewhat better now that she was able to cry and share her feelings with her mother and Daniel.

Nicolette looked down at the food left on her plate, realizing that she was still famished, so she took her seat along with the rest of them and began to eat her food once more. "I do realize that your curiosity has allowed you to have further questions about what has taken place with the Earl and me," said Nicolette. "But I do have a long day ahead of me tomorrow, and I must be feeling my best. So, if you will excuse me Mother, I shall retire to my chamber for a long and relaxing soak in the tub. If I do not see you both before I leave at the crack of dawn in the morning, I shall see you when I return in a couple of days. Please wish me well, Mother and Daniel, or perhaps a prayer or two maybe even more appropriate at this time."

"Please be safe, my dear," exclaimed Lady Elizabeth. "There is no doubt that I will be praying for your safety above all else, my dear."

The following morning the bright yellow sun had barely showed its face before Nicolette was in the Mayfield carriage on her way to the Mayfield cottage. When she arrived at the cottage, the Earl's private coachman helped her to the door and unlocked it so Nicolette could step inside. Just like the Earl said when they last saw each other at the Mayfield horse stables, the cottage will be quiet as a mouse. She was the only one here, and she felt a slight eerie knowing that. She continued up the stairs, trying to follow the Earl's previous instructions. After walking down a long hallway, she finally found the chamber where she would slip out of her gown and dress herself as Nicolas Pendleton. Once again, she was grateful that she wore the corset that was laced in the front so it would be faster and easier for her to undress herself. Now that she was fully dressed as a horse jockey, she took one last glance into the mirror and was pleased with what she saw. She placed her gown, undergarments, shoes and bonnet on a leather chaise lounge near the large poster bed and practically ran down the stairs and out the door where the carriage was waiting to escort Nicolas Pendleton to Lingfield Park.

"Good morning, Lady Anne," said Lady Miranda when she first saw Lady Anne step foot into the Mayfield dining room the morning of the day before they left for the Derby Trial Stakes. Lady Miranda was feeling thankful at this very moment that Lady Anne agreed to stay at Primrose Estate and go with the Mayfield family to the horse race. Lady Miranda had almost completely forgotten that Lord Jared had asked her kindly if she would do him a large favor. And now she could take Lady Anne with her to

London in order to pick up a leather pouch of money that Lord Jared left on his bed in the Mayfield cottage. After she agreed to follow through with his request, she asked him what the money was for. Although Lord Jared was reluctant to tell her, he decided that she had a right to know since she was doing him a favor. He told her that he was placing a large wager on a particular horse and that horse happened to be Blubelle.

But hasn't the French horse they call the "Gladiateur" had all the major wins so far? She remembered asking him. But she knew from past history that there was no need to argue with her brother.

"Please come sit with me, Lady Anne," Lady Miranda kindly asked Lady Anne. "I have a small favor to ask of you, and perhaps it will be to your liking." After Lady Anne was sitting comfortably in the chair next to Lady Miranda, she told Lady Anne about the favor that she had promised Lord Jared that she would do for him. "Well, I would be delighted to accompany you to the city today, my lady; I have been feeling a bit restless lately. Perhaps we can do some light shopping while we are there," replied Lady Anne with a little more vigor in her voice. "That sounds like an excellent idea," replied Lady Miranda with a smile on her lovely face. "So let's hurry and finish our breakfast so we can leave right away." Lady Anne thought about Lord Jared while she was finishing up her morning meal. She remembered the other afternoon when they took the horses out for a ride and how much fun they were having just enjoying each other's company. She felt as if she could relax with Lord Jared and talk about anything that she wanted to talk about when she was in his company since he was so attentive to her every need. *I suppose the Earl is right; I am beginning to see that his brother is smitten with me. I must admit he is as handsome as the Earl of Primrose in his own gentlemanly way. After all, he is a Mayfield, and I am an Ashton, and isn't that the bloodline our fathers want? But I can't help but feel like there is something other than the fact that the Earl says he doesn't love me is why he doesn't want to marry me. I almost feel like there is someone or something else that he is keeping a secret and I am determined to find out one way or the other.*

Lady Miranda and Lady Anne couldn't have asked for a nicer day to take a trip into the city. They could definitely see that fall was in the air. The sky was a bright blue, and the air was crisp and cool. There were vibrant red, gold, yellow and orange leaves everywhere on the tall trees. The Mayfield carriage continued to stroll along the cobblestone streets of London, heading for the Mayfield cottage. Lady Anne and Lady Miranda, along with one of the lady's maids, sat comfortably inside the carriage while Lady Anne made the time pass by quickly with her continuous chatter. Suddenly, the carriage pulled up in front of the Mayfield cottage before they even realized it. The footman who was riding beside the coachman hopped down, helped the ladies step outside the carriage, and led them inside the cottage. Lady Anne followed Lady Miranda up the stairs to Lord Jared's bed chamber. Lady Miranda opened the door and stepped inside the chamber while Lady Anne stood in the hallway waiting. Lady Anne suddenly noticed another bed chamber that was directly across from Lord

Jared's chamber, and it appeared to be the Earl's chamber. So, Lady Anne took it upon herself to enter the chamber that looked like it would belong to the Earl and peep around the room. When she saw the leather chaise lounge on the other side of the large bed, she noticed what looked like a lady's gown and undergarments lying across the chaise lounge. So, she decided to walk over there and take a closer look, and when she looked directly down at the gown, she realized that the gown and undergarments belonged to Nicolette. She had seen these items in Nicolette's possession once before. Besides, Nicolette was the one who designed the front laced corset. There was no doubt in her mind that these items belonged to Nicolette, but what she wanted to know was, what in heaven's sake were they doing here?

"Oh, there you are, Lady Anne; I thought I heard your voice coming from this room. It sounded as if something frightened you, my lady," said Lady Miranda with a puzzled look on her face. "Well, I suppose you can say that I sounded that way, my lady," replied Lady Anne as she quickly walked away from the chaise lounge to the entry of the chamber where Lady Miranda was standing. "I thought I heard someone behind that dressing screen on the far side of the room. I suppose I am imagining things, my lady, because when I looked, no one was there," replied Lady Anne as she began to giggle out loud.

"I suppose I can see why you would imagine such things, Lady Anne; after all, it is unusually quiet here when no one is occupying the premises at the moment. But I assure you there is no one except us here at this time, my lady," said Lady Miranda with a reassuring smile on her face. "I found the leather pouch with the money, so let's be on our way. We can do a little shopping before the carriage takes us to Lingfield Park where I will leave the money with the owner of the hotel on the premises of the horse track. Lord Jared and the owner are long-time friends, and he will see to it that Lord Jared gets the money right away."

"You are a good sister to Lord Jared, my lady, and perhaps you will be a good sister to me and me to you one day."

"You are already a dear friend to me, and I am most grateful," replied Lady Anne with her heart racing, wondering what to make of what she just witnessed. She was still in total shock, and she had made a quick decision to keep what she just found to herself. Lady Miranda would be even more devastated to see Nicolette's gown and belongings in the Earl's chamber than she was at the moment. He was her brother, and she didn't know anything about what was going on between her and the Earl. But she was bound to find out soon enough because she was more determined than before to find out what was going on with the Earl of Primrose, and she got a feeling that it had something to do with her cousin Nicolette.

When Nicolette arrived at Lingfield Park, the carriage escorted her straight to the race track, where the Earl was waiting on her arrival. The coachman pulled up in front of the very large horse stables where the racehorses were located. Nicolette sat nervously inside the carriage dressed as Nicolas Pendleton while waiting for the Earl to arrive. Once she saw the Earl walking her way, she began to relax. The feeling of being able to relax seemed rather odd to her for a moment because normally, when she was dressed as Nicolette when she was near the Earl, her heart began to pound, and she felt any way but relaxed. Nicolette stepped outside the carriage and greeted the Earl as Nicolas Pendleton. "Please follow us to the stall where Blubelle is located, Mister Pendleton; it won't be much longer before you will be taking Blubelle out for a practice run around the track," said the Earl with a half grin on his handsome face.

Nicolette followed the Earl into the stables, and they continued until he stopped in front of the stall where Blubelle was located. Nicolette was so thrilled to see Blubelle that she couldn't wait to rub her beautiful, shiny white coat and whisper in her ear. She hated to have to be so quiet that she couldn't talk around the Earl or the others like she normally would. But she knew how risky this was and the last thing she wanted to do was to mess things up for the Earl. But she couldn't help but blush from her head to her toes while the Earl was standing on the other side of Blubelle. He moved to her side and gently whispered in her ear that if she had to relieve herself, he would cover for her. In other words, he would hand her a chamber pot to use, and he promised not to look as if he was standing guard, making sure no one came around them. Then, he would go and empty the pot when no one was looking. "I suppose you thought of everything, my lord, and I guess I should be thanking you for that," Nicolette whispered into the Earl's ear with a red face and a half grin. "Perhaps it is my duty to remind you, Nicolette," he whispered in her ear once more. "You are still a lady underneath all those garments, my dear, and a most desirable one, may I add." Nicolette's cheeks were on fire now as she softly whispered back, "You have no shame, my lord."

"It is time for us to bring Blubelle to the front, my lord," exclaimed Lord Watson as he approached the stall where the Earl and Nicolette were standing beside Blubelle. "Blubelle is good to go, Lord Watson," replied the Earl as he motioned for Nicolette to lead Blubelle from the stall and follow him and Lord Watson to the front of the track. "This will be your first practice run with Blubelle, Nicolette, and ride her as you do at Primrose Estate, and you will do just fine. She is a fast runner, Nicolette, and you are the one who can ride her that way", said the Earl as he watched Nicolette mount Blubelle and suddenly take off around the horse track as fast as Blubelle could run. Nicolette was relieved to know that the ladies' stocking that she chose to put over her hair after it seemed like a million hair pins she used to keep it in place was working for her. At that very moment, she felt and obviously looked like Nicolas Pendleton, and she was thankful. Once she crossed the finish line, she headed back to where the Earl and Lord Watson were waiting to hear how fast Blubelle's time was. They waited a short while to hear the results, and they were satisfied with their first run. Nicolette slowly rode Blubelle back to the stables with the Earl and Lord Watson walking that same way.

The day seemed to have dragged by slowly. They were only allowed one more practice run with Blubelle, and her timing was even faster than before. The Earl seemed pleased with the results, and that made Nicolette breathe with a sigh of relief. The day at the track was coming to an end, and Nicolette was glad when the carriage escorted her and the Earl over to the hotel suite that he was allowing her to stay in while she was there. The Earl had already had her belongings taken to the room by Lord Watson. The Earl was relieved to hear Lord Jared would be helping a dear friend out at the track since his friend's trainer came down with a much contagious sickness at the last moment. The Earl insisted on Lord Jared helping his friend since he really didn't want to have to tell his brother about Nicolette and her disguise as Nicolas Pendleton.

The Earl headed up the stairway with Nicolette still disguised as Nicolas Pendleton, unlocked the door to her hotel suite, and entered the suite when no one was around. "You do not have to worry, my dear; you can feel safe here with me," said the Earl with tenderness in his voice. "I am not worried, my lord; I do feel safe here with you."

"I shall wait a moment, and then I shall leave you here for the night," said the Earl. "Please look around; I believe you will find everything you requested earlier, Nicolette. I am looking forward to seeing Nicolas at the track tomorrow morning. I hope you sleep well, my dear," said the Earl as he quietly slipped out the door where the carriage was waiting to take him to the Mayfield tent.

The following morning was race day, and the Mayfield family, along with Lady Anne, Lord Atticus and Lady Luisa, all left early this morning to attend the Derby Trial Stakes at Lingfield Park. Lady Anne was feeling rather fatigued this morning since she could hardly sleep the night before. She tossed and turned in her large canopy bed for most part of the night wondering over and over in her mind why Nicolette's belongings were in the Earl's chamber at the Mayfield cottage in London. The only time that she knew that the Earl had spent the night at the cottage recently was the evening that the Earl met Lord Atticus, Lady Luisa and me at the Rainbow Restaurant for dinner. But then she remembered that it was the same night that they all saw Nicolette and George at the Rainbow Restaurant. It was the same night they all saw George down on one knee proposing marriage to Nicolette, and it appeared as if her answer to George was a big yes, but she found out later from Nicolette that she did not give George an answer. Instead, Nicolette told her that she told George she would give him an answer when he returned to England after his trip to Charleston. All she could do at this moment was to shake her head and tell herself that none of this made any sense at all. When Lady Anne turned her pretty face to glance outside the Mayfield carriage, she realized that they had already arrived at Lingfield Park. And then she told herself that she would not let anything or anyone stand in her way of finding out why Nicolette's gown and other items were doing in the Earl's chamber at the Mayfield cottage in London.

When the Mayfield carriage pulled up beside the Mayfield tent facing the horse track, Lady Anne saw the Earl quickly walking towards them. Once the Marquis and Lady Constance stepped out of the carriage, the Earl helped his two sisters and Lady Anne step from the carriage. Lady Anne couldn't help but notice how handsome the Earl looked today in his not-so-formal attire. She always thought he was even more handsome when he was wearing a white shirt with open buttons to show off his bronzed muscular chest. "Welcome family and Lady Anne to the Derby Trial Stakes," said the Earl with a big smile on his face as he leaned over and placed a light kiss on the top of Lady Anne's gloved hand. "I am delighted that you are here."

"We are delighted to be here, my lord, but I do not see Lord Jared anywhere, my lord," asked Lady Anne while glancing beyond where the Earl was standing. "Lord Jared will not be joining us here at the Mayfield tent today, my lady," replied the Earl. "He is here at the track, but he will be helping out a dear friend of his today, and he wants to extend his deepest apology to all of you."

"Well, he will truly be missed today, my lord," said Lady Anne in a somewhat sad voice. "My groom will lead all of you to the Mayfield tent now to find your seats," said the Earl. "Will you please excuse me? I must leave and go to the horse stables; I shall return soon. Please help yourselves to the refreshments inside the tent. I'm sure you will find them to your liking."

The Earl turned around and headed straight to the horse stables, where he knew Nicolette and Lord Watson were patiently waiting. But it didn't escape his mind that Lady Anne had just asked about Lord Jared, and he also noticed the sad look on her face when she found out that he wouldn't be joining them today. *Could it be that she is beginning to warm up to the idea of Lord Jared becoming her husband? Soon, I will inform my brother that I am aware of his feelings for Lady Anne and that I have already informed Lady Anne that I do not have those feelings for her, and I think it would be better if you, my brother, and Lady Anne marry. Surely, Lord Jared will want to marry Lady Anne with my blessing, but Father and Lord Ashton's blessing is still the one that I'm not sure of. A bloodline is what they want, and a bloodline is what they shall get.*

CHAPTER 13

Autumn 1865

"Ah, there you are, my lord," exclaimed Lord Watson. "Why are you acting so jittery, Lord Watson," asked the Earl with a curious look on his face when he arrived at the horse stables at the track.

"Well, it has something to do with Nicolette, or I mean Nicolas, my lord," replied Lord Watson while turning red in the face.

"Well, go ahead and tell me, or does the cat have your tongue," said the Earl. "We can't seem to find the chamber pot anywhere, my lord, and Nicolette is desperate to… you know what I mean, my lord,"

"May I remind you that I mentioned that I needed to hide it away? If you go look between those few stacks of hay in the corner of Blubelle's stall, you shall find it. So, where is Nicolette now? I told her to stay near you while I was gone," said the Earl with a stifled laugh on his face. "I'm over here, my lord; I find it to be much easier to sit over here on the bench since I'm feeling distressed."

"Hurry, come quick, I will get what you need," said the Earl. Nicolette rose from the bench and ran as fast as she could to a hidden corner in Blubelle's stall to finally relieve herself. "And by the way, I heard your laughter, my lord," said Nicolette out loud. "Now, it is my turn to remind you that I find none of this to be a laughing matter, my lord."

Once the Earl returned from emptying the chamber pot, he handed Nicolette the curry comb and told her to brush Blubelle. "I will stand next to Blubelle also, I believe that will be the best way for us to speak without anyone hearing our conversation. We have been very discreet, my dear, and so far, it seems to be working. When the Earl stepped closer to Nicolette, he did not smell her womanly scent mixed with a strong scent of white Jasmine, but instead, he only smelled her womanly scent since she agreed with him it would be better not to wear any fragrances while she was disguised as Nicolas Pendleton. But he had to admit her scent was even more intoxicating than before. And at this very moment, he wanted to strip away this Nicolas Pendleton attire until he saw her naked body. He wanted to kiss those pink lips of hers and feel her naked breasts against his bare chest. "My lord, did you hear what I asked you?" asked Nicolette, suddenly trying to get the Earl's attention. "Oh, sorry, Nicolette, my mind must have wandered off. Now, what is it you asked me, my dear?"

"When your family and everyone arrived at the track earlier, did Lord Ashton, Lady Margaret and Lady Anne arrive as well, my lord?" curiously asked Nicolette. "Lady Anne arrived at the track in one of the Mayfield carriages since she was still visiting Primrose Estate, and as far as Lord Gerald and Lady Margaret, I'm sure they have arrived by now," replied the Earl. "I am just curious if anyone has mentioned to them that Mother, Daniel, and I were not planning to attend the Derby Trial Stakes since I forgot to tell them. I believe they might have thought we were attending, and they may have sent one of the Ashton carriages to the Ashton cottage this morning," said Nicolette with slight concern in her voice.

"Even if that is the case, Nicolette, there is no need to worry, my dear. I'm sure your mother or Daniel will inform them that all of you decided to stay behind since you are so busy with work at the shop," replied the Earl while staring into the big blue eyes of Nicolette.

"It is time, Lord Mayfield," exclaimed Lord Watson as he stepped inside the stall of Blubelle and announced it was time to bring Blubelle to the front and place her inside her starting gate. Nicolette took off her hat, placed her helmet on her head, put on her gloves, grabbed her horsewhip and mounted Blubelle. She was starting to feel somewhat nervous inside, and it wasn't because of how Blubelle would do on her run; it was because she was hoping that she would remain as Nicolas Pendleton and that no one would find out that she was Nicolette. "You do not have to be nervous, my dear; I have all the confidence in the world in you, Nicolette," said the Earl with a most tender voice. "I'm glad you do, my lord, because I'm not quite as sure as you are, my lord," replied Nicolette with a deep voice.

When Nicolette and Blubelle stepped inside their own starting gate alongside the other racehorses in their starting gates, you could see the number 5 on their stall. The bells rang, and it was time to open the gate and race the horses around the track. The Earl, Lord Watson and the entire crowd there cheered out loud while watching their favorite horse race around the track. Blubelle was among the front runners while the Gladiateur pulled slightly ahead of them. When the horses made their last and final turn around the track, it was not a short distance to the finish line. Blubelle began to pull out in front of the other horses, and she crossed over the finish line with a close second place to the Gladiateur, who finished the race in first place. Nicolette wasn't exactly sure that she had finished the race in second place until the Earl and Lord Watson came running towards her as she guided Blubelle to where the winner boxes were located.

"Oh, for heaven's sake, that is exciting and frightening at the same time, my lord," said Nicolette as she leaned over to whisper in the Earl's ear. "You did so outstanding, my dear; I have never felt as proud of anyone as I do you at this moment," said the Earl as he whispered back into her ear but realized she still had to wear her helmet. When Blubelle and Nicolette arrived in the box for a second-place winner, she was greeted by people who placed a second-place ribbon on her and handed her flowers and a second-place winner's cup. She stayed mounted on top of Blubelle while a photographer took some tintype photographs. Nicolette let out a huge sigh of relief when that was over. She felt as if she could breathe a lot better now until she looked out and saw all the Mayfield and Ashton family standing outside the box, staring her way. Suddenly, they were allowed inside where she was, and they were coming towards her, the Earl and Lord Watson, to congratulate them on their second-place finish; when she immediately glanced over at the Earl, she noticed that the Earl was beginning to walk with them and moving them away from her and Blubelle. She was grateful that the Earl did not allow anyone to get too close to her; she could hardly breathe already. Now that the Earl had them occupied with his attention after a while, it made room for Lord Watson to lead her and Blubelle past them and head towards the horse stables where she could spend some private time with Blubelle. At that moment, she was so proud of Blubelle and herself; she could tell that the Earl was very pleased with both of them.

"You might want to go sit for a while and take a rest, Miss Braxton," said Lord Watson. "They may call you back to the second place winner's box for more photographs and publicity, but right now, all the attention is on the Gladiateur since he is the winner of the race and, therefore, he has won the "English Triple Crown." That is the best and most prestigious award you can win. I can almost envision the Dark Knight or even Blubelle having earned that honor one day, Miss Braxton. But as for now, the Gladiateur is getting all the attention along with his owner, Count Frederic de Lagrange and his trainer, Tom Jennings Sr., whom I have acquainted with in the past. Therefore, this helps to take the spotlight off of us, and the Earl seems quite pleased with a second-place finish since he will be able to retain most of his wager and maybe profit from a second-place finish. Ah, speaking of the Earl, here he is now, Miss Braxton."

"You may go ahead and start packing up everything now, Lord Watson. My family and the Ashton family are heading over to the Lingfield Park Hotel to join us for dinner. Nicolette, you may excuse yourself to your hotel suite until I call on you once our families leave to go home after dinner. I will inform them that Nicolas Pendleton had to leave Lingfield Park immediately once he arrived back at the stables. Word had come that there was an emergency in the Pendleton family. Therefore, they will understand why he wasn't able to join everyone for dinner. Don't worry, my dear; I have already requested the hotel staff to bring food to your room as we speak, So please make haste and go before my family makes their way there," said the Earl with a very pleased look on his handsome face.

Nicolette stepped closer to the Earl, gazed into his sapphire blue eyes, and quietly said. "I thank you, my lord; it appears as if you have thought of everything."

"No, it is you. I should be thanking Nicolette; not only have you made me a proud man today, but you have made me a much wealthier man as well. And you will indeed be rewarded for your brave and generous efforts my dear," said the Earl with a kind and loving tone in his voice. "There is no need to reward me, my lord; it is my pleasure to help out," replied Nicolette.

Suddenly, a carriage pulled up, and the Earl and Nicolette stepped inside the carriage and took their seats across from one another. "I will see to it that you make it safe to the hotel suite, my dear. I'm sure you are famished by now, and there will be food in the suite when you arrive. Please be ready when I call on you later. I have a Mayfield carriage on standby to escort you and me back to the city. We shall go to the Mayfield cottage first so you can change your attire. I'm sure you are rather anxious to discard this Nicolas Pendleton disguise, Nicolette," said the Earl with a smile on his face. "I must say so, my lord. The clothes are rather comfortable, but the fabric that is tightly wound around my chest is what's so uncomfortable. I am most anxious to remove it, my lord," said Nicolette as she was beginning to blush from head to toe. Immediately, the Earl had a vision of Nicolette's full breast and taut nipples, and he began to be aroused thinking about that night in the Mayfield library at Primrose Estate. He remembered how warm and soft her bosom felt in his hands and how she responded when he squeezed her hard nipples. And at that very moment, all he could think of was stripping off her garments and kissing her in places that no man had ever gone before.

"We have arrived at the hotel, Nicolette, so let's hurry, my dear before we attract anyone's attention."

Nicolette and the Earl pulled their hats as low as they could over their heads to cover their faces and walk as fast as they could to the Earl's hotel suite. They were both relieved when they arrived at the suite and stepped inside. Before the Earl could bid goodbye to Nicolette, he noticed that the food had arrived, and she seemed very pleased. They both were standing very close together, staring into each other's eyes, when the Earl came very close to kissing the rosy lips of Nicolette, but he decided that it would be best to wait until later. But he was not sure that she would even allow him to kiss her again since she still thought that he was marrying Lady Anne. Instead, the Earl said, "Thank you once again, Nicolette; I am forever in your debt, my dear." Before Nicolette could utter a word, the Earl quickly slipped out the door.

Nicolette stood completely still for a moment, thinking about what almost took place a moment ago between the Earl and her. *Am I imagining things, or did the Earl almost kiss me, she said out loud. How dare he even think about kissing me now that he has proposed marriage to Lady Anne! I do not regret helping him by racing Blubelle in the Derby Trial Stakes. He may have stolen my heart, but he will never have my body as long as he is promised to another.* But then it just occurred to her that the Earl had witnessed George proposing marriage to her as well. So, therefore, he must be thinking that she was promised to another. Quickly, she shook her head as if to rid herself of any thoughts of the Earl and glanced over at the table in the front room of her hotel suite. The food she saw on top of the table looked so delicious she hurried to the table to take her seat and quickly began to devour it. Once she finished eating, she felt very sleepy. All she wanted to do was to lie across the large poster bed in the adjoining room and fall asleep, but she had to stay awake and be ready to leave when the Earl returned. So, she decided to take a soak in the large tub behind the large screen in the corner of the room.

Nicolette was thankful that the Earl had left clean Nicolas Pendleton attire for her to wear. But this time, she decided not to wear the fabric underneath her shirt that so tightly and uncomfortably held her breast flat to her chest. There was no need to be uncomfortable once more. After all, she would be heading straight to the Mayfield cottage, where she left her gown and undergarments. The Earl still hadn't returned quite yet, so she decided to lie across the large poster bed after all. But as soon as her head touched the soft feather pillow, she fell fast asleep, dreaming of a knight on a dark horse with shiny black hair and sapphire blue eyes.

"You do not have to keep apologizing for waking me up earlier, my lord. I tried not to fall asleep since I knew you would be coming back to the hotel suite, but I obviously couldn't help myself, my lord," said Nicolette in between yawns as the Mayfield carriage continued to stroll down the dirt roads on the outskirts of the city. "But I can see that you are still sleepy, my dear," replied the Earl in a deep masculine voice. "Why don't you lay your head right here on my shoulder and take a few winks since we still have some distance ahead before we arrive at the Mayfield cottage," said the Earl as he slid closer to Nicolette in the carriage seat. Nicolette lay her head on the shoulder of the Earl, closed her eyes and immediately realized that she had just made a mistake by doing so. Her heart began to beat faster, and her body began to tremble slightly, with his body being so close to hers. She could feel his warm breath on her face and smell his manly scent mixed in with the musk fragrance that they were both wearing on their bodies since that was the only fragrance she had in the hotel suite when she took her bath earlier.

The Earl waited a few minutes to see whether Nicolette had fallen asleep on his shoulder, but by the way she kept moving around, he could tell she was still awake. Then suddenly, she raised her head up and gazed into his sapphire blue eyes, and he completely lost control. He lifted her chin, placed his warm lips on her lips, and parted her mouth so he could thrust his tongue inside and kiss her with all the pent-up passion he had kept inside his body for so long. All of a sudden, he could feel her trying to pull away and resist the passion that was consuming both of them. "We must stop doing this, my lord," whispered Nicolette while trying to catch her breath. His opened mouth was still lowered to hover closely above hers. "Why must we stop Nicolette," replied the Earl while his lips were trying to find her warm lips once more. "You very well know why, my lord," replied Nicolette in a soft, trembling voice. "If you are referring to our marriage proposals, then I am going to repeat myself once again, my dear. I do not plan on marrying Lady Anne in the near future or never, and as far as you marrying George, you know as well as I know that will never happen," said the Earl as he pressed even closer to Nicolette.

"But that is not what Lady Anne believes, my lord," said Nicolette. "Lady Anne knows the truth since we have talked to each other. I told her that I did not love her and I did not want to marry her. I told her about my brother having feelings for her and that a marriage between her and my brother should be sufficient enough to satisfy our fathers. We have an agreement between us and I feel confident that she will now honor this agreement."

"What makes you so sure that I will not marry George, my lord," asked Nicolette with a slightly curious look on her face. "Because George cannot kiss you like this, my love." Nicolette's lashes trembled downward as she yielded to the fiery heat of his kiss, and it was a long moment later before the Earl lifted his head. He could tell that they were inside the city by the horse's hooves galloping across the cobblestone streets of London. There was a streak of light that beamed inside the carriage from the street lamps, and her big blue eyes glowed smilingly into his as she willingly pressed toward him with lips eagerly parting as she sought his mouth once again. His kiss delved so deeply that it aroused every sense of her womanly desires. While his lips pressed upon her lips, he reached inside the manly shirt that adorned her lovely body and slid his masculine hand across her soft shoulder and below to touch her bare breast. She was not wearing anything underneath the shirt, but the buttons on the front were making it impossible to hold her breast in his hands, so he ripped a few buttons from her shirt.

Nicolette gasped out loud for a fleeting moment, clasped her fingers behind his neck, and peered up at him in the meager light.

His gaze flicked down so he could stroke her pale, silken breasts underneath the torn shirt. His warm hands slid across the valley between her bosoms and found her taut nipple. He playfully squeezed her nipple until she moaned out loud with pleasure. Encouraged by her response and lack of resistance, he lowered his head and captured a breast in his mouth to cast warm, lingering kisses on the hardness of her taut nipples. The delicately hued fullness of her breast gleamed pale and lustrous in the faint light and was as enticing as any lavish feast he had ever encountered.

"Please! You mustn't!" she gasped while wedging her arm down between them. Then he raised his head since he realized that she sought to halt his advancing intrusion. "You mustn't! Not here!"

It took every measure of restraint for the Earl to curb his ardor. Nicolette pulled her manly shirt over her bosom and tied her shirt together the best she could at that moment. "Here are your coat and your hat, Nicolette," said the Earl while he was staring at the golden curls that had fallen loose from the hairpins in Nicolette's hair. "I will help you with the hairpins, my love since we are almost to the Mayfield cottage."

"It will not be necessary, my lord; I can safely tuck my hair underneath the hat without using the pins, my lord." Before the Earl could speak a single word, he heard the coachman outside the carriage announcing their arrival at the Mayfield cottage. The Earl immediately stepped outside the carriage and quickly helped Nicolette outside the carriage.

"Come quickly; we must make haste to enter the cottage before anyone sees us." Nicolette walked as fast as she could behind the Earl with her hat pulled down to cover her face.

When they entered the cottage, the Earl practically ran up the large stairway, only pausing a time or two so Nicolette could catch up with him. "Please slow down, my lord; you must have forgotten that I am not wearing my usual corset underneath this shirt. I am struggling to keep up with this pace of yours," said Nicolette when she stopped walking when she reached the top of the stairway. The Earl stopped walking and turned around to look at Nicolette and said with a grin on his handsome face, "I must have forgotten for the moment that your bosom is bare underneath those garments, but I assure you I will not forget for long."

"You have no shame, my lord," replied Nicolette as she picked up her pace and followed the Earl until they arrived at the bed chamber where she had previously left her gown and other belongings. When the Earl went to turn the door knob to enter the room, he realized that the door was locked, so he reached underneath a vase sitting on a small table beside the door. "I don't remember locking the door when I left that morning," said Nicolette with a curious look on her face. As a matter of fact, I don't believe I even closed the door to your chamber that morning when I left."

"I do believe I left the door opened for you to easily find this chamber the day I left the cottage," replied the Earl with a puzzled look on his face. "I suppose someone else must have been here, my lord," said Nicolette as she and the Earl stepped inside his chamber.

"There is no one that I know of, Nicolette; Lord Jared has been at the race track the past few days." Before Nicolette could walk around the huge poster bed to get her gown and undergarments from the large leather chaise lounge where she left them when she changed into the Nicolas Pendleton attire, the earl reached out and put his arms around Nicolette. He brought her body close to his until she could feel the heat from his loins. She only slightly had to raise her mouth to his since she was rather tall in stature. Then she moved her mouth to nuzzle the ridge of his jaw, working slowly to his earlobe. Suddenly, she had an enticing image of shoving off these form-fitting clothes and nuzzling every inch of him. The thought that he had just a moment ago when he first put his arms around her, that she would slap his face and kick him out of the chamber, disappeared. And here she was reveling in lust, and he found it to be quite intoxicating. Their bodies were chest to chest as she glared into his eyes, and her mouth found him once again. He parted her lips with his tongue and kissed her until her body was weak and her legs began to tremble. He must have felt her body tremble and shudder beneath his body, so he lifted her up into his arms and placed her on the large poster bed.

He immediately sat on the bed beside her, took what was left of her hairpins from her golden hair, and watched as the curls fell over her shoulders, cascading down her back. He came closer, ran his trembling hand through her beautiful hair and lifted her chin to kiss her now swollen lips. When he slid his hand down to reach inside her shirt, she stopped him long enough to lean forward and raise her shirt over her head to expose her bare breast. But she didn't stop there; she unbuttoned her breeches and slid them and her undergarments from her long legs. The Earl reached out to remove them from her hands and threw them on the floor beside the bed. When he stood up to remove his garments and take a look at her, he saw a beauty like none other. How many nights had he dreamed of her beauty, but nothing could match the beauty his eyes were beholding at this very moment. While he was still standing beside the bed, he reached over and lit a candle so he could watch how the candlelight flicked over the soft sheen of her naked body. It was whetting his senses until it felt like fire was flowing through his veins. "I just wanted to tell you right this moment how beautiful you are, Nicolette."

When he lay down on the bed beside her, he continued to gaze down at her and spoke out loud, "Your body is as sweet as honeydew and so soft and tempting, and it makes me want to make love to you." Nicolette could not subdue the blush that crept into her cheeks as she allowed her imagination to conjure such an event. The Earl bent over and bestowed another passionate kiss on her warm lips and delved his tongue into her sweet mouth as his hands stroked her swollen breast, lifting and kneading the soft globes with his fingers. His breathing was slow and thick, and he did not seem hurried in any way. Her nipples grew hard and tight, and he bent his head and suckled her nipple. She shivered in anticipation as his hand slid down to her thighs and skimmed up her thigh to part her legs. With one hand, he reached between her legs, parting her sex.

She was already wet there, and his fingers slipped easily enough between the folds. He explored her gently while his breathing and her breathing grew rough. But then his thumb found that sensitive nub at the crest of her sex, and her back arched, thrusting her breast upward. And with a low moan escaping her lips, he bent over, took her nipple in his mouth and continued to circle her needy spot with his thumb. He slipped his finger inside of her and felt how tight she was when her intimate muscles clenched around his finger. She moaned as he began to work his finger in and out. She was so aroused and so wet that he told her he must have her now. He forced her thighs wide and thrust his manhood into her quivering sex. She gasped at the pain that mingled with a wave of pleasure as he pushed further and further into her. Kissing her once again, he began to gently thrust again and her body began to adjust to his. He moved easily, gliding in and out with smooth strokes. Within a few moments, her hurting began to cease, and it began to feel warm and quite pleasant.

And at that very moment she was feeling desired and so needed by him. She could tell that there was nowhere on earth that both of them would rather be, and they knew that they had and would still go through hell, but it was worth every moment of it. Then suddenly, he made a gruff sound and started to take her hard and fast. *Yes, yes, yes...Yes.* She climaxed so fiercely that it jolted her hips upwards, and the pleasure went on and on in wave after wave.

He made a loud moan that sounded like a growl, and then he collapsed on top of her, shuddering in his release. She was holding him now as he was making a pillow out of her breast. They were feeling as close to one another as two people could feel at that moment. He raised his head, gazed into her big blue eyes, and tenderly said, "I hope that I did not hurt you too badly."

"Not terribly, my lord, I will be alright."

"And it will get better, I promise. It only hurts once, and you shall see," replied the Earl sleepily.

They both were aware that they couldn't stay there holding on to one another. Nicolette was going to have to leave right away, so she first found the chamber pot since she was in desperate need. Then she walked over to the wash basin and washed her face. She brushed her hair, swept it up on top of her head and placed the hairpins in her hair. When she walked over to the leather chaise lounge where she left her gown, undergarments and other belongings, she noticed her gown and corset lying on the floor beside the chaise lounge. She didn't recall leaving her gown and undergarments lying on the floor since that was not like her to do that. She even remembered turning around and looking at her gown lying on the chaise lounge as she walked out the door that she left open. There was no doubt in her mind now that someone had been at the cottage inside the Earl's chamber. *But who could it be? She asked out loud.*

The Earl was fully dressed, and he grabbed his hat as he led Nicolette, fully dressed in her gown and undergarments, down the long stairway where he found his coachman. "It is time to take Nicolette to the Ashton cottage, and please see to it that she gets there safe," said the Earl to his coachman. "I believe I shall stay at the Mayfield cottage for the rest of the night. After you escort Nicolette to her home, you may come back here to sleep. You will be taking me to Primrose Estate first thing in the morning."

"Yes, Lord Mayfield, I will see to it that she arrived safely, and I shall see you in the morning, my lord," said the coachman as he slipped outside the door of the cottage with Nicolette lifting her gown and running as fast as she could towards the Mayfield carriage.

254

CHAPTER 14

Autumn 1865

It was still pouring when Nicolette hurried inside her seamstress shop the following morning. She was beyond grateful to her mother for opening the shop earlier that morning. When the Mayfield carriage escorted her home to the Ashton cottage late last evening, she was more than glad that her mother and Daniel had already retired to their bed chambers for the night. She was feeling exhausted and overwhelmed with what had taken place between her and the Earl last evening. At the moment she wasn't quite sure how to feel about what happened. There was a part of her that wanted to feel ecstatic and alive, and there was another part of her that felt confused and afraid. So many thoughts were racing through her head right now, but she had to keep her mind on her work.

"Good morning, Mother," said Nicolette as she placed her wet, dripping umbrella in the corner of the shop. "Sorry I'm late getting here this morning, Mother; I can see that you have made a lot of progress with our workload. I am most grateful for all you accomplish here, Mother."

"You are so welcome, dear, but as you well know, this is what I love to do. I have known that I enjoy sewing since I was a young girl. I can see that you are even more gifted than I am, Nicolette. If you look over there on the corner of the sewing table, you will see that our orders for new gowns have expanded tremendously, my dear," said Lady Elizabeth with slight concern in her soft voice. Nicolette quickly walked over to the corner of the very large sewing table and began to read the list of orders when she heard the front door of the shop open.

"Hello, is anyone here?" asked the young lady who stepped inside the shop. Nicolette placed the list back down on the sewing table, walked into the front room of the shop, and kindly greeted the young lady. "Welcome to Nicolette's Seamstress Shop and how may I help you?"

"I am looking to speak to Miss Nicolette Braxton. Are you Miss Braxton?" asked the young lady. "I am Nicolette Braxton," replied Nicolette. "My name is Willow Smith, and I was sent here to your shop by Lord Austin Mayfield. He sent a messenger to my home quite early this morning informing me that there is a job opportunity for my sewing skills at your establishment, Miss Braxton,"

"Well, it is a pleasure to meet you, Miss, or is it Mrs. Smith?" curiously asked Nicolette. "It is Miss Smith and you may call me Willow if you like."

"Willow, I may not be able to afford your services at this time, but if you check back with me in a few weeks, I may be able to afford your service at that time, replied Nicolette. "Well, hold on one moment, Miss Braxton. The Earl did mention in the message that he would be paying my salary and not you, Miss Braxton. He mentioned something about paying you back for a large favor that you had recently done for him, but he did not mention to me what that favor was, and I did not ask. He went on to mention that he knew that your mother and you are quite busy making new gowns for the Regency Ball this season, and you could use my help. I assure you that I have much experience since my mother trained me as a young girl, but sadly, she has passed away, and I do not have the means to keep her shop open, so I sadly had to let it go."

Nicolette just stood in front of Willow, staying quiet for a brief moment, thinking about what the Earl had done this morning. She remembered the Earl mentioning to her that he wanted to give her the money that he obtained from his wager on the Derby Trial Stakes and she had refused his offer. Evidently, he was trying to think of a way to repay her for the favor. But after what happened between them last evening when she gave him all of her body and soul, he surely must have known by then that he owed her nothing. Nicolette was beginning to turn red in the face because of her thoughts from the previous evening. "Will you please excuse me for one moment, Willow? I would like to speak with my mother," Nicolette walked to the back room where her mother was sitting at the sewing table. "Mother, the Earl has sent a young lady by the name of Willow Smith here this morning to work for us, and I wasn't aware that he intended on doing so until her arrival," said Nicolette with somewhat of an anxious look on her face. "So why would he do that, my dear, without you being aware of it, my dear?" curiously asked Lady Elizabeth.

"It's because he thinks he owes me a favor since I raced Blubelle in the race, and we finished in second place. He keeps telling me that if it weren't for me, he would have lost his entire wager," replied Nicolette. "Since you got back, dear, we haven't had a chance to speak about what happened at the race. So you are telling me that you finished in second place, and you were able to get away with your disguise?" asked Lady Elizabeth with a slight grin on her lovely face. "I must say you are full of surprises, my dear, even though I thought it would be much too risky."

"Hush, mother! Don't forget we are not alone at the moment," said Nicolette. "So, what are you trying to tell me, my dear?" asked Lady Elizabeth.

"I am trying to tell you that the Earl sent Willow here to help us in the shop, and he plans on using the wager money to pay her salary," replied Nicolette. "Why, I think that is an excellent idea, Nicolette. As you can see, with all these orders for new gowns, we can certainly use the help," said Lady Elizabeth while staring into her daughter's blue eyes and wondering why she saw a bit of hesitation there. "Why do I sense some reluctance to accept the Earl's help?" asked Lady Elizabeth.

"Perhaps it is an excellent idea, Mother, since we both could desperately use the help, but I do not want to feel obligated to the Earl in any way, Mother," said Nicolette with a slight tremble in her soft voice. "The Earl is not offering us an obligation, my dear;

it appears to me that he is repaying a favor," replied Lady Elizabeth. "And I must say it is a very kind offer, my dear."

"Well, I suppose you are right, Mother. It is very kind of him to offer help. I will tell Willow Smith that she can start to work right away." Nicolette left the back room and told Willow that she was their new seamstress.

"Please follow me, Willow; I shall help you get familiar with our shop."

It was late morning when the Earl arrived at Primrose Estate. It was still raining outside when he stepped outside the Mayfield carriage heading towards the manor to let his mother and the Marquis know that he was home. "Good day to you, Lady Katherine," said the Earl when he stepped inside the manor. "Where is Mother, sis? I want her to know that I've returned home before I head out to the horse stables."

"She is in the parlor with the piano, my lord," replied Lady Katherine. "Miranda is practicing a new song on the piano since the Duke and Duchess requested Lady Miranda to perform at the October Regency Ball. I had no choice but to make myself absent from the room moments ago; I presumably do not have quite the patience for such an endeavor, my lord."

The closer the Earl and Lady Katherine got to the parlor, they could hear the sounds of Lady Miranda's voice and piano playing in their ears. "I see what you mean sister. I am most grateful I do not have to stay in there very long," said the Earl, trying to hold back his laughter.

"I'm home, Mother; I decided to stay at the cottage in the city last evening since I had some important matters to attend to first thing this morning. Greetings Lady Miranda! Is that a new tune I hear, sister," said the Earl as he walked over to accept the cup of tea his mother poured for him. "Thank you, Mother," politely said the Earl as he took a seat in his favorite chair. "Congratulations, son, for your second-place finish at the Derby Trial Stakes," said the Marquis in a deep masculine voice when he entered the parlor.

"I must say I am quite impressed with that mare of yours. Blubelle certainly came through in place of the Dark Knight. That wasn't Teddy Pendleton racing Blubelle, was it? Lord Jared mentioned that Teddy's cousin Nicolas Pendleton was racing Blubelle. Well, he certainly got Blubelle to run fast around the track, but I don't recall seeing him riding Blubelle here at our track. He must have taken her out when I wasn't around because he sure knew how to ride her." The Earl quickly gulped down the rest of his tea and stood up from his chair. "Sorry, Father, to leave so soon, but I must get down to the stables since I just now returned home. I shall see to it that I join everyone for the evening meal." The Earl quickly left the parlor, thinking about the look he just noticed on the Marquis's face. It was as if he could read his father's mind, and it appeared that his father might have an inkling that the person who was racing Blubelle in the race was none other than the lovely Nicolette Braxton.

When the Earl stepped out of the carriage in front of the stables, he must avoid a few mud puddles along the path to the stables. The heavy rain had finally eased up but it left some deep mud puddles in the ground. When he entered the stables, he walked straight over to the stall of the Dark Knight to check on his progress. He was greeted by his groom and a veterinary doctor standing next to the Dark Knight. "Oh, there you are, my lord," said the Earl's groom when they saw the Earl. "Your timing couldn't be any more perfect. I just now finished examining the Dark Knight's leg, and it appears that he is fully recovered, Lord Mayfield," said Dr. Lewis. "I must tell you, though, that your choice to pull him out of the race was the best decision, my lord. Now that the racing season has ended, he should be in excellent shape to start next season." The Earl began to smile and thankfully replied, "This is excellent news, doctor, and I am extremely pleased to hear this. Now, have you had a chance to look at Blubelle since you arrived at Primrose Estate, Dr. Lewis?"

"No, I haven't, my lord," replied Dr. Lewis. "I think that is an excellent idea, my lord. Wasn't it Blubelle that raced in the Derby Trial stakes and had that second-place finish, my lord," asked Dr. Lewis. "Yes, my sweet Arabian mare Blubelle made us all proud, doctor," replied the Earl. "Well then, we must take a look at her and make sure she is fairing well, my lord, after a fast run like she just encountered," said Dr. Lewis as he followed the Earl over to Blubelle's stall. When the Earl approached Blubelle, he immediately thought of Nicolette and all the passion between them last evening. It was still fresh in his mind, and his body was graving her touch. He never knew that it would be possible to desire another human being as much as he desired to be in the presence of his lovely sea goddess with her big blue eyes. *Not only has she stolen my heart, but she has captured my body, mind, and soul. We belong to one another now, and I will not stop until I make her my bride.*

"Hello, brother," said Lord Jared as he suddenly approached the Earl. "Congratulations once again, my lord," said Lord Jared. "I did not know for sure that we had another winner until Blubelle surprised me. I am looking forward to the next horse racing season, and I know you are as well. The groom just informed me that the Dark Knight is good to go for next season. I am certainly glad now that I asked Lady Miranda and Lady Anne if they would do me that big favor I asked of them."

"And what big favor was that brother?" asked the Earl with a slightly curious look on his face. "When I first got to the race track, I noticed that I left my wager money on my bed at the Mayfield cottage in the city. So, I sent a messenger to the manor asking our sister if she would go to the cottage and bring the money and drop it off at the hotel at Lingfield Park the day before the race. I am most grateful to her and Lady Anne whom I found out later accompanied her. I put my wager on Blubelle for a second-place finish, and I am happy to say that it certainly paid off," replied Lord Jared with a happy grin on his face.

"I can see that you are pleased, brother, and I am also pleased with our sweet Blubelle here," said the Earl after hearing what his brother just told him about Lady Miranda and Lady Anne going to the cottage. That might be the answer to why the door to his chamber was locked when Nicolette swore that she had left the door open when she changed her clothes and left her gown and undergarments in the bed chamber. So that means that someone did go into that room, and they would have seen Nicolette's gown and undergarments that were left there. "It appears that everything looks in tip-top shape with Blubelle Lord Mayfield," said Dr. Lewis. "She is also ready to breed, my lord if that is something you are considering in the near future," says the doctor as he was leaving. "I will take that into consideration, doctor; you have a good day now," replied the Earl as he motioned for Lord Jared to follow him to his private study in the back of the stables.

On the way to his study, the Earl realized that he had so many things he needed to tell his brother. But he decided to only tell him one thing now, and the other information that he needed to tell him could wait till later. When they got inside the small study, he asked Lord Jared to be seated, and he took his seat behind his desk. "I'm not exactly sure how you are going to respond to what I am about to tell you, brother," said the Earl in a not-too-calm voice. "But first, I want you to know that I do not have a mad bone in my body about what I am about to tell you. As you well know word has gotten around that Lady Anne and I are to be married come December."

"Well, my lord, the news actually came from Lady Anne's own mouth, is what I hear," said Lord Jared. "Well, that happens to be true," said the Earl. "But there is a problem with that Lord Jared. I never proposed to her; she blurted that out in front of all the ladies at breakfast the morning of the hunt, and I wasn't even aware of such a thing," said the Earl with a slight look of anger on his face.

"And why would Lady Anne do that if you did not propose marriage to her, my lord?" asked Lord Jared with a puzzled look on his face. "When I found out that morning, I was angry, so I asked to speak with her. She told me that she was sorry, but she was tired of all the gossip surrounding whether the Earl was ever going to marry her or not, and when she was asked that question at breakfast, she couldn't help but blurt out loud that they were getting married," replied the Earl. "Do you plan on proposing marriage to her any time soon, brother?" asked Lord Jared.

"I do not plan to propose marriage to Lady Anne now or ever, Lord Jared," replied the Earl.

"And why did you come to that decision, my lord?" asked Lord Jared with a curious look on his face. "Did something happen between you and Lady Anne, brother? Is there something I'm not aware of? Does Father know that you plan on not honoring your agreement?"

"Perhaps you need to allow me to answer all your questions, brother," said the Earl, standing up from his chair behind his desk. "First of all, I have a simple answer to why I'm not proposing marriage to Lady Anne; I do not love her Lord Jared. But right now, at this very moment, I am staring into the face of the man who really loves Lady Anne, and that man is you, Lord Jared."

"And what makes you think that, my lord?" asked Lord Jared with a startled look on his red face. "I see the way you look at her when we are all together," said the Earl. "I can see how both of you are always smiling when you are together and how easy it is for both of you to strike up a conversation with one another."

"Well, I do find her to be a beauty among the debutantes, my lord," said Lord Jared. "She is most pleasant on the eyes and I know that you would even have to agree to that brother. And as far as Lady Anne and I found it pleasant to talk to one another, you have to remember, my lord, that when you were an emissary for the government, you were gone for a long while. Lady Anne and I became close friends over a period of time. But I always knew that you and Lady Anne would marry one day, and I know my boundaries, brother."

"Well, perhaps you do not have to consider those boundaries any longer, brother," replied the Earl with a slight grin on his face. "So, what are you trying to tell me?" exclaimed Lord Jared. "I am trying to tell you that you are free to pursue the one you really want to be with, brother. You will also be doing me a huge favor if there is an upcoming December wedding between you and Lady Anne. Therefore, Father and Lord Ashton will still get their blood line, but not through Lady Anne and me but with both of you. So, what do you say, brother? You can't deny your feelings. I have spoken the truth."

"Well, I must say, my lord, it seems as if you have given this marriage proposal much thought," replied Lord Jared with a surprised look in his eyes. "Does Lady Anne agree with this new plan of yours, brother?" Lord Jared asked as he rose from his chair. "The last time Lady Anne and I spoke about this matter, she agreed to be your bride come December if that is what you wish as well, Lord Jared," replied the Earl.

"I do not know what to wish right now, brother; you have truly caught me by surprise. This is a very complex situation you find yourself in, my lord, and it seems as if you are asking me to come to your rescue, brother," said Lord Jared with slight hesitation in his voice. "Well, I must say you have caught me by surprise as well, Lord Jared," exclaimed the Earl while pacing back and forth.

"Can you look me in the eye, brother, and tell me that you are not willing to take Lady Anne as your bride? I thought you would jump at the chance to be with her and you can't tell me that is not so!"

"This is not easy admitting to my brother that I want to marry the lady that has been promised to him all these years," replied Lord Jared.

"Perhaps I can understand how you must feel, Lord Jared, but believe me when I say that you and Lady Anne have my sincere blessing. All I want is for the both of you to be happy, and that will make me happy as well, brother," said the Earl as he walked over and patted his brother on his shoulder in a loving manner. "You give me a lot to think about, brother, and I must say that this news does happen to lift my spirits, but what are you going to do, brother?" asked Lord Jared as he stared into his brother's blue eyes.

"Who will you marry, my Lord? Do you have any prospects? The October Regency Ball is coming up in a couple of weeks, and I suppose most of this season's debutants will be attending. Maybe you will find a new suitor among the ladies at the ball my lord."

"Don't you worry about me, brother, since that is among the other things that I mentioned earlier that I need to discuss with you, but that can wait until later," replied the Earl. "Now, if you will excuse me, Lord Jared, I have a pile of papers on my desk that need my attention." Lord Jared smiled at his brother as he turned around and quietly left the room.

"I'm certainly glad you brought food with you today for our noonday meal, Mother," said Nicolette as she sat at the sewing table along with her mother and Willow. "Yes, dear, but I can see that you did not eat very much, my dear," replied Lady Elizabeth. "I know, Mother, but I want to get as much work done as possible. After all, we only have a couple more weeks until the Regency Ball," said Nicolette as she began to yawn. "Don't you worry, my dear; it appears that Willow is quite skilled and has exquisite taste like you, my dear. We will manage just fine as always, my dear," said Lady Elizabeth with a reassuring smile on her lovely face. Nicolette glanced over at Willow and smiled before she spoke, "We are most fortunate to have you join us here at our shop, Willow."

"I am delighted to be here, Miss Braxton, but it is Lord Mayfield you should be most grateful to," replied Willow with a smile on her lovely dark skin face.

"I cannot deny that the Earl has done us a tremendous favor, and I am most grateful," said Nicolette as she suddenly heard her father's blue bell ringing in the front room. "I will go see who has come inside the shop, Nicolette," said Lady Elizabeth as she rose from her seat at the sewing table and entered the front room. "Oh, what a pleasure to see you, Lady Anne," said Lady Elizabeth. "You must be here for your final fitting for your new gown, my dear."

"Yes, Lady Elizabeth, I am here for my final fitting, but while I am here, I would like to speak with Nicolette privately if that shall be possible," said Lady Anne as she looked past Lady Elizabeth into the sewing room where she saw Nicolette seated at the sewing table. Nicolette couldn't help but hear what Lady Anne requested, so she got up from the sewing table and walked into the front room, where her mother and Lady Anne were standing at the counter.

"Good day, Nicolette," said Lady Anne. "I must speak with you right away if you have the time Nicolette?"

"As you can see, Lady Anne, we are loaded down with orders for new gowns for the ball," replied Nicolette with a curious look on her face. "Is it that urgent that we speak, or can we wait until later?" asked Nicolette. "I insist that we speak now, Nicolette; I feel it is most urgent. I have a carriage outside waiting, and since it is still raining outside, we can talk privately in the Ashton carriage since Mother and Lord Atticus are doing some shopping at this time," said Lady Anne with urgency in her voice. "Well, if you insist, Lady Anne, I shall grab my umbrella and follow you. I will return soon; Mother and Lady Anne can do her final fitting before she leaves," replied Nicolette as she followed Lady Anne outside into the cool, damp rain.

"What is so urgent that you have to drag me outside into this pouring rain, Lady Anne?" asked Nicolette as she dragged the bottom of her wet gown and took her seat inside the carriage. "I have made quite a discovery, Nicolette," said Lady Anne with a slight devilish look in her dark brown eyes. "And what discovery might that be, my lady?" asked Nicolette with the same devilish look in her big blue eyes. "Well, it so happens that Lord Jared left his wager money at the Mayfield cottage and noticed that he had done so and asked Lady Miranda if she would go to the cottage on the morning of the day before the Derby Trial Stakes and bring it to the hotel at Lingfield Park that day. So, I happened to be still visiting Primrose Estate, and Lady Miranda asked if I would accompany her to the cottage to do a favor for Lord Jared. I agreed to go with her, and once we got to the Mayfield cottage, I happened to wander into a bed chamber that looked as if it might have belonged to Lord Austin. Would you like to take a wild guess on what I saw lying across a rather large leather chaise lounge, Nicolette?" asked Lady Anne with a mean tone in her voice. "I have no idea what you are talking about Lady Anne," replied Nicolette. "Of course, you know what I'm talking about Nicolette since it was your gown, undergarments and other items I discovered lying across the leather chaise lounge. I would recognize that gown anywhere, Nicolette. It happens to be one of your originals; I have seen it hanging in your armoire at Old Wood

Manor. And you cannot deny that the corset does not belong to you since it is one of your designs that lace up in the front. What I want to know is why these garments happen to be in the bed chamber of the man that I plan to marry."

"First of all, Lady Anne, how do you know that I haven't made that exact same gown and front laced corsets for other ladies to wear since I established my seamstress shop here in London? And I can see why you would think that they belong to me, and if the shoe were on the other foot, I would be asking the same question. And second of all, you don't have to keep up this pretense around me, Lady Anne, because it does so happens that I know what is really going on between you and the Earl," said Nicolette with a sarcastic tone in her voice. "What are you talking about, Nicolette?" asked Lady Anne. "I am talking about the fact that the Earl never officially proposed marriage to you, Lady Anne. You were not telling the truth at breakfast the morning of the hunt at Primrose Estate," replied Nicolette. "And how would you know that Nicolette?" asked Lady Anne.

"The Earl is the only one who could have told you that and you two would have to be awful close in order for him to share that with you."

"I can honestly say that the Earl does consider me a dear friend, and he has confided in me from time to time, my lady," replied Nicolette. "Well, I see. I would like to know what else he has told you, Nicolette," asked Lady Anne. "He has told me that he does not want to marry you since he knows that it is his brother, Lord

Jared, who is smitten with you, my lady, and I happen to agree with him. It has been rather obvious when we see you and Lord Jared together at various times. I believe you feel the same way about Lord Jared, but you don't happen to know it since you can't see beyond the Earl's title," said Nicolette. "Oh, so it is you that is putting these silly notions in the Earl's head," replied Lady Anne with anger in her voice. "He did mention that I do not love him as much as I love his title," replied Lady Anne. "Well, how dare you and he both imply such a thing about me, Nicolette? I am quite sure that it is your belongings that I found at the Mayfield cottage, and I am also sure that you will not like the word to get out that I discovered your belongings in the bed chamber of the gentleman I am to marry come December."

"The only gentleman that you will be marrying come December will be Lord Jared, my lady. And as far as your threats are concerned, I could say that those garments do not belong to me. And how will it look if everyone is gossiping about the Earl having another lady in his bed chamber when he is engaged to you my lady? So, if you will excuse me, I must get back inside the shop where I can breathe much fresher air." Nicolette opened the door to the carriage, and while she was opening her umbrella, she heard Lady Anne say out loud, "I do not plan to marry Lord Jared Nicolette. I will be marrying the Earl come December, and there is nothing you can do about it, my dear," replied Lady Anne as she stepped outside the carriage behind Nicolette.

When Nicolette walked back inside the seamstress shop, she nearly closed the door on Lady Anne and walked straight back to the sewing room where her mother and Willow were still hard at work. "Would you mind showing Willow where Lady Anne's new gown is hanging, Mother, so she can give it to Lady Anne to try on so she can do the final fitting," quickly asked Nicolette to her mother as she took her seat at the sewing table. "Is everything alright with you, my dear? Your face appears to be rather flushed," asked Lady Elizabeth with a concerned look on her face. "I'm alright, Mother. I shall explain later, but for now, Mother, I'd rather not talk about it," replied Nicolette as she picked up her scissors and began to cut the silk fabric that was spread out on the table in front of her. And immediately, she thought about the Earl and wondered how it was going to be possible to speak with him any time soon.

CHAPTER 15

Mid-October 1865

"Jackson, please tell one of the coachmen to have a carriage ready first thing tomorrow morning. I need to make a trip into the city," said the Earl to his groomsmen after coming from the horse stables into the manor to freshen up for the afternoon tea in the front parlor. He was feeling slightly more at ease now that he had at least gotten one thing off his shoulder. He wanted to tell his brother that he did not plan on marrying Lady Anne and that Lord Jared had his blessing to marry Lady Anne come December. But Lord Jared never really gave him a direct answer as to whether he would propose to Lady Anne, but at least he did not say no to the idea. But Lord Jared did leave his study at the stables earlier with a smile on his face and that gave him much hope indeed. But at the moment, what was foremost on his mind was the fact that Lord Jared had mentioned that Lady Miranda and Lady Anne were at the Mayfield cottage the morning Nicolette had changed her clothes and left them there. Now that he was about to partake in the afternoon tea with Lady Miranda in his presence, maybe he would have a chance to find out more information about what took place when they went to the cottage to pick up the wager money for his brother.

"Good afternoon, family; I think I might join you for the afternoon tea," said the Earl as he entered the front parlor and took a seat in his favorite chair. "I've been knee-deep in paperwork most of the day, and now that the racing season is officially over, I also closed the books for this season. I am very much looking forward to next season since I will be able to get an early start next season. And by the way, Dr. Lewis gave the Dark Knight and Blubelle a thorough exam and they both are in excellent condition. Dr. Lewis even mentioned that Blubelle is ready to breed if that is something I want to do in the near future. Lord Jared must not be joining us for tea this afternoon?" the earl asked the Marquis. "Your brother happens to be in his study busy with paperwork," said the Marquis, standing near the large fireplace in the parlor. "He is going over some architectural drawings for making some new improvements to the wheat field locations. It's something I've wanted to talk to you about, my lord, but right now is not the time. We can discuss that later because right now, we are all looking forward to the upcoming October Regency Ball, and most important, we are looking forward to a December wedding between you and the lovely Lady Anne."

Suddenly, the Earl started toying around with his tea, the cup swirling in his hands. As he went to take a sip, the room grew much quieter than before.

"Are you alright, my lord?" asked Lady Miranda as she suddenly rose from her chair, making sure the Earl was okay. "I'm perfectly fine, I must have drank too much tea at once," said the

Earl after he stopped coughing. "Since you are the one who has spent more time with Lady Anne than I have lately, has she mentioned any plans about the wedding, sister?" asked the Earl with a fake smile on his face.

"Well, now that you have mentioned it, brother, I do find it to be rather odd that she has hardly mentioned anything at all about the wedding. But now that you have more free time my lord, perhaps you should be asking Lady Anne that exact question. I'm sure she would enjoy a visit from you any time," replied Lady Miranda as she took her seat on the blue velvet settee.

"I suppose you are right, lady Miranda; I shall call on Lady Anne very soon. Perhaps I will make a trip to Old Wood Manor after an early morning trip into the city," said the Earl while walking over to a small table in the parlor to write a message to Lady Anne and tell her to expect a visit from him tomorrow afternoon.

"Oh, there you are, Lord Atticus and Lady Luisa," said Lady Constance when Lord Atticus and Lady Luisa entered the front parlor. "Good day, everyone. Lady Luisa and I just returned from taking the horses out for our afternoon ride, and a hot cup of tea is exactly what we need at the moment," replied Lord Atticus as he took his seat beside Lady Luisa. The Earl finished writing his message to Lady Anne and placed it into the hands of one of the footmen and told him to make sure this message got to Old Wood Manor in the hands of Lady Anne immediately. "I was just about to excuse myself and go look for you, Lord Atticus, but I can see that you are in the company of the lovely Lady Luisa," said the Earl as he returned to his seat. "I would like to say this one thing: I am free to spend more time focusing on the cotton industry these days, and I have a few ideas I would like to discuss with you, my lord."

"I suppose I do have some free time, my lord; I am quite sure Lady Luisa and Lady Miranda have their own plans for the rest of the day," replied Lord Atticus. "Perhaps you can read my mind, Lord Atticus. I am working on a birthday gift for you, and Lady Miranda needs to practice on her piano playing a new tune for the upcoming Regency Ball," said Lady Luisa in her sweet Scottish accent. "Well then, it is settled," replied the Earl as he rose from his chair. "We can go to my study to discuss some business, Lord Atticus, and maybe we can have something much stronger than this cup of tea to drink," said the Earl with a half grin on his face.

But before he and Lord Atticus left the parlor, the Earl turned around and glanced over at the lovely Luisa and spoke out loud, "I pity you, my lady, if this birthday gift you happen to be working on requires you to be in the piano parlor with my sister!"

"And why is that, my lord?" asked Lady Luisa. "It's because you are going to need something to plug up your ears if you don't already have something," replied the Earl as they left the room with laughter in the air.

Nicolette couldn't remember a time when a nice soaking in this large copper tub at the Ashton cottage felt any better. Her whole body was aching from bending over all day doing final fittings for the new gowns they were making for the upcoming October Regency Ball. She was glad when Willow and her mother took the initiative to do Lady Anne's final fitting since she wanted to keep her distance from Lady Anne after what had taken place earlier between them. There was no doubt in her mind that Lady Anne suspected that the gown and undergarments she saw in the Earl's bed chamber at the Mayfield cottage belonged to her. Lady Anne might be somewhat naïve, but she was not a complete nincompoop. But I could not tell Lady Anne why the gown and undergarments were there at the cottage in the Earl's bed chamber. I wonder who else knows about the gown and undergarments by now. I'm sure Lady Miranda must know since she was there with Lady Anne, and that makes me wonder if the Earl knows by now that his sister and Lady Anne saw the gown and undergarments when they were there. Oh my, she spoke out loud. I must find a way to see the Earl, and the sooner, the better.

It wasn't long after Nicolette finished her bath and put on her nightgown when her ladies maid Sally and she heard a knock on her chamber door. When Sally opened the door, she saw Daniel standing there with a letter in his hand. "This message just arrived for Nicolette; please see to it that she receives it right away." Sally took the message and closed the door. "Who is at the door, Sally?" asked Nicolette while sitting at her vanity, brushing her long, damp hair. "It is your brother, miss. He has brought a message that has just arrived at the cottage, and it is for you, miss," replied Sally as she handed the sealed envelope and a letter opener to Nicolette. "That will be all Sally, except you can bring me a warm glass of milk or no, I change my mind, and instead of milk, you can bring me a large glass of wine," asked Nicolette as she sat staring at the unopened message lying across her lap. Quickly, Nicolette opened the letter with the message and read it to herself. The Earl was requesting to meet with her tomorrow morning at the Mayfield cottage. He would have a carriage to pick her up from the Ashton cottage and escort her over to Mayfield cottage before she went to work. He told her that he couldn't wait to see her and that he had something important to tell her.

Thank goodness for the long soak in the tub and her choice of a glass of wine for her nightcap last evening; Nicolette would not have gotten any sleep at all last night. She obviously was excited about her meeting with the Earl this morning since she hadn't seen him since they shared their passion with one another. She was starting to blush and felt desire in places on her lovely body that only the Earl could make her feel when she suddenly said out loud, "No Sally, I don't desire to wear my hair all pinned up on my head today, perhaps I prefer the long side braid today." Nicolette knew that on more than one occasion the Earl had complimented her on the long braid in her hair. "And when you finish braiding my hair, I believe the pink and gray satin day gown will do just fine to wear today, Sally."

"That gown will be fine if you say so, miss," replied Sally while staring at Nicolette with a curious look in her eye.

"Now that I'm dressed, I must hurry downstairs and tell Mother about the message I received last evening," said Nicolette to Sally as she grabbed her matching bonnet and hurried down the stairs to the dining room where her mother and Daniel were waiting. "Good morning, Nicolette," said Lady Elizabeth when Nicolette entered the dining room and took her place at the dining table. "You seem to be rather chirpy this morning, my dear," said Lady Elizabeth as she gazed into her daughter's big blue eyes. "And it appears you have dressed rather well for just a normal workday at the shop. Is there something happening today that I'm not aware of, my dear?"

"Yes, Mother, there is something I need to tell you; I will be leaving soon when a Mayfield carriage comes here to escort me to the Mayfield cottage where I am to meet up with Lord Austin this morning before I go to work," replied Nicolette as she hurriedly spoke to her mother.

Before her mother could utter a single word, Daniel cleared his throat and suddenly asked, "Why in the world would you be meeting the Earl at the Mayfield cottage, Nicolette? Why can't the Earl come to the seamstress shop to see you this morning, sister? It does not appear to be the appropriate thing to do if you both are meeting one another in privacy, Nicolette. Don't you agree with me, Mother?" asked Daniel. "I suppose you are probably right, Daniel," replied Nicolette. "But the message I received from the Earl late last evening says that he has something to tell me, and if he is taking a risk to do so, then it must be important."

"I agree with Daniel, Nicolette," said Lady Elizabeth with concern in her voice. "I do not think it is appropriate behavior, and you are taking a big risk, my dear."

"I'm quite sure that the Earl is well aware that this is somewhat of a risk, and he will be taking every precaution to speak with me in private without any repercussions," replied Nicolette as she finished eating her breakfast and got up from her seat when the butler announced that a Mayfield carriage was waiting for Miss Nicolette Braxton.

The Earl was already waiting outside the Mayfield cottage for the lovely Nicolette to arrive. At least it was a clear and sunny day, not like the previous day, when it had been pouring rain all day. The Earl was very much looking forward to being in the company of his lovely sea goddess with the big blue eyes. *She has put a spell on me*, he thought to himself, *and I desire her like none other before her*. He was just about to take a seat on a wooden bench when he heard the horse's hooves and the carriage wheels pulled up in front of the cottage. When he opened the carriage door and stared into Nicolette's blue eyes, his manhood began to swell slightly. "Good morning, Nicolette," said the Earl in a deep, masculine voice. "Good morning, my lord," replied Nicolette as she witnessed the desire in the Earl's sapphire blue eyes. "It is a pleasure to see you, my dear. I shall take my seat beside you in the carriage, and the coachmen will take us for a nice carriage ride if that agrees with you, Nicolette," asked the Earl with much tenderness in his masculine voice. "That will suit me fine my lord, but you must tell me why you have requested me to take such a risk to come here for this morning. I also have something I need to tell you as well, my lord," said Nicolette as she felt the manly presence of the gentleman who was making her heart skip a beat at the moment.

"I must tell you that I had a chance to speak with Lord Jared, and he mentioned to me that Lady Miranda and Lady Anne went to the Mayfield cottage the morning of the day before the Derby Trial Stakes and retrieved the wager money that Lord Jared had accidentally left on his bed in his bed chamber. There was no mention of them seeing a gown and undergarments at the cottage, but that answers the question of why the door was locked when we got to the cottage. Then, I went on to tell my brother that the engagement between Lady Anne and me was a total farce. I told him that I have no intention of marrying Lady Anne and that I think he is the one that should be marrying Lady Anne come December," said the Earl while tenderly staring into Nicolette's lovely face. "And what did Lord Jared have to say about that, my lord?" asked Nicolette.

"He never said that he would marry Lady Anne but he also never said no either. I could tell by the smile on his face that hearing such words from me made him a happy gentleman," replied the Earl as he began to inch closer to Nicolette. "Now it is my turn to tell you what I need to tell you, my lord," said Nicolette. "While I was working in my shop yesterday, Lady Anne came in for the final fitting for her new gown. But first, she told me to go and sit in the carriage with her so we could talk privately. She told me about seeing a gown and undergarments and mentioned that they looked as if they belonged to me. It appears that she had previously seen them in my bed chamber when I was staying at Old Wood Manor."

"So, what did you tell her, Nicolette?" asked the Earl as he reached out to hold the slender, cool hand of Nicolette. "I told her that I have made other gowns that look identical to some of my gowns since I've been here in England, and it doesn't mean that the gown and undergarments were mine."

"Ah, so you didn't mention anything about the horse race and your disguise as Nicolas Pendleton. So now she possibly thinks I have been entertaining someone at the Mayfield cottage," said the Earl as he reached out and lifted her chin and stared into her big blue eyes. "I suppose she would think that, my lord, but she knows that they probably belong to me," replied Nicolette as she locked eyes with the Earl's sapphire blue eyes. "And that is another reason why I have asked you here, Nicolette," said the Earl as he lowered his mouth against Nicolette's warm lips and delved his tongue into her mouth. He kissed her with so much passion that her body began to tremble, and when he let go, she could hardly catch her breath.

"I want you to come to me, Nicolette since I have made you mine, and I want to tell you that I want to marry you, Nicolette. I want to live the rest of my life making you happy, and I want you to have my children. These feelings that I have for you are the feelings that I want to have for someone when I marry and you are that someone, my love. Please say that you will marry me, Nicolette," asked the Earl. Nicolette just sat there staring into the face of the Earl without saying a word. "I do not know what to say, my lord," replied Nicolette with a tear in the corner of her right eye. "I never told you what else Lady Anne told me yesterday when we were sitting inside the carriage," said Nicolette as she turned her head to stare out the carriage window. "What did she tell you, Nicolette?" quickly asked the Earl.

"She told me that she will not be marrying Lord Jared come December; instead, she will be marrying you, my lord," replied Nicolette as she tried to hold back a tear from sliding down her warm cheek. "Well, Lady Anne can say what she wants, but I shall repeat myself once again," said The Earl as he moved a loose curl from Nicolette's face. "I shall not marry Lady Anne, Nicolette, now or ever, my dear. You are the lady I want to marry, Nicolette Braxton. You are the sea goddess that I want to share my bed with," said the Earl as he leaned over and found her warm lips once more.

"What about George?" asked Nicolette when they stopped to catch their breath. "What about George?" replied the Earl

"As you well know, my lord, George did ask for my hand in marriage," replied Nicolette, suddenly feeling the Earl's warm breath on her skin. But when she looked into his eyes, she saw a look of anger like she had never seen before. "When George returns to England, he will know right away that you are mine; he will have to live with that fact, my dear," said the Earl. "After all, I made him a most generous offer before he left for America; I offered him a position at the Mayfield-Ashton Cotton Industry. But whether he wants to accept the offer when he returns to England is up to him. I suppose he can return home to Charleston, but it will be without you, Nicolette."

"Perhaps I say yes to your marriage proposal, my lord," said Nicolette as she turned and slid back into the carriage seat. "So how are we going to be married when everyone by now has probably heard that you and Lady Anne are getting married come December? You got to remember that I am just a poor seamstress from Charleston, South Carolina my lord."

"Then I shall take a poor seamstress from Charleston, South Carolina, to be my bride, and we shall live happily ever after," replied the Earl. "Then we are going to have to encourage a union between Lady Anne and Lord Jared," replied Nicolette. "Your father and Lord Ashton are set on a bloodline between the Mayfield and the Ashton families, and they will accept nothing less. But as of now, Lady Anne is being spiteful since she suspects that something is brewing between you and me, my lord. She has always been somewhat jealous of me. I even noticed that when we were children. But I do not know why she would be jealous of me, my lord," replied Nicolette. "She will not care about our happiness or your brother's happiness; she will make it hard for us, and I know her well."

"You are exactly right in what you say, my dear. I have on occasion noticed her jealousy towards you, but I can understand why, Nicolette. There is no one like you, my dear Nicolette; you are a diamond among pearls," replied the Earl as he placed his warm hand on her thigh. "But there is one thing that I do know for certain about Lady Anne," said the Earl as he felt the heat of her thigh on his hand. "She hates a scandal more than anyone I know and the idea that the Earl would discard her for another lady and she would be left desolate without a beau to take his place would be her undoing. That's why I know when she sees that she can not win, and then she will come to her senses and realize that she can also marry for love. There is no doubt in my mind that my brother adores the ground she walks on, and he is the man that will make her happy," said the Earl as he lifted the chin of Nicolette and asked one more time, "Will you marry me, Nicolette?"

"Yes! Yes, my lord, I will marry you," replied Nicolette as she felt the Earl's lips against her pink, swollen lips and his hand moving up her thigh to a place where she yearned for his touch.

CHAPTER 16

October 1865

"See, that didn't take as long as you thought it would, Mother," said Nicolette as she took her place at the large sewing table in her seamstress shop. "Well, I must admit that I am glad to see you return with a smile on your face because you and Lord Austin are well on your way to creating quite a scandal, my dear," replied Lady Elizabeth. "Speak quietly; Mother Willow might hear us," said Nicolette as her eyes glanced around the shop. "By the way, where is Willow? I don't see her here," asked Nicolette.

"She has gone to pick up some buttons and a few other sewing materials since we are running out of supplies rather quickly," replied Lady Elizabeth. "I'm truly sorry, Mother; I should have taken care of that sooner," said Nicolette as she picked up her scissors to cut some ivory-laced trim from a bolt of fabric.

Suddenly, Nicolette and Lady Elizabeth heard a loud young gentleman's voice coming from the front room of the shop, "I have a message from the Ashton family for the Braxton family." Nicolette quickly rose from her seat and walked into the front room, and the messenger handed her the message. She picked up the letter opener from the counter, opened the message and saw that it was an invitation from the Ashton family to join them in a couple of days at Old Wood Manor for Lord Atticus's birthday celebration. She took the message and handed it to her mother before she took her place at the sewing table. "I suppose we can take the afternoon and evening away from work in order to attend Lord Atticus' birthday celebration, my dear," said Lady Elizabeth as she stared at her daughter hard at work. "Of course, we can; you and Daniel have been working harder than anyone, and you absolutely deserve to enjoy yourselves, Mother," said Nicolette with admiration in her big blue eyes.

"Now, Mother, I must tell you the news of what happened when I met with the Earl this morning before Willow got back to the shop," said Nicolette as she moved to a chair next to where her mother was sitting. "The Earl has informed Lord Jared that he did not propose to Lady Anne. You remember the morning of the hunt at Primrose Estate when Lady Anne blurted out at breakfast that the Earl had proposed marriage and they were to be married come December? She was not being truthful. The Earl told Lord Jared and me that he has not proposed marriage to Lady Anne and that he never will. Even though he knows that a marriage between him and Lady Anne is what both their father's desire and he had promised to honor their request, he has changed his mind."

"And does this change of mind have anything to do with you, Nicolette?" asked Lady Elizabeth with a devastated look in her eye.

Nicolette just sat there quiet for a moment and stared at her lap before she could speak, "I suppose it has a lot to do with me, Mother; the Earl has taken it upon himself to ask for my hand in marriage," replied Nicolette with a trembling voice. "Oh, my Nicolette, have you and the Earl done what I think you have done, my dear?" asked Lady Elizabeth. "I remember you telling your brother and me that you have strong feelings for Lord Austin, but I never dreamed it would come to this, Nicolette. I hope you realize what a serious scandal this could cause for the Ashton and the Mayfield families, and they will regret that we ever stepped foot here in England. What are you and the Earl thinking, Nicolette? I am wondering what you are going to do to make this right without hurting so many others, Nicolette?"

"Lord Jared is in love with Lady Anne, and he has been feeling that way before we ever came to England, and he wants to be the one to marry Lady Anne come December," replied Nicolette. "And does Lady Anne know about Lord Jared wanting to marry her and do you think she will marry Lord Jared?" asked Lady Elizabeth.

"At first, when the Earl told Lady Anne that he would not marry her, she was very upset, of course, but then when she realized that he was dead serious, she agreed that she would marry Lord Jared. But when she saw my gown and undergarments thrown over the leather chaise lounge at the Mayfield cottage, she changed her mind about marrying Lord Jared. I suppose she is angry at me and the Earl since she obviously suspects that something is brewing between the Earl and me. Now she is only being hateful and spiteful," said Nicolette, with tears sliding down both her pale cheeks. "But you can hardly blame Lady Anne, my dear," said Lady Elizabeth as she watched the tears flow from her daughter's eyes. "She has known for a few years that there is an agreement for Lord Austin and her to marry. She probably has been counting on this proposal to take place since he no longer has to leave Primrose Estate for long periods of time any longer. But yet he chooses not to ask for her hand in marriage and tells her that he no longer wants to marry her and then she discovers that there may be something brewing between you and the Earl," replied Lady Elizabeth.

"I do know what you are saying is true, Mother, but they do not love each other; she seems to be more interested in Lord Jared. Every time we are all together, she is always clinging to Lord Jared and he is mesmerized by her. They thoroughly enjoy each other's company, and the Earl and I agree that they belong together. She hardly speaks to the Earl and him to her, and you know how much Lady Anne loves to talk. I think that the Earl is an honorable man, and he doesn't want to disappoint his father, Lord Ashton or Lady Anne."

"You and I both know Nicolette that they do not always marry for love here in England," said Lady Elizabeth with much concern in her soft voice. "I do know that Mother and that is why I think that Lady Anne can have both with Lord Jared. She can give the family the bloodline they so desire and be so dearly loved at the same time," replied Nicolette as she reached inside her pocket for a handkerchief to dry her tears.

"But you forgot one important thing, my dear, the bloodline that she will have with the younger son does not come with a title like the one that Lady Anne will have if she marries the Earl of Primrose," reluctantly said Lady Elizabeth. "I do not want to say things that are making it even more painful for you to accept, my dear, but you don't seem to be thinking clearly."

"Mother, I have not been thinking clearly since the day I met the Earl; he has surely put a spell on me. Perhaps you are right, Mother. I love him, and I loathe him at the same time, and I can't help but wonder how that is possible. But all it takes is one look from those sapphire blue eyes and a kiss from his warm lips, and I fall right into his arms and now into his bed," replied Nicolette as a stream of new tears came rolling down her lovely face. "I told the Earl I would marry him, but I'm only going to cause a horrific scandal and much heartache for others if I marry him. But there is nothing to compare to the heartache I am feeling at this very moment, Mother!"

Lady Elizabeth quietly rose from her chair, placed her loving arms around Nicolette, and held her there while her daughter cried a mountain of tears.

It was the morning of Lord Atticus' birthday celebration that was to take place at Old Wood Manor. The Earl decided to have his breakfast in the Mayfield dining room with the rest of his family. The night before this morning, he hadn't got much sleep since he could not stop thinking abut his lovely sea Goddess with big blue eyes. Ever since he proposed to Nicolette a few days ago, he had been walking around with his head in the clouds. After telling his father, the Marquis, that he is planning on marrying Nicolette instead of Lady Anne, he has moped around Primrose in a rather disappointed state of mind. He wasn't expecting his father to take the news too well, but he surely wasn't expecting him to respond with such anger in his voice. Once, he told his father about the possibility of Lord Jared proposing to Lady Anne, which did help to ease some of the anger. His father made it clear that he didn't disapprove of the lovely Nicolette; as a matter of fact, he spoke highly of her and her family. But what he was most concerned about was the Ashton family and how they were going to receive the news. After all, the Ashton family was the one who brought the Braxton family to England so they could help them in a time of need. The Marquis did not hesitate to let the Earl know that there would be a scandal of the likes that they had never known before, and he asked his son how Nicolette, and he thought that they would ever survive it.

The Earl remembered telling his father that his love for Nicolette was the kind of love that he would die for and that he would never stop loving her. He made it clear to his father that he could never be happy with Lady Anne, and if a title is what he and Lord Ashton expect to go along with a bloodline between their families, then he would pass his title to Lord Jared, and she would be marrying the Earl of Primrose after all. He would never forget the look on the Marquis's face when he told him that. His father turned as red in the face as he ever recalls and told him point blank that he would not allow his firstborn son to do such a thing. Obviously that was the last of the conversation that day because his father left his study quickly and slammed the door. And now he was showing up at breakfast wondering if he would have a second chance to speak with the Marquis before they left later that day to attend Lord Atticus's birthday celebration at Old Wood Manor.

"Mother, I cannot believe that we finally finished sewing the last piece of fabric for this lovely gown for the Queen. I am happy to hear that the Queen has accepted the invitation to the Duke and Duchess of York's October Regency Ball. I hear that Queen Victoria has not attended any balls or social events since the passing of her husband, Prince Albert. It has been four years since his passing, and she still mourns his loss as if it were yesterday," said Nicolette as she was in deep thought about the Earl and how they both shared a love as deep as the Queen and King shared for one another. "Yes, my dear, I am delighted that I might get a glimpse of the Queen, especially since she will be wearing this lovely gown," said Lady Elizabeth as she watched her daughter hand-stitching the ivory lace around the bodice of the pale gold silk gown.

"I want you to go on home to the cottage after you finish with the gown my dear; you have been working day and night on the Queen's gown. I would like for you to get some rest before we go to Old Wood Manor for Lord Atticus' birthday celebration," said Lady Elizabeth with kindness in her voice. "I want you to come soon, Mother, and you can close up shop early, Willow," said Nicolette as she rose out of her chair to walk over to Daniel's tailor shop to see if the coachman could get free to escort her to the Ashton cottage.

"I suppose I should make up my mind soon, Sally," said Nicolette as she sat on the window seat of her bed chamber at the Ashton cottage. She needed her long golden hair to dry quickly because soon she would be dressing for Lord Atticus's birthday celebration. "Perhaps the sapphire blue satin gown with the gold trim and low cut front bodice will do, Sally," said Nicolette as she rose from the window seat to open one of her wooden boxes where she found her gold and pearl necklace and matching earrings. "And if you look over there in the trunk on the other side of the armoire, you will find the matching bonnet to the gown I shall be wearing this evening, Sally," said Nicolette as she walked over to the mirror and held her necklace and earrings up towards her neck and ears. Instantly, she thought about the Earl and the fact that she would be seeing him at Old Wood Manor that evening.

She couldn't remember ever feeling this way about anyone or anything that had ever taken place in her life. There was a part of her that was so excited about the Earl wanting to marry her, and then there was this other part of her that felt afraid and sad that if she did marry him, she would be hurting so many others. *But then, if I don't marry the Earl, will he be pushed into marrying Lady Anne, or does he mean it when he says that he will never marry Lady Anne now or ever? Oh my,* thought Nicolette, *I can't think of this right now, or I will go crazy. Perhaps I shall get a chance to speak with the Earl this evening since I have so many things to say, and I'm sure he has many things to say to me as well.*

"I'm ready for you to help me with my hair now, Sally; I believe wearing it up with a few curls cascading down will look lovely with the pearl necklace and the matching earrings," said Nicolette as she took her seat in front of her vanity mirror. "I believe you are right about that, miss; I'm sure the Earl will like it as well," said Sally as she allowed a giggle to escape from her mouth and caused both ladies to fill the air with laughter.

It had been several days since the Earl last saw Nicolette, and he was hoping that he would have a private moment to share with her this evening. When he was not with her, he couldn't help but think about her all the time. He couldn't wait to feel her in his arms once again; he missed her warm touch. The past few days, he had been in the company of his sister on several occasions, and Lady Miranda had not mentioned anything about seeing a gown and undergarments in his bed chamber. He couldn't help but think that was rather odd since any other time, she would have been teasing him about that very thing and asking him questions about who the gown belonged to. *And if she chose not to mention it to him, she would have surely said something to Lord Jared, and without a doubt, he would have mentioned it to me.* So now he was beginning to wonder if Lady Anne was the only one who saw the gown and undergarments, and for some reason, she had chosen not to tell anyone other than Nicolette she saw them.

"You can step out of the carriage now, my lord," suddenly said Lord Jared. "What are you in such deep thought about brother? It looks as if you are a million miles away. We have safely arrived at Old Wood Manor, and it looks as if we are right on time," said Lord Jared as he stepped outside the carriage to help the ladies step down. "You can be certain that I will inform you later, brother, but right this moment, we are here to celebrate our dear friend's birthday." Both gentlemen quickly turned their heads when the Ashton carriage escorting the Braxton family pulled up in front of the manor. The Earl and Lord Jared immediately walked over to the carriage to help Nicolette and Lady Elizabeth from the carriage.

"Good Evening, Daniel, Nicolette and Lady Elizabeth," said the Earl as he took the lovely gloved hand of Lady Elizabeth to help her step out of the carriage. After that, he placed his hand in the white-gloved hand of Nicolette and helped her step outside the carriage. "I must say that you ladies look quite lovely this evening; I have to admit that I am rather partial to the color of blue you are both wearing, ladies," said the Earl with a slight smile on his handsome face. "I suppose you are rather partial, my lord since the color matches with your eyes rather well," softly replied Nicolette as she gazed into the sapphire blue eyes of the Earl. Nicolette, Lady Elizabeth and Daniel stepped ahead of the Earl after greeting Lord Jared and started walking towards the front entrance of Old Wood Manor. And then, without further hesitation, the Earl and Lord Jared swiftly followed behind.

When they entered the manor, they were escorted to an elegant room with musical instruments and a small dance floor adjacent to a very large dining room where they would be seated once the entire guests had arrived. When Nicolette first entered the room, she saw Lady Anne and Lady Miranda standing near a small black piano close to a very large window. Lady Margaret and Lord Atticus started heading their way to greet them. "Good evening, sister, Nicolette and Daniel. How lovely to see you," said Lady Margaret with a smile on her face. After Lord Atticus bid them a good evening, he turned around and started talking to the Earl and Lord Jared. A moment later, some other guests approached Lord Atticus, and they started talking to him while the Earl turned his attention back to Nicolette once her mother and Lady Margaret walked away in deep conversation.

The Earl stood close enough to Nicolette so he could whisper to her. "When the evening meal starts to come to a close, I want you to meet me in Lord Atticus' study. I will excuse myself first, and then you will wait a few minutes and excuse yourself from the table and come to the study."

"I shall be there, my lord," whispered Nicolette and then they both went their separate ways. But Lady Anne was standing behind both the Earl and Nicolette, and she overheard what the Earl requested Nicolette to do. Lady Anne was hidden discreetly between other guests and the Earl, and Nicolette did not see her there. Lady Anne knew immediately how she could get back at Nicolette for betraying her, and Nicolette would be in for a big surprise before this evening was over. Then Lady Anne began to glance around the room until she laid her eyes upon Lord Jared and quickly headed in his direction. Nicolette was standing near Lord Jared, speaking with the lovely Lady Luisa, when a servant approached her and handed her a letter that had just arrived at Old Wood Manor from North America. She quickly walked over to a small table found a letter opener, and quickly opened the sealed envelope. It was a message from George in Charleston, South Carolina, telling her that he had decided to stay in Charleston to help his father with the cotton plantation. He continued to say that his father had developed poor health recently and needed his help, so he was asking her to come to Charleston to marry him, and hopefully, they could return to England once his father's health improved.

When she looked up from reading the message, she noticed everyone was moving towards the dining room to take their seats at the large dining table. The servants led her to her seat, and she discovered that her seat was next to Lord Jared's seat and across from the Earl and Lady Anne's seat. Immediately, she asked her mother if she would change seats with her so she didn't have to be directly across the table from Lady Anne and the Earl. The Earl of Old Wood Manor and Lord Atticus were seated at the head of the table when he got everyone's attention as he rose from his chair and raised his wine goblet up in the air to wish his son Lord Atticus a Happy Birthday and to thank all his family and guest for attending the celebration. Then, immediately, everyone raised their wine glasses, and cheers went up in the air to wish Lord Atticus a

Happy Birthday. Once the Earl of Old Wood Manor picked his utensil to begin eating, everyone else began to eat their dinner. Nicolette joined in ever so often with a comment about the conversation at hand, but mostly, the Earl and Nicolette's attention was on each other as they continued to glance at one another from time to time.

As time went by, Nicolette noticed that Lady Anne was the second person to excuse herself from the dining table. The first person to leave the room was one of the children of a family guest. It wasn't long after that Lord James Mayfield and Lord Gerald Ashton both left the dining room. After Nicolette noticed that the Earl refused to partake of his dessert, he rose from his seat and excused himself from the table and left to go to Lord Atticus' study to wait for her arrival. She remembered him telling her to wait a short few minutes before leaving the table, so she decided to eat her dessert. When she finished eating it, she excused herself from the table and left the dining room to walk down a hallway leading to Lord Atticus' study, where the Earl was waiting for her arrival. On her way there, she heard voices coming from what appeared to be Lord Gerald's study.

When she got closer, she saw that the door was not closed all the way, so she stopped walking and stood behind the door where no one could see her. Then she began to hear Lord Ashton say to the Marquis, "How dare the Earl of Primrose dismiss my daughter to marry a commoner? Her father had no title and even though Lady Elizabeth is the sister of my wife and their father is an Earl,

Lady Elizabeth did not retain a title when she married. For God's sake, they are only dressmakers, my lord!"

"You know how my son is, Lord Gerald. Once he makes up his mind about something or someone, there is no turning back. My son's happiness is important to me and so is the Mayfield and Ashton's family future important as well. But I have to say, my lord, that Nicolette is a lovely lady no matter what you think of her right now," replied the Marquis. Nicolette couldn't tolerate hearing anymore, so she quietly tip-toed to Lord Atticus' study and slowly opened the door to find Lady Anne and the Earl standing face to face. She stared in horror when she saw Lady Anne reach up to pull the Earl's lips to hers and kiss him suddenly. When the Earl pulled away from Lady Anne, the Earl and Nicolette's eyes locked with one another. Within the blink of an eye, she quickly lifted her gown and ran as fast as she could to the bed chamber where she stayed when she visited Old Wood Manor.

When she entered the bed chamber, she locked the door behind her, flung her body across the large canopy bed and allowed herself to sob many tears into her feather pillow. Moments later, she heard a loud knocking on the chamber door. Then she heard the Earl asking her to let him in, but she only told him to go away. But he kept knocking on the door and kept insisting on her to let him come inside the chamber. "Please allow me inside the door so I can explain what just happened, Nicolette," shouted the Earl as he continued to pound on the chamber door. "Go away, my lord, you cannot explain what I just saw with my own eyes," said

Nicolette between sobs. "But it's not what you think, Nicolette," replied the Earl with desperation in his voice. "Please go away, my lord; I do not want to see you," exclaimed Nicolette.

The Earl continued to knock on the door when he suddenly saw Lady Elizabeth coming towards him. "What is all this commotion about, my lord?" asked Lady Elizabeth when she saw that the Earl was pounding on the chamber door. "I was in the ballroom after leaving the dance floor with Lord Chamberlain when Nora found me and informed me that she heard Nicolette crying out loudly in the bed chamber where she stays upon our visits. Nicolette, it's your mother, and I want to know if you are alright, dear; please let me come inside the chamber, my dear," asked Lady Elizabeth with concern in her voice. "Only if you can make the Earl go away, Mother, will I let you in the door," replied Nicolette as she raised her head from the pillow. The Earl stopped pounding on the door and stood completely still for a moment. When he glanced into the face of Lady Elizabeth, he saw a look of slight agitation in her eyes. At that moment, he realized that Lady Elizabeth wasn't quite pleased with him. "I think it will be best if you leave us for now, my lord," replied Lady Elizabeth. "I do not know what is happening between you and Nicolette, but I can see that my daughter does not want you here right now." With a slight nod of his head, the Earl left and headed back to the study, cursing under his breath and hoping to find a bottle of Lord Atticus' favorite brandy.

"Please unlock the door, dear; the Earl is not here any longer. You need to tell me what you are so distressed about," said Lady Elizabeth as she stood anxiously waiting at the chamber door. Nicolette rose from her bed, grabbed a clean handkerchief from the vanity drawer, and unlocked the door for her mother to enter the chamber. "Perhaps you should tell me what is going on between you and Lord Austin, dear. I have never seen him look so distraught, my dear," said Lady Elizabeth as she stood there staring at her daughter's pale face and swollen eyes.

"I saw them kissing earlier, Mother," said Nicolette as she continued to wipe the tears from her eyes. "You saw who kissing?" asked Lady Elizabeth. "When I came to Lord Atticus' study to meet the Earl there upon his request, I saw the Earl and Lady Anne kissing, Mother," replied Nicolette.

"Oh, for heaven's sake, dear, I can see why you are so upset," said Lady Elizabeth as she walked over to the small basin that was on the dresser and poured some water from the pitcher in order to wet cloth for Nicolette to wipe her face and her swollen eyes. "Here, Nicolette, let me help you clean your face, and you can tell me why the Earl would do such a thing," said Lady Elizabeth. "Is that why the Earl kept pounding on the chamber door and kept pleading with you to let him explain what happened between him and Lady Anne?" asked Lady Elizabeth while she took her daughter's arm and led her over to the seat at the vanity facing the mirror. "Now I want you to sit here and let me fix the hairpins in your hair, and then you are going to put a tad of this rouge on your pale cheeks," said Lady Elizabeth. "After that, we are going back downstairs to join the others in the ballroom. You will dry up these tears and show Lady Anne and the Earl both that you are a strong lady of integrity and not a frightened little girl who runs away. I'm quite sure that there is an explanation for what took place between the Earl and Lady Anne and I don't doubt that the kiss was all of Lady Anne's doing."

When Nicolette and her mother arrived downstairs, they entered the small ballroom, where they heard music and saw several guests dancing to a lovely tune. Nicolette noticed Lady Miranda, Lord Jared, Lady Anne, Lord Atticus and Lady Luisa right away, but there was no sign of Lord Austin anywhere. Nicolette couldn't help but wonder where he might be, but then she told herself, *why should I even care? As a matter of fact, I do not care to see him at all.* Then she remembered the message that came from George earlier, and suddenly she realized that she would go back home to Charleston and marry George. *I shall tell George the truth about the Earl and me and if he doesn't want to marry me, I shall go and visit with my aunt and uncle where we were living before we left for England. I will leave Mother and Willow to run the shop until George and I return to England.*

With that thought in mind, she held her head up high and made her way over to the refreshment table for a glass of champagne to calm her nerves before her mother, Daniel, and she left soon to go to Ashton cottage for the rest of the night.

CHAPTER 17

October 1865

It wasn't that late when the Ashton carriage pulled up in front of the Ashton cottage. The cobblestone streets still shone bright with all the gas-lit lamp posts and bright stars shining up above in the night sky. But Nicolette wasn't feeling very bright at the moment. As a matter of fact, she was feeling rather dark and sad. She hardly said two words in the carriage on the way to the cottage. She politely told her mother and Daniel that she did not want to talk about what happened earlier at Old Wood Manor. The last thing she needed to hear right now was *I told you so* from Daniel. Nicolette remembered Daniel warning her that whatever was brewing between her and the Earl could end up in a disaster, and boy, was he right. When Daniel took her by the hand and helped her step down from the carriage, Nicolette said to him, "I am sorry, Daniel, that I did not listen to you when you warned me that whatever was taking place between the Earl and me may not end well. You couldn't have been more right, brother."

"But that is not what I wish, sister; I can see that you are deeply heartbroken by what has taken place. I only want you to be happy, and I know now that the Earl is the gentleman that you truly want to be with. And I can tell by the way the Earl looks at you, Nicolette, he feels the same way," said Daniel with concern in his voice. "Whatever you saw in Lord Atticus' study may not be what the Earl wanted to take place, dear. You must give the Earl a chance to explain," said Lady Elizabeth as Daniel helped his mother from the carriage.

"I know what I saw, Mother, and I never want to speak to him again. Now, if you will excuse me, I need to be alone," replied Nicolette as she lifted her lovely sapphire blue gown and ran as fast as she could inside the Ashton cottage and up the stairway to her bed chamber.

Nicolette was pacing back and forth in her chamber when Sally entered the room. Sally could tell that Nicolette was extremely upset, so she hurried to help her undress and get ready for bed. Before leaving the chamber, Sally said, "I hope that whatever is making you so sad, miss, shall pass away and that you shall feel much better in the morning."

"Don't leave yet, Sally," said Nicolette in a very low tone of voice. "There is something I need your immediate help with. I want you to come back to my chamber in a few minutes, and I will explain."

"I shall return very soon, miss," replied Sally as she walked out the chamber door.

Nicolette strode over to a small table in the chamber and began writing a letter to her mother and Daniel. When she finished writing the letter and sealed the envelope, she looked at a calendar in the drawer of the small table and saw that tomorrow after lunch, the Royal Princess Ship would be leaving England for North America. Immediately she started thinking about making plans to board the Royal Princess Ship to North America tomorrow. But first, she needed to go to her seamstress shop first thing in the morning and finish sewing the lovely gown that she had made for Queen Victoria. And while she finishes Queen Victoria's gown, Sally could be packing her trunk and baggage with her belongings so she could have them sent to the ship. When she gets ready to leave the shop for her mid-day meal, she can go to where the ship is docked and buy her ticket to sail to North America.

Not being able to say goodbye to her mother or Daniel was the last thing she wanted to do, but she knew if she told them that she was leaving, they would try to stop her. But the letter she was leaving for them to read explained that she would be returning to England. She knew that her mother would be truly upset about her leaving, but she told her to please keep the seamstress shop open and allow Willow to continue to help her since she knew that the Earl would continue to pay Willow's salary even with her gone from England. She also told her mother and Daniel to please take good care of Biscuit since she sadly had to leave him behind. Nicolette heard a soft knock on the chamber door and quietly unlocked the door so Sally could enter. Nicolette handed Sally the letter and began to explain her plans to her, but Sally didn't look too pleased with her mistress at the moment. "Are you sure this is what you want to do, Nicolette?" asked Sally while turning back the covers on the large canopy bed. "Maybe running away from here will only make you unhappier in the long run," said Sally as she noticed the sadness in her mistress's eyes that she had never seen before. "I have made up my mind, Sally, and I shall be leaving on the Royal Princess tomorrow. So please do as I told you to do, and I shall see you first thing in the morning," said Nicolette as she slipped inside the covers of her large canopy bed and dreamed of a knight on a dark horse with shiny black hair and sapphire blue eyes.

"Are you awake, Lord Mayfield?" asked Mobley, Lord Atticus' groomsman, when he entered Lord Atticus' study at Old Wood Manor. "Yes, Mobley, I woke up when I first heard you knock on the door. I suppose I must have fallen asleep in this chair after partaking of this nearly empty bottle of brandy," replied the Earl as he rubbed his eyes. "I see daylight peeping through the window behind the closed silk drapes Mobley. I assume it must be morning, and I must have slept here all night."

"Yes, indeed, my lord, it certainly appears that way," said Mobley as he handed the Earl a glass of water.

"Well, what do we have here?" asked Lord Atticus as he entered his study and glanced down at one of his nearly empty bottles of brandy. "I didn't see you in the ballroom last evening, so I asked Lady Anne and Lord Jared where you were, and they said that they weren't sure, but they thought maybe you had left earlier. But here you are, my lord, tucked away in this chair in my study with a nearly empty bottle of brandy."

"Did something happen that I don't know about my lord?" suddenly asked Lord Atticus with a curious look on his face. "Maybe you should take a seat and let me explain," replied the Earl as he finished gulping down the last swallow of water, handed the glass to Mobley and started to speak as Mobley left the study. "I apologize for what I am about to say; I chose to keep from you until now, Lord Atticus," said the Earl. "I do not want to marry Lady Anne; my heart belongs to another, Lord Atticus," said the Earl. "I see, my lord; so is it the lovely Nicolette, the lady that stole your heart, my lord?" asked Lord Atticus with a half grin on his handsome face. "Perhaps I saw this coming for a long time, my lord, and this news does not surprise me," said Lord Atticus. "I tried to keep it a secret, and so did Nicolette because we didn't want to hurt anyone or cause a scandal and hoping maybe that these feelings we have for one another would disappear, but they kept growing stronger until I gave into the passion between us and made her mine."

"Are you saying what I think you are saying, and does my sister know of this shared passion, my lord?" asked Lord Atticus with a more serious look on his face. "I did not tell Lady Anne anything at all about Nicolette and me, but I did tell her that I do not want to marry her. I also mentioned to her that I am certain that Lord Jared is quite fond of her and that he would be honored to take her as his bride. I have spoken to my brother, and he never said yes to marrying her, but seeing the wide grin on his face when I made the suggestion was proof enough. They seem to be the perfect match, and she can still give our fathers the bloodline they so desire to have between our families, but just not with a title," said the Earl as he rose from his chair to pour himself another glass of water.

"So, let me ask you, my lord," asked Lord Atticus. "Who else knows about this, my lord? Do our fathers know, and what do they say? I can imagine that they're not too happy about this even though Nicolette is a lovely lady, and I can see why you are quite fond of her, my lord."

"Yes, our families all know by now, and I can't speak for Lord Gerald; my father is not too pleased, but he will come around since he only wishes me to be happy," replied the Earl as he pulled his pocket watch out and saw what time it was. "So, what happened last evening to cause you to consume one of my best bottles of brandy? And by the way, you owe me one, my lord?" asked Lord Atticus.

"Right before the evening meal, I whispered to Nicolette to meet me here in your study towards the end of the evening meal. Lady Anne must have overheard the conversation and went to the study before Nicolette arrived and when she saw Nicolette open the door, she pulled me towards her and kissed me passionately on the mouth. When Nicolette saw us kissing she turned away and ran to the bed chamber where she stays upon her visits at Old Wood Manor. I ran after her and headed to the chamber and knocked on the door so I could explain to Nicolette that it was Lady Anne who kissed me, not the other way around, but she would not let me in. She told me to go away and that she did not want to talk to me ever again."

"I kept knocking on the door for her to let me in, and then Lady Elizabeth showed up at the door, and Nicolette said the only way she would allow her mother to come inside the door would be if I would leave. So, I left without anyone else seeing me, and I came straight to your study, and here I am with a shattered heart and a terrible headache. If you would be so kind as to call for me a carriage, Lord Atticus, not only will I have one bottle of your favorite brandy sent over to you, I will have two bottles, my lord."

"It was merely a joke, my lord; you do not have to send me brandy. A dear friend like you with a broken heart and a tangled web he's found himself in recently, I would say that you deserve a bottle of my favorite brandy," said Lord Atticus.

"I must get to the city right away and go after a lovely sea goddess in distress, or I will forever regret it if I don't, my lord."

"Well, don't let me stand in your way, my lord," replied Lord Atticus as he rose from his chair. "Please follow me, and I shall get you a carriage to take you to the city immediately, my lord."

"Oh, dear, I can't praise you enough for the magnificent work you have accomplished. The Queen's gown for the October Regency Ball is by far your best work yet, my dear," said Lady Elizabeth as she went to hang up the Queen's gown among the other finished gowns. "Thank you, Mother, but I couldn't have finished it without you and Willow's help," replied Nicolette with a slightly nervous tone in her voice. When she stared up at the clock, she noticed that she had finished earlier than she thought she would, so she decided to go ahead and take her break and get a bite to eat.

"Are you feeling alright, dear?" asked Lady Elizabeth. "You happen to look rather pale, my dear." Nicolette and her mother both knew that they couldn't discuss what happened last evening with Willow present, but Nicolette was glad not to talk about it anyway. "If I look pale, Mother, it's probably because I am famished since I did not eat my breakfast earlier. I believe I will go out and get me a bite to eat now if that so pleases you, Mother," said Nicolette as she grabbed her cloak and her drawstring purse heading towards the front door.

Nicolette walked down the cobblestone street until she found a carriage to take her to the dock where the Royal Princess ship was waiting. In the meantime, Daniel left his tailor shop and found a carriage to escort him to the Ashton cottage to have his mid-day meal. When he got to the cottage, he ran upstairs to his chamber to get some more money from his chamber. When he walked past Nicolette's chamber, where the door was left open, he noticed that all her belongings were missing from the chamber. When he walked inside the chamber and opened the Armoire, he noticed all her gowns were missing. He immediately ran down the stairway to find Sally, and when he saw her, she handed him the letter that Nicolette had left for him and his mother. He found a letter opener and read the letter with a look of devastation on his face. Then he ran back outside and jumped into the carriage, and the coachman went as quickly as he could to Nicolette's Seamstress Shop to see his mother and to give her the letter.

When the carriage pulled up in front of the seamstress shop, Daniel quickly jumped out of the carriage and ran towards the front door of Nicolette's Seamstress Shop with the letter in his hand. Suddenly, the carriage that was escorting the Earl to the city pulled up behind the other carriage. When the Earl looked out the window of the carriage, he saw Daniel running towards the door of the shop with something in his hand that resembled a letter. So, the Earl decided to step out of the carriage quickly and followed Daniel inside the seamstress shop. The Earl immediately sees Lady Elizabeth and Daniel standing in the front room of the shop and Lady Elizabeth is reading a letter with a look of horror on her face. She let out a loud gasp and then caught her breath as she looked up at the Earl and asked him if he could please help them go find Nicolette. "Nicolette had Sally to pack her belongings, and now she has gone to board the Royal Princess Steam Ship leaving for North America, my lord," said Daniel as they quickly followed the Earl out the door to get inside the carriage that would escort them to the dock where the Royal Princess Ship was waiting.

When they arrived at the ship dock, the Earl handed the coachman some money and told him to stay put while Daniel, Lady Elizabeth, and he went to find Nicolette. Lady Elizabeth and Daniel decided to check all up and down the dock while the Earl asked to board the Royal Princess Ship to look for Nicolette. Normally, no one except for family members would be allowed to board the ship without a ticket, but since he was the Earl of Primrose Estate, the staff believed him when he told them he was only boarding to look for a passenger. The Earl noticed a sign that said that the Royal Princess would be leaving England around three o'clock today. He was relieved to know that because that gave him plenty of time to find her and to tell her how much he loved her and that he wanted to marry her. That also gave him plenty of time to make sure her belongings were not on the ship, and if they were, that gave him time to get them off the ship and loaded into a carriage. So, he continued to walk the top deck of the ship until he saw her towards the front of the ship wearing a blue velvet cloak with her golden curls cascading down her back, standing near the ship rails staring out at sea. At that very moment, he had to catch his breath and stare at the loveliest lady he had ever seen. She was every bit the sea goddess he had dreams of every night since the day he first laid his eyes on her.

"To see you here, Nicolette, reminds me of the time we used to meet here in this very spot," said the Earl out loud as he stopped several feet behind his lovely sea goddess. "You are even more beautiful now as a woman than when I saw you standing here before as a young girl."

"What are you doing here, my lord?" angrily asked Nicolette as she continued to stare out to sea. "Please go away, my lord; I do not need your flattery. Why waste your flattery on me when it is Lady Anne you are with, my lord?"

"But you are wrong, Nicolette; I am not with Lady Anne now or ever," said the Earl as he started to inch closer to Nicolette. "That is not what I saw last evening, my lord. I saw you kissing Lady Anne, and that tells me that you are not being honest with me. Do you take me as a complete fool, my lord," asked Nicolette as she slowly turned around to face the Earl and stared into his sapphire blue eyes.

"I see you as a woman like none other, Nicolette; I do not see you as a fool," replied the Earl with a loving, tender voice. "The kiss that you saw last evening was not any of my doing at all, Nicolette," said the Earl. "Obviously Lady Anne must have overheard us last evening when we were waiting along with the other guests to enter the dining room for Lord Atticus birthday dinner. I was waiting for your arrival in Lord Atticus' study when Lady Anne entered the study and caught me by surprise. I asked her why she was there, and I told her to leave immediately. She refused to leave and started walking towards me, and when the door opened and she saw you standing there, she pulled me forward and kissed me without my consent. I was furious at her when I saw you standing there and then suddenly running away as fast as you could run. That is when I came after you to explain to you that I do not want her, Nicolette. She only did what she did so she could get back at you and me. So please believe me, Nicolette, I will never want to hurt you," said the Earl as he came up to where Nicolette was standing and got down on one knee.

"You are the lady that has stolen my heart, and I will never love another. So please do not leave me here without you, Nicolette; I want you to stay here and be my wife. Will you please marry me?" asked the Earl as he stared into her big blue eyes. Nicolette just stood there staring at the Earl for a brief moment and began to realize that many people were starting to gather around them. "I have already told you once that I will marry you, my lord, and then look what happened," replied Nicolette as she held back a tear in her eye. "I overheard the Marquis and Lord Ashton talking last evening, and Lord Ashton is not too pleased with the idea of you marrying me instead of his daughter."

"But as I told you before, Nicolette, it is my title he most seeks for his only daughter," said the Earl. "And as far as the Marquis goes, he will come around to accepting the fact that you are the one I want to marry. So, what do you say, my dear? My knees are beginning to feel the hardness of this deck floor."

"Yes, my lord, I will marry you," said Nicolette as the tear began to slide down her lovely cheek.

Quickly, the Earl stood on his feet, swept his sea goddess into his arms and passionately kissed her as her feet found the wooden planks on the ship's top deck. The Earl hadn't even noticed that several of the passengers aboard the ship had gathered around them until he heard the sweet voice of Lady Elizabeth approaching them. "There you are, Nicolette; I am so grateful that the Earl has found you, my dear," exclaimed Lady Elizabeth as she hugged her daughter. "We need to hurry if we are to find your belongings,

Nicolette," quickly said the Earl. "Nicolette, you go with your mother and Daniel to find the Ashton family carriage that is carrying your baggage, and I will go to the staff room on the ship and see if your belongings have been delivered to your stateroom yet and if they are on board I will have them sent back to the carriage right away," said the Earl as he let go of her hand and kissed her on the cheek. "Yes, my lord, we shall see you back at the Ashton family carriage soon," replied Nicolette as she lifted her gown and cloak and hurried to find the Ashton family carriage.

"I am so glad you decided to join us for breakfast this morning, my dear; I did notice that the Earl stayed quite late last evening. It was rather nice of Lord Gerald's brother to allow you and the Earl into his grand library in the main house on the property, my dear. I am happy to know that the Earl shares your profound interest in Literature, my dear. The servants are telling me that Lord Ashton's brother is quite ill, and he is mostly confined to his chamber these days. I have recently noticed that I have not seen him up and about as in the past," said Lady Elizabeth as Nicolette handed the bowl of sausage gravy to Daniel. "Yes, Mother, I suppose you are right about Lord Ashton. The Earl and I did not see him. It was the butler who escorted us to the library."

"Perhaps we could finish our breakfast soon and head to the shop earlier than usual this morning," said Nicolette as she hurried to finish her breakfast. "Now that we have finished all the new gowns for some of the ladies to pick up at the shop to wear to the October Regency Ball, we will have a few days to take some time for ourselves," said Lady Elizabeth as she rose from her chair to go get their cloaks. "After witnessing all the attention that you and the Earl received on board the Royal Princess Ship, I'm quite sure there is lots of gossip in the air at this moment," said Lady Elizabeth as Daniel, Nicolette, and she swiftly walked to the carriage that would escort them to the seamstress shop. "But do not allow it to put a damper on your plans with the Earl, my dear; I am truly convinced that the Earl will fight tooth and nail to have you as his bride," said Lady Elizabeth as she placed her slender hand on her daughter's rosy cheek. "I suppose this time I can fully agree with you, dear Mother," replied Nicolette as she stepped inside the carriage.

Since it was getting late last evening when the Earl left the company of his lovely bride-to-be, he decided to spend the night in his bed at the Mayfield Cottage in the city. When he got to his bed chamber and stripped off his garments, he began to have memories of him and Nicolette sharing their passion with one another as he slid into his big poster bed. He was having visions of her lovely body lying next to his naked body, and his manhood began to swell slightly with just the thought of her. Then he began to straighten his pillows, pull the bed covers over his half-naked body, and he fell fast asleep when his head touched his feather pillow.

The following morning, when the Earl woke with dark clouds in the sky, he decided to leave the cottage much earlier than he first anticipated. Since he didn't have a groom or a footman to attend to him, he decided to take it upon himself to do some shopping. First thing, he would go to the shop that sells brandy and have two bottles of Lord Atticus' favorite brandy sent to Old Wood Manor, and then he would go see Daniel to have his new suit for the October Regency Ball sent to the Mayfield Cottage. And lastly, he would visit Nicolette's Seamstress Shop and take her to some place of her choosing for a lovely mid-day meal. Just the thought of seeing her again made him whistle as he ran down the stairs heading to the Mayfield carriage.

It was nearly noon when the Mayfield carriage pulled up in front of Braxton Tailor Shop. The dark clouds were still hanging low in the sky, but there was no rain in sight. The Earl stepped inside the shop and took a look at his finished tailored suit that he would be wearing to the Regency Ball in a few days. He was truly impressed by what he saw; Daniel had already gained the reputation of one of the most prestigious tailor shops on Seville Rowe in London. After speaking with Daniel and taking care of his business there, he walked out the door to go next door to Nicolette's Seamstress Shop when he bumped into Viscount Douglas Martin and his wife. "Good day," said the Earl as he spoke and nodded his head to greet the Martins. But they did not greet him in return; instead, they turned their heads and kept walking. The Earl knew immediately what was happening and why they ignored him. He was rather sure that by now word had spread around that he had discarded the lovely Lady Anne whom he promised to marry one day for a seamstress without a title. He knew deep down that he could endure this scandal, but what worried him was if Nicolette could.

At the very moment, he was about to open the front door of the seamstress shop when he looked up and saw Lady Anne step outside the Ashton carriage. They stood there staring at one another for a brief moment until the Earl decided to walk towards her. "Fancy running into you here, my lord. I guess I should have known," said Lady Anne with a smirk on her lovely face. "I suppose I should be congratulating you on your upcoming marriage, my lord; I see that you didn't waste any time. Now, if you will allow me, I must pick up my gown for the Regency Ball, my lord. Even if I have to say so, your poor seamstress from Charleston without a title does have excellent taste in design and other ladies and gentlemen," said Lady Anne as she quickly walked past the Earl and stepped inside the seamstress shop.

When the Earl stepped inside the shop, he heard Lady Anne tell Willow that she wanted Nicolette to attend to her, so the Earl decided to step outside and wait in the Mayfield carriage upon encountering even more ladies stepping into the shop. He realized that Nicolette was way too busy to leave her shop right now, so he would wait for her in the carriage. When Nicolette overheard Lady Anne requesting for Nicolette to attend to her, she asked her mother to help the other ladies who entered the shop, but when her mother approached them, they asked for Willow to attend to them. They turned their heads and would not speak to Lady Elizabeth. Nicolette could see what was happening; it was just as the Earl predicted. Nicolette walked to the back room where the new gowns that were ready to be picked up were located; she grabbed the yellow and chestnut brown silk gown with the amber gemstones on the bodice of the gown. This was Lady Anne's gown and it was one of Nicolette's favorite gowns from her autumn designs. The gowns from her autumn collection would be among the gowns that several ladies would be wearing to this season's October Regency Ball.

"Your gown is finished, my lady," said Nicolette as she held up the gown to show Lady Anne. "Well, if I must say, I am quite pleased with my gown, Nicolette. But I can't say the same for you, Nicolette; you have betrayed me in every way possible. Even if Lord Jared does ask for my hand in marriage, it does not mean that I will accept. Ah, I'm quite sure that would be ideal for you and the Earl. Either of you won't have to feel quite as guilty about your betrayal to me, my father and the Marquis," remarked Lady Anne with a mean tone of voice. "I am glad you are pleased with your gown; it shall look quite lovely on you, my lady. But the last thing I ever want to do is to hurt you or anyone else. I tried not to have feelings for the Earl, and I even tried to leave here and go back to Charleston. But the love that the Earl and I have for one another goes beyond anything that either one of us has ever known before. And you can have that same love with Lord Jared, my lady if you would only open your heart and let your feelings flow.

"Ever since we were younger girls Lady Anne, you always had more of everything than I had, yet you were never satisfied. You always wanted to try to outdo me with all the activities that we did together. Most of the time, I would let you win so you wouldn't be so jealous of me," said Nicolette in a pitiful tone of voice. "You always got your way no matter whom or what stood in your way. But this time, I'm not going to let you win and destroy the happiness that the Earl and I have found. There is a beau out there who truly adores you, and his name is Lord Jared, so if I were you, I would not let a love like that pass by, my lady," said Nicolette as she handed Nora the ladies' maid the gown and left the front room of her shop to grab her purse and head out the door to step into the carriage where the gentleman she adored was patiently waiting.

The next few days were rather cold for the last days of October. Not only was the weather quite chilly, but there was another kind of chill in the air. Gossip had already spread throughout that the Earl had chosen another bride to be other than Lady Anne of Old Wood Manor. The Earl had taken up residence until a couple of days ago at the Mayfield cottage so he could stay close to Nicolette. Today was the day of the October Regency Ball, and there was much excitement in the air. The Earl could not help but feel slight guilt over the fact that his family and the Braxton family were both getting the cold shoulder since he declared his love for Nicolette and asked for her hand in marriage.

Lord Jared visited Old Wood Manor yesterday and came back home to Primrose Estate with good news: Lady Anne had accepted his brother's marriage proposal. They were to be married come December, and if, by some miracle, Lady Anne could ever forgive him and Nicolette for falling so deeply in love with one another, then he could envision a double wedding come December. But that still left him wondering how this evening would go since everything was up in the air. There was only one thing that he was certain about, and that was that he couldn't wait to dance with his lovely sea goddess and swirl her around the dance floor that so happened to belong to the Duke and Duchess of York.

"I can't help but keep staring at your lovely gown, Nicolette. This gown and the gown you made for the Queen is your best work yet, my dear," said Lady Elizabeth, standing in Nicolette's chamber admiring her silver and garnet silk gown with the white diamonds and garnets on the fabric of the gown. Suddenly, Nicolette and her mother heard a knock at the door of her chamber at the Ashton Cottage; it was Daniel. "This package just arrived for Nicolette's mother," said Daniel as he handed his mother the package and left. "Well, open it, dear; I am as anxious as you are to see what it is, my dear," quickly said Lady Elizabeth. Nicolette opened the wooden box, and when she peeped inside, she saw a beautiful garnet and diamond necklace with matching earrings. It was a gift from the Earl to match the lovely gown she made to wear to the Regency Ball this evening. She remembered him asking about the gown she would be wearing to the ball, and now she knew why. "It is the loveliest and probably most expensive gift any gentleman has ever given me, Mother," said Nicolette with a happy but stunned look on her lovely face. "Indeed it is, my dear, but you best get used to it because there will be many more gifts in the future. I must leave and go to my chamber now; I must get ready for the ball, my dear," said Lady Elizabeth as she left the chamber.

Guest after guest poured into the large ballroom at the palace of the Duke and Duchess of York. The Earl and the Mayfield family had recently arrived at the ball, and they were already feeling the repercussions of the Earl's decision to marry Nicolette instead of Lady Anne. But there was certainly one thing that the Earl couldn't feel bad about and that was the fact that his family was standing by him and his decision to marry Nicolette. But when they announced the arrival of the Ashton family moments ago, he saw Lord Jared quickly making his way over to Lady Anne. Nicolette, her mother and Daniel had not arrived yet, and he was eagerly anticipating her arrival. He was hoping that she would like the garnet and diamond necklace with the matching earrings and that she would be wearing them that evening.

"Good evening, my lord," said Lord Atticus as he walked up to stand beside the Earl. "Are you sure you want to be seen with me, Lord Atticus?" said the Earl with a slight chuckle in his deep masculine voice. "Haven't you heard what a scoundrel I've turned out to be, my lord?" asked the Earl while glancing around the room. "But that doesn't deter me, Lord Austin; I have been known to be quite a scoundrel myself," replied Lord Atticus. "Well, it's good to know that at least one member of the Ashton family has not disowned me, my lord," said the Earl as he heard the announcement of the Braxton family's arrival. When the announcer introduced Nicolette and she entered the ballroom, all heads turned to gaze at her, and everyone stood there staring in awe at her beauty. The Earl had to catch his breath; she looked like a princess.

"Please excuse me, my lord," said Lord Atticus as he took his eyes off Nicolette and noticed Lady Luisa and Lady Miranda slowly walking toward Nicolette, Daniel and Lady Elizabeth. The Earl decided to walk over to a servant, grab two glasses of champagne from his tray, and make his way towards Nicolette. When he approached her, Nicolette slightly curtsied, and he handed her a glass of champagne and whispered in her delicate ear, "You look so lovely, Nicolette, that I want to kiss those rosy lips of yours at this very moment. But I can take you by the hand and dance this lovely waltz with you, my dear." The Earl and Nicolette quickly placed their champagne glasses on the tray of a servant who passed by them. He gently led her to the dance floor, pulling her into a warm embrace as they swayed together. When he gazed into her big blue eyes, he noticed that her eyes were sparkling like diamonds under the bright glow of the large chandeliers.

As he twirled her around the dance floor, Nicolette whispered into the Earl's ear, "Did I happen to mention how handsome you look this evening, my lord? I am very much looking forward to your kisses, my lord."

"I am quite certain that I can make that possible, my dear, and the sooner, the better," replied the Earl in a soft, quiet, masculine voice. "Do not tease me, my lord," said Nicolette as she stared into his sapphire blue eyes that were beaming with desire for her. The lovely waltz was coming to an end when he twirled her around one last time. When the music ended, he bowed, and she curtsied, and they left the dance floor together. When Nicolette and the Earl walked over to where Lord Jared and Lady Anne were standing, several guests that were standing nearby began to look their way. Nicolette was the first to speak to Lord Jared and Lady Anne, "I would like to congratulate you both on your engagement. I hear that you are making an official announcement this evening after the arrival of Queen Victoria. I am glad for both of you. I wish you great happiness." Instead of looking away, Lady Anne decided to look Nicolette in the face and reply, "Not so long ago, I would probably spit venom into your face, Nicolette. But recently, I have come to my senses and realized that you and the Earl are right. I have now opened up my heart and allowed myself to love for the first time, and Lord Jared is the gentleman who truly loves me, and I do not have any doubt that we belong together."

Before the Earl and Nicolette could utter a single reply to Lady Anne, Queen Victoria entered the ballroom upon announcement. She stood still at the entrance and let all the guests stand and admire her. Everyone there was mesmerized by how lovely she looked in the most beautiful ball gown they had ever seen. The queen and her royals walked over to where their thrones were located and took their places. And all the other guests continued with their usual activities. The Earl and Nicolette continued to savor every moment of the evening even though they were completely ignored by most of the guests. Suddenly, the Queen rose from her throne and started speaking out loud to all the guests, "As all of you are well aware, I lost my dearest husband, King Albert, to that horrible typhoid fever nearly four years ago. I have mourned his death in solitude until I received this magnificent gown from a lovely and most gifted seamstress and diamond among us. I want to give all my thanks to the lovely Miss Nicolette Braxton, who made this lovely gown for her Queen and helped her Queen feel alive once more."

Suddenly, everyone in the ballroom looked over at Nicolette and the Earl and turned their attention back to the Queen as she continued to speak out loud, "It has come to my attention that the lovely Miss Braxton has caught the attention of one of my most favorable among us, Lord Austin Mayfield of Primrose. I hear that they are to be married come December, joined by his brother Lord Jared Mayfield, and the Lovely Lady Anne Ashton of Old Wood Manor. So, raise your glasses, everyone, and let's toast to looking forward to a double wedding come December!"

"Cheers!" shouted all the guests out loud as they raised their glasses into the air.

The rest of the evening, the Earl and Nicolette hardly had a chance to dance or even talk since so many of the guests were greeting them one after another and congratulating them on their upcoming marriage. "I guess it takes the Queen's favor to get everyone's approval, my lord, said Nicolette as she whispered into the Earl's ear. "I have no doubt in my mind, my darling Nicolette, that sooner or later they would have fallen head over heels in love with you just as I have, my dear," said the Earl as he lifted her lovely chin and passionately kissed her warm lips just as he promised he would.